I0680748

Erector Set
Erected
Hammered
Nailed

Galaxy
Retrograde

Anthologies
Night of the Senses: Carnal Caresses
Christmas Goes Camo: Melting the Ice
Treble: Trouble at the Treble T
Subspace: Head Games
Bound to the Billionaire: Made for Him
Three's a Charm: Double Entry

Collections
Heatwave: Summer Spice
Feral: Black Cat Fever
Clandestine Classics: Northanger Abbey
A Little Bit Cupid: Hot Pants and Valentines

Galaxy

RETROGRADE

DESIREE HOLT

Retrograde
ISBN # 978-1-83943-935-3
©Copyright Desiree Holt 2020
Cover Art by Claire Siemaszkiewicz ©Copyright December 2020
Interior text design by Claire Siemaszkiewicz
Totally Bound Publishing

Published in 2020 by Totally Bound Publishing, United Kingdom.

RETROGRADE

Dedication

To all the great SEALs who have passed through my life and inspired this series, and to Margie Hager, friend, faithful beta reader and general all-around best friend in the world. And finally to Maria Connor, my outstanding assistant. I could never make it without you.

Chapter One

Well, didn't this just turn out to be a clusterfuck.

"They're gaining on us," John 'Rocket' Hardin called from the rear of the van.

"I'm pushing this baby as hard as it will go," Matt 'Viper' Roman ground out.

The tension inside the van was so thick they could almost see it. Disaster was always waiting for them around the corner, but Scott 'Blaze' Hamilton knew if anyone could get them to the exfil point, it was Viper. No one could outdrive him.

"Damn it," Blaze swore under his breath.

A previous rescue attempt by another group had failed and put the hostages in jeopardy. That was always when Galaxy was called. When Blaze had done his research, he'd learned that the only reason the hostages were still alive was because the kidnappers needed them to make sure the ransom was paid. At first, it had sounded like a by-the-book rescue. Jim and Nita Rosen, one of America's one-percenter couples with money to burn, had been kidnapped for ransom.

Their daughter, Angela, afraid her parents would be killed if she called in the FBI, had paid it, but the jerkoffs had come back and asked for more.

When the first people she'd hired had botched the job, that was when she'd turned to Galaxy.

For the four highly trained former SEALs, this should have been a simple retrieval. Tapping into every source, they were unhappy to learn that the kidnappers were less than sophisticated. They were offshoots of a cartel whose leader was barely second tier and had big ideas about establishing himself. Kidnapping was his prime source of income while he built up enough of a bank to take on the big cartel chiefs. These people were the most dangerous kind, since they had oversized egos and small brains. The crew who worked for him came from the dregs, which meant things could easily go wrong.

Reaching out to all their contacts, they'd gotten the location where the Rosens were being held—an old warehouse just outside the little town of San Felipe. Only two guards were on duty at any one time, an indication of the kidnappers' stupidity and arrogance. The one good thing was that the so-called brains behind this kidnapping only showed up once a day, about midday, to check on their victims. It certainly sounded like amateur hour to Galaxy, but sometimes those were the ones that went sideways.

After a drive-by to scope the place out and take pictures, the team planned the operation. They would breach the building, grab the Rosens and get the hell out of there in their borrowed van before the leader and the rest of the bad guys showed up for their daily visit.

'Saint' Francis, their official pilot, would be waiting for them at an extraction point with the helicopter.

Easy peasy, right?

Wrong.

As they'd learned in the military, if something can go wrong it will.

FUBAR.

Fucked up beyond all repair.

Especially with kidnappers like these, who were not very smart.

At first, it was smooth sailing. Only one vehicle, an old car, was parked by the warehouse. They knew from their source that this was the one driven by the two men left to guard the Rosens, so they were good to go. Using an infrared scanner, they were able to determine the location inside of the guards — away from the captives, sitting near the entrance to the warehouse. Breaching the door was kindergarten work for them, as was disposing of the guards before the two knew what was happening. They grabbed the Rosens and hustled them out to their waiting van.

Just as 'Viper', their designated wheelman, cranked the engine, a car drove up to the warehouse. Three well-armed and unpleasant-looking men tumbled out, even before the vehicle had come to a stop. One looked to be in charge, pointing at the Galaxy van, and at once the others began shooting at them. They pulled out onto the road before the doors were even fully shut, but the other vehicle was after them at once. Blaze thought there must be a hell of a motor in that thing, because they barely got out to the road before the other vehicle was practically on their tail.

Now they were racing down the two-lane road to the extraction spot with shots from the vehicle behind them peppering the van they were using. It pissed Blaze off that a cheap-ass operation like this one had managed to grab two high-value targets and get away with it. But even more, that best-of-the-best Galaxy was barely escaping a deadly showdown.

"Fuck it all," Viper cursed.

"It's true, you know," Blaze reminded his partners. "The only easy day was yesterday."

"And today will be our last," Rocket snapped at him, "if we let ourselves get beaten by these pieces of shit."

"Never fear. The Viper is here."

Viper was swerving back and forth to avoid the bullets as they sped down the road at a speed that would dry the spit in the mouth of most people.

"Yeah?" Blaze shifted in his seat. "Well, get us the fuck out of here, then."

The Rosens, thankfully following orders without question, were huddled down between the front and middle seats as directed. In the far back seat, John 'Rocket' Hardin and Vic 'Eagle' Bodine had knocked out the glass in the windows and were firing their Glocks at the pursuing vehicle.

"We need more firepower," Blaze said. "They're coming hot and fast."

He lifted his LaRue Tactical AR15 PredatAR rifle and turned so he was kneeling facing the rear. With great care, he balanced the barrel of the rifle on the back of the seat. The Aimpoint red dot optic allowed him to focus more accurately on his target, and he sighted carefully.

Yes!

He zeroed in on the man in the passenger seat. From the brief glimpse when they'd emptied out at the warehouse, he'd pegged him as the leader.

Take out the man at the top and the rest will fall apart.

The vehicle was so close to them he knew that if he hit the driver, the car could jump out of control and rocket into them.

"Heads down," he shouted.

Rocket and Eagle obediently bent forward, allowing Blaze a clear line to his target.

Crack!

The car behind them swerved crazily. It was still close enough that Blaze could see the splintered windshield as well as the blood splatter on the glass. But it still kept coming. *Are they crazy?*

Yes, he answered himself. Or they would never have done this.

He figured the tires were bulletproof, but a well-aimed bullet from his PredatAR could penetrate the special composition of the rubber.

Crack!

Now the car swerved sharply to the right and Blaze saw the flattened rubber. But the damn fucking thing kept on coming. *Shit!* The piece of crap wouldn't die.

Then they were at the rendezvous, the helicopter waiting two hundred yards away with its rotors already turning.

"Get the Rosens to the chopper," Blaze yelled as they rocketed to a stop.

He slid out and shouldered his rifle. Two men piled out of the car behind them, guns drawn, one of the men covered in blood splatters from the dead man. Blaze had thought for sure the idiot thugs would back off, but apparently they were too stupid to know that would be the smart thing to do. As Viper and Rocket hustled the Rosens toward the helo, Blaze took precise aim and fired, taking down another of the kidnappers. The last one stood frozen for a moment. Blaze was already moving toward the chopper, Eagle with his own weapon moving beside him. Then the man lifted his weapon to fire it.

Fucking idiot.

"I got it," Eagle told him. With one well-placed shot, he disposed of the last of the thugs.

Before anyone could arrive to investigate the gunshots, the two men jumped into the chopper and in seconds Saint had them in the air. They were a good fifteen minutes away from San Felipe before either of the Rosens spoke.

"Thank you." Jim Rosen was holding his wife's hand. "I don't know who you are or where you came from, but thanks is such a small word for what you did."

"Yes." Nita Rosen gave a brief nod in agreement. "What Jim said."

Blaze had his first chance to look them over carefully. They seemed to be fairly ordinary people dressed in disheveled but obviously expensive clothing. They also appeared to have somehow kept their shit together during their ordeal, which Blaze knew could destroy a lot of people.

"I'm glad you two are doing okay."

"Okay?" Jim's laugh was anything but humorous. "Trust me. We are far from okay. But we've been through a lot of tough times to get where we are. You learn that keeping it together is the only way to survive."

"The kidnappers weren't very smart," Blaze told them. "And those can be the most dangerous kind."

"Well, thank you again. We owe you a lot."

"We're just glad you're safe now."

Blaze leaned back in his seat, pulled out his cell and texted Angela Rosen that the team had her parents and was on the way back to the hangar. He was more than ready to deliver them to her, get showered, get out on the town and get laid in spades. He'd learned long ago that high-octane sex was a much better mood relaxer than any alcohol on the market. Thank god he knew plenty of women whose drug of choice was no-strings sex.

His cell dinged and he read the message, then sifted to look at the Rosens.

"I texted your daughter, Angela, earlier to let her know you were okay. She just texted back to let me know she's waiting at the hangar."

"Oh." Nina Rosen took a deep breath. "Oh, thank you."

"Yes." Jim nodded. "More thanks. I—" He paused, swallowed. "We are more grateful than you can imagine. And happy that we can come home to our daughter."

Neither of the Rosens said much after that. Blaze was pretty sure the aftereffects of their harrowing experience were finally taking over their bodies and minds. They wouldn't be forgetting this for a long time, if ever. He buckled into the seat next to Saint, his location of choice. Watching the world slip by beneath them helped settle him after one of their missions.

He leaned his head back and closed his eyes, thinking about the night ahead. He'd call Fran as soon as they landed, ready for a night of hot, unrestrained sex. Just as when he'd been an active SEAL, the work came first. When he was on a mission, he was totally focused on it. No distractions. But when the job was done and there was down time, he played as hard as he worked.

Fran was one of few women he felt comfortable with, a woman who made no emotional demands of him and wanted nothing more than a great night and hot, steamy sex. Fran was focused on her own career, as she'd told him the first time they'd had dinner, and she had neither time nor energy to invest in a relationship.

Fine by him. She had a body he could lose himself in, luscious breasts, full lips that knew exactly with to do with his cock, and —

Fuck!

As images flashed through his mind, said cock swelled and tried to push its way through the denim of his fly. He tried to shift without calling attention to himself, but Saint slid a glance at him and laughed.

"Getting a little ahead of yourself there? At least wait until we land."

"Yeah, yeah, yeah," Blaze growled.

"By the way." He glanced over at Blaze. "Your brother called while you were doing the retrieval."

Blaze lifted an eyebrow. His brother seldom called, busy as he was at the hospital. "Nolan? Called you?"

"Texted, actually. Said he wasn't sure if you were around or not but knew I could get hold of you."

"Huh. He's usually too tied up with patients to call during the day. Did he say what he wanted?"

"Just that he gave your number to someone and you should definitely take her case."

That was weird. Nolan never got involved in Galaxy business. The man's position as head of the surgical department took up enormous amounts of his time, although Blaze knew Nolan wouldn't have it any other way. Nor could he imagine who Nolan, in his very conservative world, would have come into contact with that he thought needed Galaxy.

"I don't suppose he gave you a name or anything."

"Yeah, as a matter of fact, he texted me the info." He pointed to the cell phone in a side pocket of his seat. "Go ahead. Look it up. You know the code."

One of the things they had all agreed on from the beginning was how they handled their cell phones. With no landline, by design, they'd purchased the most powerful cells made, phones that they could use to call someone on the ground and maintain a conversation from the air if necessary. They also knew each other's codes. In a high-risk situation, they needed to be able to access one another's information.

Blaze picked the phone up and punched in the code to unlock it, then hit the text icon and found Nolan's.

Hey. Can you pass along to Blaze that a woman named Peyton West will be calling his secret phone? Take good care of her.

Blaze read the message twice.

"That's it? That's all he said?"

Saint nodded. "He called me because he knew the four of you were actively involved with the rescue while all I did was sit my fat ass here in the chopper waiting for you guys."

Blaze chuckled. "That's one way of putting it." He looked at the screen again. "I'll wait until I check with my brother. I wonder if it's anything urgent?"

"Dude." Saint maneuvered the helo into a new flight path. "Everyone who calls you guys is urgent."

Blaze supposed that was true. When the four of them had gathered to celebrate becoming civilians after sixteen years as SEALs, little had they expected that their festive dinner would change their lives so dramatically. But getting a little drunk and buying a hundred dollars' worth of lottery tickets had seemed a good way to celebrate. Who knew they'd win the largest Powerball lottery ever, and wind up with almost one-point-six billion dollars?

Billion!

Blaze's mind still tripped over that every time.

But after the original craziness had settled down, the four of them had realized the sky was now the limit. They could afford their dream, and Galaxy was born. With a Gulfstream 500 that served both as their office and transportation, a luxury cabin cruiser and a small racing boat docked at Viper's home on Davis Islands, they were ready to go anywhere at any time. It suited all of them not to be tied down to regular offices and their type of clientele didn't want a paper trail.

He wondered idly what kind of woman Nolan had connected with and what her story was that he'd felt compelled to give her the phone number. Although he and his brother were close, they were also extremely busy with their own lives. He didn't think any of Nolan's patients were the kind to need Galaxy's services, but of course he never knew. But he was damn curious what had brought about the out-of-character phone call.

After they landed and got the Rosens reunited with their daughter, he'd give his brother a quick shout. If it sounded okay, he'd contact the woman to see what the deal was. Then he'd go home to his luxury townhouse on the water, call Fran and get ready for a night of unequaled sex.

Five minutes later, they touched down at the private airstrip and double hangar they'd built on land they'd bought just north of downtown Tampa. Blaze and Viper helped their passengers out of the chopper and guided them toward where their daughter was waiting on the tarmac. He loved reunion scenes like this. It made everything they did so worthwhile.

They all stood back to give the family room as Angela came running over to them. She wrapped her arms around Eagle, who had been the contact for her, and Blaze thought for a moment she'd drown him in her tears.

"I have no idea how to thank you."

Eagle grinned. "That hug was a pretty good start."

"Well, you'll like this even better. I already called my bank and had your fee transferred to the account you gave me. You just don't know…" She stopped and swallowed hard.

"I do. We all do. Thanks for the prompt payment of the fee." He grinned again. "And the hug."

At last they got everyone to Angela's car, accepted all the thanks and gratitude, and saw the Rosen family off.

"That could have turned to shit," Viper commented.

Eagle nodded. "I know this sounds weird, but I'd rather deal with professional criminals every day. Guys like these are unstable and unpredictable."

"Amen to that."

"You gonna call that woman?" Saint asked, finished now with hangaring the helicopter.

"Yeah. Forward the text to me."

In seconds, his phone dinged with the incoming message.

This is Peyton West. Your brother, Dr. Nolan Hamilton, gave me your number. I have a desperate situation involving my sister and he said if anyone could help, it was you. Please call me.

Her number was included.

For a moment, he was tempted to leave it until tomorrow. But again, he thought how unusual it was for his brother to do this. The woman must be in a very desperate situation.

Swallowing a sigh, he sent a text to his brother.

Is this woman legit?

All the way. Get on board. Please.

Please. Well. Curious to see what had put the bug in Nolan's ear, he tapped in her number. He wasn't prepared for the sound of the voice that answered. Soft, musical, something that vibrated through his blood. But it also held a heavy overlay of desperation.

"This is Peyton West."

"Yeah, this is Blaze Hamilton. You called."

"Oh. Uh, I really need to meet with you. I have a situation that your brother said you could probably handle." Pause. "I have nowhere else to turn."

How many times had he heard that? Galaxy specialized in being the last chance for people, the agency that took jobs no one else could or would do. He wasn't about to ask her for details on the phone. Galaxy clients only delivered information in person.

"Okay. I can book you on a flight tomorrow afternoon. Say one o'clock." Enough time to get his act together after this case. Hot, raunchy sex always did that for him.

Another pause vibrated across the connection. When she spoke, the tightness in her voice was evident.

"If you could make it today, I'd really appreciate it."

Today. Everyone wanted their meeting right now. Everything was an emergency. Sadly, it often was.

"Look, Miss West —" he began.

"No, you look." The musical quality was gone from the voice, replaced by intense need. "My brother-in-law is dead. My sister is in a coma she may never wake up from and everyone from the local police to the FBI are hands-off on the case. You're my last and only hope." She paused. "I have money, if that's the problem. I can pay."

Fuck. Why was everything always so urgent?

Because you and the other guys have made a habit of dealing with urgency. That's what you wanted, right? Right.

He sighed and mentally said goodbye to a night of dirty, raunchy sex. The SEAL in him took over.

"Fine. Okay. We just finished a…situation. Let me check with my pilot and see when he can be ready to go again."

He muted the phone and walked over to Saint, who was leaning against his car, watching.

"I figured I'd better hang around. I can be set again by four this afternoon as long as we make it a short hop."

Blaze nodded. "Thanks, big guy. She sounds desperate."

Saint cocked an eyebrow. "Don't they all?"

Blaze unmuted the phone.

"I'm going to text you an address. Use your GPS to find it. Be here at four sharp."

"I'll see you then." She disconnected.

When Galaxy had been formed, the partners had determined that they did not want a cookie cutter private contractor agency. They wanted the clients no one else would handle. The jobs others turned away from. Maybe it was the adrenaline rush, or the challenges presented by off-the-book situations, or maybe it was just a commitment to keep using the skills they'd learned as SEALs. Whatever it was, they'd become the go-to place for those who had exhausted all other channels.

They'd agreed from the beginning on having no formal office. They didn't want to be confined to a building, hemmed in by the walls. Their meetings would be held where there was no chance of eavesdropping or wiretapping or any other listening device. When they'd bought the Gulfstream 500, they'd outfitted it with every electronic device they might conceivably need. Meetings were held in the air so there was no way anyone could eavesdrop or interrupt.

He drove home to shower and change and run the name of Peyton West through all the databases he had access to. What he found didn't sound any alarms. She'd had three tickets for speeding over the years, but so what? Who didn't have at least one? Not married. Not in a relationship that even his deepest search could find. She lived in Texas—San Antonio—and was a multi-published author of romantic suspense novels set mostly in Texas.

Was she looking for help with a book? Galaxy didn't do that kind of stuff. It made them too visible.

He learned her sister and brother-in-law had recently been in a car accident, hit by a speeding vehicle in front of a hotel. The brother-in-law had been killed and the sister was still in a coma. Blaze vaguely remembered reading about it online when he was idly skimming—just three paragraphs, and there hadn't been anything that rang his chimes. Hit and run, that was it. He hated those, because no one was ever made to answer for it, but nothing had seemed out of the ordinary.

Besides, Galaxy didn't investigate auto accidents. That was what the cops were for. Did that mean she had an overactive imagination and there was little substance to whatever she wanted from him? He mentally shook his head. No, his brother was too much of a pragmatist to send him someone who saw shadows where there were none.

Before he checked further, he decided to reach out to Nolan and get the skinny on Peyton West and her situation. His brother shocked him by having five minutes free at that particular moment.

"She's not a nutcase," he said at once. "This isn't something she made up for one of her novels, I promise you that. This is some serious shit and everyone everywhere is stonewalling her. If you can find out who the driver was, that ought to open up the whole can of worms. But I believe her, Blaze."

He couldn't ask for better validation than that.

He was waiting when the black sedan headed down the gravel drive exactly at four o'clock and parked by the hangar. All four of them tried not to prejudge clients before interacting with them. Appearances, as they all knew, could be very deceiving. But the woman who exited the Mercedes, tense and buttoned-up as she was, made every bit of saliva in his mouth dry up.

She was of medium height, the slacks and sweater she wore doing little to disguise the mouthwatering curves of her body or the natural sway of her hips as she walked. Thick, glossy chestnut hair was pulled back tightly into a ponytail. When she came close enough, he could see her eyes were a rich dark green that looked out at him from beneath chocolate lashes. Out of nowhere, he was seized with a desire to strip off her clothes and run his hands over her body.

Dickwad! Asshole!

Where the hell had this come from, anyway, and what the fuck was wrong with him? He never, ever reacted to clients like this. He'd better get his shit together in a hurry. And figure out why he had lost his brain somewhere on the tarmac.

But then his common sense caught up with him. He saw the rigid way she controlled herself, the look of strain etched into her face and the mixture of rage and panic that swirled in her eyes. It was a look he'd seen in so many of the clients who came to Galaxy. And that was enough to make his hungry dick, the one that had been looking forward to some action tonight, deflate in a hurry. This was business. A mission. This was what they did. What she was here for. Thank god for his SEAL discipline.

He held out a hand to her. "Scott Hamilton, but please, call me Blaze. We're all used to our military code names."

They had decided to use those with clients, since they addressed each other that way and there'd be less confusion.

"Peyton West. I have a desperate need for your help, and I can't stress that word enough."

He nodded toward the plane, waiting in front of the hangar. "All right. Let's take a little flight to nowhere and you can tell me all about it."

Chapter Two

Peyton studied the man waiting for her as she walked toward the plane with him. When Dr. Nolan Hamilton had given Peyton his brother's phone number, she hadn't been sure what she'd expected when she called. He hadn't told her a lot about his brother's company, just that they were an unorthodox group of men, all former SEALs, who did things no one else wanted to touch. That they took jobs no one else would, jobs often conducted in a thick cloud of secrecy. Whatever problem she was wrestling with, he was damn sure that if anyone could help her, it was them.

She sure as hell hoped so, because at the moment she was convinced her life was in retrograde. Yeah, retrograde. Literally meaning 'backward step'. She knew it usually referred to a planet moving backward, and that was exactly what everything seemed to be like at this point in time.

Driving to this meeting, the past few weeks had raced through her mind like a movie on steroids. An unsolved hit-and-run had left her brother-in-law dead and her sister in a coma from which she might never emerge. Peyton's publisher was not happy with her latest book and her editor was pushing for major revisions. Of course, the last situation was at the bottom of her list of important things. She was sure ignoring phone calls and sending cryptic messages would probably end up with her contract being yanked, but she couldn't worry about that now. It was the least important thing in her life.

She was pissed off and terrified at the same time. It was bad enough that Dane and Brianne had been victims of such a deliberate crime, but worse that the police were not only acting as if they had no leads but didn't seem to be doing anything about it. She could smell money and political pressure scattered through everything. Too bad for whoever that was. She damned well wasn't going to allow people to sweep this under the rug while verbally patting her on the head and expressing fake sorrow.

So, just as when she plotted a book, she had made a plan, an outline, then attacked this problem and gotten...nowhere. She felt like some avenging angel, but one that needed help breaking down doors. After three investigative agencies she'd approached had turned her down, she knew that what she needed were people not afraid of anyone or anything.

And every hour she wasn't fighting this battle, she sat beside her sister and talked to her, hoping and praying that something would elicit a reaction. An eyelid tic. A muscle twitch. Anything at all. And the continued lack of response only made her angrier and more desperate.

When Dr. Hamilton had approached her about some possible help, she'd had many questions. Who were these people, anyway, who had their office in a plane?

What kind of men were they? What was his brother like? Nolan, as he'd suggested she call him, had given her one of his rare smiles and pointed out that the kind of clients they had wanted everything under the radar. Galaxy was usually the client's last resort, he'd told her, and covert was the best description of what they did.

Well, she was certainly looking for all that. The more she'd asked questions on her own and the more people had resisted her, the more convinced she'd become that at least one of them — Dane or Brianne — had deliberately been targeted.

While she'd waited for her call-back, she'd done a search for information about them. It was better to learn as much as possible about the people she was meeting, but the web was devoid of information about Galaxy. She'd then turned to finding out as much as she could about SEALs. It was critical that the people she hired fit all the qualifications. She'd learned they were an elite Special Operations Force, warriors trained in, among other things, counterterrorism. That they completed assignments against the worst possible odds and they did not know the meaning of defeat. *Well, okay, then.* Just what she was looking for, although she didn't necessarily think counterterrorism entered into it.

Then she'd thought, but who knows? Something was very wrong here and it could be anything.

Watching Scott Hamilton walk across the tarmac to meet her, she knew at once he was exactly what she was looking for. He was the very image of what she'd imagined a SEAL to be, a seasoned veteran, a warrior with a take-charge attitude and a quiet air of power and confidence. Nothing would deter this man from completing his mission. He might as well have been wearing a T-shirt that said *Don't fuck with me.*

Her instincts, which she liked to think were good, told her he was a man who meant business. Who didn't shy away from trouble but gave it in spades. A man whose enemies feared him. That was exactly what she needed. Someone not afraid of anyone.

"Mr. Hamilton." She nodded at him. "Blaze."

She certainly wasn't prepared for his overwhelmingly powerful presence, the sheer aura of masculinity and control — and, yes, the sexual magnetism — that radiated from him. She judged him to be over six feet with a lean, muscular body, a face marked by a square jaw and high cheekbones, a well-trimmed scruff of beard and a nose that looked as if it had once been broken. Maybe more than once. Whiskey-colored eyes looked out at her from beneath lashes a shade darker than the thick head of black hair. He was like a glass of smooth, fine whiskey with a sharp bite to it.

And oh, god, she felt as if she'd been bitten, and her body reacted accordingly. When he took her hand, her nipples hardened into tight peaks and the pulse between her thighs set up a wild throbbing. She had the wildest urge to strip off both their clothes and attack him right here on the runway. *Damn!* That definitely was not her. And sex was the last thing she should be thinking about in this situation. She had to focus on what had happened to Dane and Brianne, and was willing to do anything to get the answers she wanted.

The image of her brother-in-law's body and Brianne's pale face came alive in her brain, reminding her there was no time to think about sex right now. She needed to focus on why she was here. She had a mission to complete and she hoped these men would help her. After all the doors slammed in her face, she needed someone who wasn't afraid of political fallout.

Blaze gestured toward the plane and followed her up the pulldown stairs into the cabin. She'd never had a meeting like this before and certainly hadn't flown in style like this. Commercial first class was nothing compared to the absolute luxury of the Gulfstream 500. From the way the interior was outfitted, it was obvious no expense had been spared. She marveled at the rich scent and feel of the padded leather of the seats, the thick carpet on the floor, the polished mahogany of the trim and the built-in tables, the damask curtains on the windows. It was like having a meeting in someone's living room.

They certainly must make a boatload of money doing whatever they do. I hope I can afford them.

Nolan hadn't mentioned their fees and she'd been so excited that she might have found someone who wouldn't be stonewalled in the search for the truth that she hadn't asked. *Well, no matter.* She knew she'd somehow find whatever she needed to pay these people.

And to that end, if she really wanted their help, she'd damn well better control her unexpected and unwanted impulses. Blaze Hamilton probably had women climbing all over him. And much sexier women than she was. She'd do well to remember that.

"Take any seat where you think you'll be comfortable," he urged, gesturing. "I'll be back in a minute. I just need a second with my pilot."

"Of course." She chose one of the upholstered armchairs and settled herself into its softness.

Blaze strode forward to the cockpit, then after just a few minutes rejoined her. She'd thought he'd take the seat across from her, but instead he dropped to the couch against the other cabin wall. His presence dominated the confined space, making her feel as if he consumed nearly all the air. Before she could analyze what she was feeling, however, the roar of the powerful engines increased and they were rolling down the runway. She took a deep breath, telling herself to settle down and get her thoughts in order. Once they were aloft, she'd have one chance to tell her story and convince Galaxy to take her case. She'd better make it good.

Blaze smiled at her, the curve of his lips like a warm blanket, easing her tension just the least little bit. "We'll have coffee as soon as we're at cruising altitude and maybe you can relax a little. Then we can talk about why you're taking this plane ride."

"Thank you. And thanks for agreeing to meet with me."

He dipped his head in a brief nod. "My brother never recommends anyone to us, so I figured it had to be very important."

"It is." She wanted to blurt it all out now, but she knew he'd let her know her when he was ready to listen.

"Do you live in Tampa?"

She shook her head. "San Antonio. But my sister and brother-in-law live here." *Maybe lived, past tense, would be more appropriate,* she thought.

"You said this has to do with them?"

"It has everything to do with them."

If she weren't so focused on the situation she was here to talk about, how easily she could be seduced by that voice, she thought. It was deep and husky, the kind that made a delicious shiver race over her skin. It shocked her that in the middle of this unbelievable crisis, such thoughts would even enter her mind. She certainly wasn't here for sex, something that had been absent from her life for longer than she cared to remember. She was here for Brianne. And Dane. To get answers and, hopefully, punish the people who had done this. She'd just have to keep her brain focused and her panties on tight.

She was restless, fidgety, eager to begin the conversation but forced to wait until they reached cruising altitude. At last the pilot's voice broke the silence.

"Blaze? We're at thirty thousand feet."

Blaze unbuckled his seat belt and rose with an easy grace. "That's our cue. Coffee? Or something stronger? Wine?"

"Coffee is fine," she told him. "Black, please."

He lifted a table from a slot in the wall, turned it and her chair so she faced the couch and locked it in place.

"Let me know if you need to adjust this thing. I'm more comfortable if I take the couch. Easier to stretch my legs. Hope you don't mind."

"No, of course not. Anything is fine. Truly."

I don't care if you stand on your head as long as I can tell you what I need.

He strode to the back of the cabin, where she assumed the galley was. She spent the intervening moments until he returned organizing her thoughts. Not that she needed much time. Since Nolan Hamilton had given her his brother's number, her brain had been focused on nothing but the situation and how she'd present it.

"Miss West?"

She looked up to see Blaze standing beside her chair, holding two cups of steaming liquid.

"Oh. Thank you."

She wondered if he noticed that her hands had a faint tremble as she took the coffee from him. She needed to keep it together here. So much depended on him agreeing to help her. Otherwise, she had nowhere to turn. Dane would have died for nothing, and Brianne might never awaken from her coma.

Stop. Think positive.

He lowered himself to the couch and sat facing her, then took a swallow of coffee.

"I Googled you this afternoon."

"No less than I expected." She tried to smile. "Good thing I don't have any deep dark secrets."

He laughed and the sound warmed her chilled body. "Not unless you count being a successful published author one."

"Hardly. And before we start, please understand this isn't something I'm embroidering with my creative mind. This is very real."

"We'll see." He crossed his legs. "Anyway, after I ran the check on you, I called my brother. It doesn't appear that you're nuts or a scam artist and he speaks very well of you, so why don't you tell me why Nolan thought you needed to get in touch with me? Galaxy only takes cases that either no one else will touch or the authorities have screwed up in some way. Something that needs our particular skills. Is that what we're looking at here?"

"I'm pretty sure I fit the bill." She fortified herself with another sip of coffee before setting the cup down.

Make it good, she told herself.

"Let me start with the last Skype conversation I had with my sister. She told me Dane had been very tense and edgy the past couple of weeks. She thought it may have had something to do with some pictures she took that she showed him. Pictures that Owen Kendrick, the son of the senior partner in the law firm where Dane worked, was in. He had her forward the pictures to his phone, but he hadn't said a word about it since then.

He kept brushing it off when she mentioned it, even though she could see he was upset."

"Did he ever explain to her?"

Peyton shook her head. "No, and that surprised me. They didn't have the kind of relationship where they hid things from each other."

"There's always a first time," Blaze pointed out.

"No. Not with them."

She had always envied their marriage, the connection they'd had and the unrestrained love they'd felt for each other. Her own life was devoid of anything like that. She had just been too busy with her writing and dealing with everything that went with growing success to spend time on a relationship. Oh, she never lacked for dates if she wanted them, and she'd even had her share of interesting sex. She'd never, though, even come close to the connection Dane and Brianne had had. Mostly, she figured, because she hadn't been looking.

"I'm sure if I could ever find out what Dane was bothered about, I'd have the answer. I just feel that's a priority. It's got to be connected with the hit-and-run." She paused, organizing her thoughts. "I mean, think about it. For me to be shortstopped at every turn is an indication, at least to me, that some pretty powerful people wanted Dane eliminated and his death swept under the rug."

"I'm not saying no to that. Not yet, anyway."

"I need someone who knows how to conduct investigations like this as much under the radar as possible. None of the people who have been so busy covering up their shit can be tipped off until I have the proof I need."

"Tell me about the incident."

"At least you didn't call it an accident like everyone else." She blew out a breath, steadying herself again. She wished she could get a better read on this man. Was he buying this? "Okay. Three weeks ago, on a Friday night, my sister, Brianne, and her husband, Dane, were having a late dinner at a favorite restaurant. Relaxing, I guess. Anyway, after they'd eaten, they were crossing the road from the restaurant to the lot where their car was parked. A vehicle came out of nowhere and ran them both down."

"Jesus!" Blaze blew out a breath.

Jesus is right. At least she now knew she had his attention.

"Dane is dead and Brianne is in the hospital with a broken leg and arm, and in a coma she may never wake up from."

She watched his face for some reaction. God, this was like trying to read a blank page.

"That's both unfortunate and sad, but not exactly the type of case Galaxy takes on."

"If I told you there was something weird about the whole thing, would you be more interested?"

"Maybe. Depends how weird, and why the police aren't handling it."

Okay, so he wasn't ready to commit to anything yet. But she hadn't given him all the facts.

"When Peter Kendrick, the senior partner at Dane's law firm, called me to tell me about my sister, I jumped on the first plane I could get. Our parents are dead, so Brianne and I only have each other. Of course, she has Dane." She paused to take a breath. "*Did* have. Damn it. Anyway, that was all he told me except for the name of the hospital. Said he was sure Brianne would want me to be there. Damn straight she would."

"That's sad and depressing, and I'm sorry for your loss, but it still doesn't sound like anything that needs our attention."

"I'm getting there. That's only the beginning." She swallowed some coffee and gathered her thoughts.

"Take your time."

"Does this flight have a time limit?"

He gave her a reassuring smile. "Yes, but we aren't even close."

"Good. When I got to Tampa, of course I went right to the hospital. I nearly lost it when I saw my vital, bubbly sister lying in bed with a broken arm and leg and barely a breath of life. She had not yet regained consciousness, which scared the hell out of me. I just broke down. I couldn't help it."

"Understandable."

"Then I got my shit together, if you'll excuse my language. After I made sure Brianne was getting the care she should, I called Dane's parents to offer my condolences. Questioning them was hard, but they didn't know anything more than I did."

She had to stop for a moment. She made her living from words, but this was incredibly hard for her to describe.

Blaze just sat on the couch, waiting for her to continue.

"They said the funeral would be in a few days. I promised them I'd be there. They were just so upset that they couldn't wait for Brianne. After we got through that disaster, I found out which police station had taken the call and went to get a copy of the report. That's when it got interesting."

He dipped his head once. "Go ahead."

"The report wasn't in the computer. Everything goes in the computer, right? At least I assumed so. They told me the cop writing it up probably still had all the notes on his desk. And no, he wasn't in at the moment."

Blaze arched an eyebrow. "So you never saw the information?"

"Only after three days of making a pest of myself. Then they told me it had finally been entered, but the damn information is so sketchy it tells you nothing. First of all, they were still trying to find the car and its driver. They said they had conflicting descriptions and they were all hazy anyway. It happened so suddenly, they told me. It was late at night when Dane and Brianne were crossing the street from the restaurant where they'd had dinner."

"And?"

"The report said there were a few people on the sidewalk at the restaurant entrance, plus the man who ran the parking lot across from the place. But everyone had a different story. Yes, they heard Brianna scream, but it all happened *so fast*! No, they have no details. The car was gone before anyone realized what had happened."

"Was there any description of the car at all? Any identification of the driver? License plate, at least?"

"If only. I kept asking the traffic cop who talked to me, but I might as well have saved my breath. Yes," she recited, "they checked the traffic cams and no, they hadn't found the car. They put out a call for it, but they believed it was long gone. Someplace. Someplace? Give me a break."

"And no trace of the driver, I'm guessing."

"That's what they told me. I went back twice to see that cop and find out if he'd learned anything, but that was a dead end. Every time I went there after that first time, I was told he was gone. Off for a week, they said. Not available."

"Off. Yeah, that sounds weird."

"Especially when I got the feeling they'd closed the case and moved on from it. No car, no driver, shaky witnesses. Bam. Done."

Something flickered in Blaze's eyes and Peyton was sure she'd caught his attention now.

"What did you do after that?" he urged. "I'm guessing you didn't stop there."

"Absolutely. I asked again about witnesses and was told they'd been no help. The traffic detectives had questioned everyone and assured me they were very thorough. However, the stories were all mixed. Different people remembered different things."

"That's not unusual in a situation like this," Blaze pointed out. "Especially if it happens very quickly. People aren't prepared to see something like that, and by the time their brain catches up with their eyesight, it's over and done with."

"That's what the policeman said. He told me it was like blowing in the wind. People said it happened so fast they didn't get a good look. Some people said the car was brown, others gray and one even said she thought it was black."

Blaze shrugged. "So basically, they have nothing."

"Right," she agreed. "The next thing I did was track down the paramedic who had been called to the scene. The one who took Brianne to the hospital. Blaze, she got very nervous. Said if the cops told her no one saw anything, then no one did. Her whole attention was focused on Brianne. Then she excused herself in a hurry and said she had to get ready for her shift."

"Okay." Blaze nodded. "What did you do next? You don't strike me as someone who'd just let something like this go."

"You're right. I didn't. After that I went to see Peter Kendrick, the senior partner in the law firm Dane was with. As I told you, he's the one who made the calls to Dane's parents and me after it happened. I had thought for sure he'd be able to get some information. Get them to at least question everyone again. He's very well connected, both in the corporate world and politically. Even all the way to Washington."

"Was he able to help you?"

"Far from it." She scowled. "Oh, at first he was very solicitous, very concerned. Promised he'd check into it. But the next time we talked, he told me he wasn't able to find out anything more than I had. Agreed with me this was a terrible disaster. How awful that it happened so fast no one was able to give a good description of the car. And wasn't it terrible that the traffic cam videos blurred so there was no clear picture of the car or driver. I was shocked when, after he apologized, he urged me to drop it. Said the firm was saddened by the tragedy and disappointed at the lack of information, but the important thing for me was to concentrate on my sister. To help her get well."

"Did you get the feeling he's involved in whatever this is?"

A bitter taste flooded her mouth. "At this point I think everyone's involved. I told him thanks for his efforts, but I wasn't about to let it go."

"What did he say to that?"

"He got very testy with me. Told me the police can get nasty if you doubt their word and they could make my life miserable. Repeated that he'd talked to them and whoever did this is in the wind. Again, he said I should concentrate on Brianne and praying she comes out of this coma. That she had a long road ahead of her if she did and she'd need me with her. That's where my energy should be, not on chasing some wild-ass theory."

"Do either the restaurant or the parking lot have outside security cameras?"

She nodded. "Both of them. The cops assured me, and not too pleasantly, I might add, they looked at both videos, but the car was a blur and the cameras didn't catch the license plates."

"Okay." He studied her face as he spoke. "Let me see if I've got this straight. A car comes racing down a street at a time when it's pretty deserted. And even though the victims had just walked out of a restaurant and there's a parking lot across the street, the car hits two people and not a soul has any details."

"That's correct." She rubbed her forehead, trying to stave off the beginning of a headache. "Believe me, I was plenty skeptical, too, but the more I asked, the more irritated they got."

Telling the story always made her edgy and upset. She wished she had something stronger to drink than coffee. It would also help a lot if she could read Blaze Hamilton better and judge his reaction. She was sure his years as a SEAL had taught him how to keep his face expressionless, but she needed to know what he was thinking.

"Have you spoken to anyone else?"

"I tried talking to the people who work at the restaurant, but they were as skittish and distant as everyone else. They gave their reports to the cops and that's all they know. And no, they couldn't give me the names of any customers without their permission. They are very sorry and wish they could be more help." She snorted. "Yeah, right."

Blaze cocked an eyebrow. "I have to admit, this definitely sounds more than a little weird."

"I had all that trouble getting a copy of the police report. When I did, I was stunned that it had nothing of use in it." She rubbed her forehead. "They must think I am very dumb."

"I agree what they told you is a crock of shit."

"That's why I wouldn't leave it alone. As a matter of fact, they weren't even going to print out a copy of the report for me until I threatened to get an attorney. I mean, a traffic accident report? Get real. Here. Tell me what you think of it. My grocery list gives more information." She took it out of her purse and handed it to him, watching as he studied it in silence.

He shook his head. "This tells you nothing. Did you point that out?"

"I might as well have saved my breath. They kept saying they were very sorry but that was all the information they had. They're very good at expressing condolences but not so much at giving straight answers." She took a deep, calming breath. Falling apart wouldn't help this situation. "Dane was buried the week after I got here. We had to have his funeral without Brianne there."

"That's tough."

"As I mentioned earlier, Dane's parents couldn't wait any longer. They were just so destroyed by the whole thing and no one knows if or when my sister will wake from the coma. They needed to bury their son. His father wanted to sue the police, but I think it was just empty talk on his part."

"Do they live here?" Blaze asked.

"South of here, in Sarasota. They took Dane back there to be buried because—" Peyton stopped and pulled in a breath. "Because obviously no one knows at this point if my sister will even wake up or what shape she'll be in. It was so depressing going through the house with them so they could pick out clothes for him to be buried in." She rubbed her face. "I don't think I'll ever get the memories of that funeral out of my mind. And how am I going to tell Brianne if we're lucky and she does come out of this?"

If only she could wake up and this was all a very bad dream.

"They have to be devastated."

"They are. Apparently, they were very close. I insisted they take the time to pick out any of his things they wanted to keep as mementos, but they said they'd wait for Brianne. They were sure she'd want a lot of his things."

"That was very kind of them."

"They're very nice people," she agreed.

"So no one's followed up on it since then?" Blaze asked the question again. "The police aren't doing any more?"

"You're kidding, right?" She waved a hand in the air. "They're pissed off at me and just want to be done with the whole thing. They have no way to identify the driver because the pictures are blurry. They did their best, everyone is sorry, but just go away and leave them alone. According to the report, there wasn't even anyone who could describe the car. If they interviewed anyone, they all had to be stupid or brainless or…" She lifted her hands in a helpless gesture, then let them drop.

"Or bought off," Blaze finished for her.

"That's what I'm thinking."

She narrowed her eyes. "If you ask me, I think there's a huge conspiracy in place here. A big coverup. But I'm just one person with little power, which is why I can't get anywhere."

He was quiet for a moment, studying her. "You may be right. A hot young attorney gets run down, he dies, and his wife is left in a coma. You'd think people would be burning the midnight oil to find whoever did it."

"Yes." His tone of voice had been very noncommittal. "You'd think."

"I take it you're not leaving it alone, though."

She shook her head. "No, nor do I intend to. I want justice for my sister. And for Dane. That may be all I can ever give her from now on." She set the empty coffee cup on the tray table.

"I understand."

"What would you do if you were me?" She paused, as if gathering herself. "This is the situation. No one can identify the driver. Nobody has come forward with any information except the paramedic, who gave it very reluctantly. Now she seems to have disappeared, along with the traffic cop. And everyone from the police to the law firm Dane worked for keeps telling me to focus on getting my sister well and letting Dane rest in peace. Don't create stories where there aren't any."

Blaze took a swallow of coffee then set the cup down.

"I'm sure I'm not the first person you've come to about this. Galaxy is rarely first in line on anything."

"You get the impossibles, right? But yes, I tried to hire three different private investigators, all with excellent references and credentials. Each one in turn said they'd check into it, then after just a few days returned my retainer. They politely assured me Tampa has an excellent police force that had done its work and was as baffled by the situation as everyone else. Of course, they didn't mention who the 'everyone else' is. They just said sometimes things like this happen, they were sorry about Dane and I should concentrate on helping my sister get better. Same old, same old."

Needing to do something with her hands, she picked up her coffee cup to take a sip, but all that was left were dregs, so she set it back down.

Blaze was silent for a long moment while he studied the report in his hands.

Peyton would have given every penny in her purse and then some to know what he was thinking at that moment.

"What still puzzles me, just as it confuses you," he said at last, "is how not one person could accurately describe the car. I know it happened fast, but not everyone is shell-shocked stupid. Someone had to see something that registered, even if just for a few seconds. You said there were others leaving the restaurant, plus the guy in the parking lot. Why wasn't anyone suspicious at the similarities in the stories? I can understand a couple of people not looking into it, but all of them? The more I think about it, the more I get the idea there's more going on here that we don't know."

"That's the thing that keeps eating at me. And believe me, it's not for my lack of trying to get answers. I think if I showed up at the police station again or pestered — well, tried to pester — city officials, they might have me arrested."

"How much of this does Nolan know?"

She shrugged. "Probably more than I should have told him. We talked several times whenever he came in to check on Brianne. Or maybe I should say I ran off at the mouth. I spent a lot of time in the chair next to my sister's bed and he was the only other human I saw for more than two minutes at a time. He's a good listener."

"That he is. The reason I ask is because it's unusual for him to send someone to me. He must have really connected with your sister and the situation."

"I think he did." She nodded. "He's really great. Very caring. Very patient-oriented. I think he gave me your number after seeing me sit beside her bed for so many hours and destroying myself because nothing about the accident made sense and nothing was being done. That's where I am at the moment and why I'm here."

Peyton leaned back, limp, as if all the air had suddenly left her body. She'd been carrying this with her from the moment she'd walked into the hospital and seem Brianne lying in bed, so still, barely breathing. Rage and shock had helped her keep it together so far, along with a need to be strong for her sister and Dane's parents. But sitting here, in the ultimate in luxury aircraft, with a man who was her last hope, she felt herself fraying badly around the edges.

She studied Blaze Hamilton's face, trying to read what was going through his mind. Did he think she was a nutcase? Obsessive? Imagining things? A maniac chasing ghosts? She'd exhausted all her options. If he said no to her, she had no idea where she'd go next.

He rose and lifted her coffee cup. "Let me get you a refill."

Was he softening her up to tell her no? In any event, she realized she needed the caffeine to keep herself going. When he was seated on the couch again, holding his own cup, he studied her again for a long moment. She was ready to jump out of her skin but forced herself to sit still and wait out Blaze Hamilton's silent assessment of her.

"I'm so tired of banging my head against a wall trying to get information. And angry. I am so damn angry." She accepted the fresh coffee. "I just want to get at the truth. Is that so wrong of me?"

Blaze shook his head. "Not at all. Everyone deserves the truth."

"There's one other thing. I don't know if it relates to this at all." She told him about Dane and the pictures Brianne had taken. "All she said was he thought he might know the people, but he wasn't sure. Now I'm thinking those photos might somehow figure in all of this. But I have no idea who was in those shots, where they were taken and why, and my sister never mentioned it again."

"She's a commercial photographer, right? Maybe it had to do with one of her clients."

"Maybe." She shrugged. "But why would it upset Dane?"

"Good question. And she never mentioned it again?"

"No. Not a word. Well, that's it. That's all I can tell you." She took a slow sip of the coffee, pulled herself together and studied him. "What do you think?"

He leaned forward, a serious expression on his face, his intent gaze on her. In the telling of her story, she'd forgotten for the moment how electric his presence was and how her body responded. What an inappropriate time for her sleeping hormones to decide to wake up. She just hoped he wouldn't notice, since she was doing her best to control herself as she waited for his answer.

"I think you got royally screwed," he said at last. "I did a search on the accident and found very little on it. Dane's obituary was longer than the news items."

"I know, right? Weird, although it wasn't the biggest news item of the week."

"Just another part of the puzzle. I think—no, strike that—I'm sure we're going to sign you on as a client.

Something stinks to high heaven here and going through regular channels accomplishes nothing, as you've found out. If someone is covering something up, especially if they've been paid to do it, that's a hard wall to break through. The thing is to find out why."

"So, you'll take this on? Nolan also said you and your partners really like to cherry pick your cases."

"We do because we can afford to. We decided that right from the beginning. I'll have to run this past them, but we have never turned away a client when one of us gave approval. We know what kind of cases all of us will get into."

Relief surged through her. She had to restrain herself from throwing her arms around him. Then she remembered her other concern.

"This will sound stupid, but I have no idea what your fees are. Nolan didn't tell me and I was just so glad he was sending me to someone who might help me, I didn't even think to ask. I can handle anything reasonable." She flashed a tiny grin. "Or even unreasonable, as long as it's not too far over the line. I do quite well as a published author, but—"

He held up a hand. "We can negotiate to whatever you're comfortable with. We won't bankrupt you. I can promise you that. We're lucky to be in a situation where we can be flexible now and then. And you definitely need our help. That's obvious. Something smells to hell here, and I want to find out what it is."

"Thank you." She wetted her lips. "I can't tell you—"

He shook his head. "No need to. But we have some work to do. I'm going to get some fresh pastries from the galley. And would you like wine rather than coffee? I'm sure telling the story again took a lot out of you."

"Thank you again. And yes, wine would be nice. But..." She paused. "We're going to talk up here?"

His grin would have turned her inside out if she weren't such an emotional wreck.

"Best place for an office. No one can overhear anything. Let me fetch the goodies and we'll get started."

Chapter Three

Blaze studied the woman across from him as she slowly chewed the pastry and sipped her wine. At first blush, he'd assumed she was like any other uptight client facing an emergency that they needed help to handle. She looked so tightly strung, struggling to keep it together, he was afraid she might break apart at any moment. But then he took a closer look and saw that along with the fine tension running through her was a healthy dose of anger. He was sure it was the latter that made her posture so rigid, even seated, and the muscles in her jaw so tight he thought the bone would crack. There was definitely a lot more to this story than she'd told him, otherwise Nolan wouldn't have sent her to him. He'd have to ease it out of her little by little, put the pieces together.

This wasn't exactly a high-concept case like a hostage rescue or finding a company executive who'd disappeared along with a hefty portion of company funds. But they'd decided at the outset that they'd consider cases where the usual avenues either didn't work or had already been explored with no results. This was even worse, because it looked like there was a massive coverup.

He had a really bad feeling about it. On the surface, someone could write it off as a drunk losing control and not even registering two people crossing in front of him. If that was the case, why not pursue it further, find the drunk driver and stick him in jail? Cops didn't write off hit and run as a practice. Oh, sure, it took a lot more work, especially if no one had any idea who the driver was. Still, Blaze had seen situations with less information than this being pursued.

If this turned out to be a massive coverup, he could be sure there was power and money involved and people who would stop at nothing to protect what was theirs. How in the fucking hell did someone like Peyton West and her family get mixed up in that kind of stew?

Just to complicate things, he was still fighting the attraction that had blasted through him the moment he saw her. It wasn't just unprofessional. It was completely unexpected and he had to figure out a way to deal with it. Here was where he hoped his SEAL discipline would help him, because he seemed to be on the verge of breaking his own rules. He hadn't been this close to losing his discipline since he was sixteen years old. He was just damn glad his partners couldn't see him now. They'd yank his balls out and roll them down the runway. No playing with the clients was a hard-and-fast rule.

Shit.

A little color had come into her face now and her hands were a little steadier. He'd been afraid when she unclenched them each time she picked up the coffee cup that she'd drop it, but the wine was settling her. Nolan had told him he was not optimistic about the outcome for the sister, but he was trying everything he could think of to bring her out of the coma.

Blaze refilled Peyton's wineglass.

"First things first. Each of us has the ability to accept a client, and whoever brings in the case is the lead on it. That means you'll be working primarily with me. I hope that's okay."

"Of course." She frowned. "Why wouldn't it be?"

"Just checking." He opened his phone to the notes section. "I hate making you go through all of this again, but—"

She held up her hand. "I'll tell it a hundred times if it means you can find out who did this and make them pay."

"That's what we do." He gave her what he hoped was a reassuring smile. "Okay, let's go back before that night. It would be too easy to write this off as some crazy drunk behind the wheel of a car. If that was the case, everyone wouldn't be trying so hard to cover it up. No, there has to be an underlying reason for this whole thing. Tell me about Dane. What kind of law does he practice? And how long has he been doing it?"

"Trial law. Litigation. And ten years. Since he graduated from law school."

"Where did he get his degree?

Blaze knew that type of law could lead to any number of complicated situations. It could be manipulated in any number of ways. Someone who specialized in it certainly knew the ins and outs. What he needed to find out was if Dane Hollister was a straight arrow or someone who could be persuaded to bend the law with the promise of hefty rewards. And if that had gotten him in trouble.

Was that where the problem was? Did he have a client with some funky business that he had maybe double-crossed?

"Do you know much about his clients? Anything at all?"

The look she gave him was apologetic but uncomfortable. "It just wasn't a subject we discussed."

Blaze shrugged. "No, it's about what I expected. I figured if you knew more about his clients, something might have rung a bell and you'd mention it."

"I'm not much help. I didn't really get into that whenever I visited him and Brianne and I never discussed Dane's clients. I mean, why would we, right?"

"I don't know." Blaze shrugged again. "Maybe if the three of you were having dinner or something when you visited. He might have mentioned something."

"Oh! Yes. A couple of times we ran into a client of Dane's, only I couldn't tell you much about them. I just didn't pay much attention. He did say one time that the firm handled litigation for some pretty high-profile clients." A tiny sigh escaped her lips. "I guess I'm not much help."

"I'll take anything I can get. I wonder if those photos Brianne shot involved any of the firm's clientele? Dane's, specifically."

She frowned as she nibbled her lower lip. "I wish I knew."

Blaze was shocked to feel his balls tighten at the sight of it. *What the fuck?* Maybe he should have gone out and gotten laid before doing this, but his discipline had never failed him before. Today it was taunting him.

"No," she said at last. "I'm sorry. It just wasn't a subject that came up. I had the feeling that when he was away from the office, he didn't want to discuss anything."

"That's okay. There are other ways to get that information."

Peyton cocked her head. "You think there's something with one of his clients that could be at the base of this?"

"I don't think anything yet. I'm just trying to get as much information as I can so I have an idea where to start digging. Tell me about their social life."

"Social life?"

"Peyton. I truly believe that whoever did this has to have a connection with Dane somewhere, somehow. The two places people make connections like that are work and socializing."

"Okay, let me think." She nibbled her lip again, the unconscious habit driving him crazy. "Whenever I visited them, the three of us usually went out to dinner. A couple of times, we were joined by another couple. I swear, though, they didn't talk about anything that sent up flags. Mostly sports, events they attended, stuff like that. Both guys were big sports junkies."

And on it went. But at the end of two hours, he realized he'd have to go way back and dig heavily into Dane Hollister's life. Track what he did at work, which could be a bitch since so much would be confidential. And shit like this could be twisted and complicated and have its roots in something years ago. He squeezed every drop of information out of Peyton that she had in her brain before closing out his Notes app.

"I'll need to go through all this, put it in some kind of order and find the best starting place." He leaned forward. "There's no telling how far in the past the beginning of this might be, but I'll dig until I find it. Did you program my number into your phone?"

"I did." She wetted her lips.

The sight of her tongue just peeping out made his cock cry out for relief.

Jesus Christ, Hamilton. This is a client. You better go stick your dick in the freezer.

But there was something so appealing about Peyton West, so tempting, something that affected more than his cock. And that was the last thing he needed to think about right now. *Where was he? Phone number. Right.*

"And I've got yours."

"I'm easy to find, anyway. I'm either at the hospital or the hotel." She rattled off the name of one familiar to him.

"I'm surprised you're not staying at your sister's house."

"I wouldn't be comfortable there. I'm fine at the hotel, and it's close to the hospital, where I spend most of my time anyway."

He pushed himself off the couch. "I'll tell Saint he can land us now. As soon as we're down, I'm going to get on with some research, starting with your brother-in-law and his law firm. Tomorrow morning I'll hit the police station in the area where the accident occurred."

"You really think Dane is somehow mixed into what happened?"

"I don't think anything yet, but I'm going to look at every single thing."

"Whatever you think best. This is what you do."

He nodded. "Yes, it is. And I'll do it as fast as I can."

"Speed isn't important." Sadness washed over her face. "Dane isn't going anywhere, and at the moment, neither is Brianne."

"We'll get it done. We always do."

"Can we get back to your fee for a minute? I'd really like to get that out of the way. I assume when you checked me out you know I'm a multi-published author. I make good money, Mr. Hamilton. I can pay you. I want to pay you."

"I know you can but, again, let's see what all the job really entails. What all is involved here. We have sort of a sliding scale for fees." He grinned. "Depending on how much we like the client."

"I want this to be fair," she protested. "I have resources. I'm not a charity case, just because your brother recommended me."

Blaze inched forward, reached over and took one of her hands in his. The contact nearly fried his nerve endings. All he could think was, *What the hell?* His second thought was, *Thank fuck for my control or I'd embarrass myself.* But he forced himself to look directly at her, capturing her attention.

"Please. Let's forget money for the moment. Okay?"

She sighed and nodded.

"How much did my brother tell you about Galaxy?"

She shrugged. "Just that you all won some money and decided that you wanted to take the skills you learned as SEALs and put them to use helping people in civilian life."

He chuckled. "That's a pretty basic way of looking at it, but I think my brother is not at all impressed with us."

She frowned. "Oh, no. He couldn't say enough good things about you. He told me that if anyone could get to the truth here, it was you and your partners."

"I'll have to be sure and thank him. But here's the deal. Obviously, we don't spread the details around, but since you came recommended by Nolan, I feel comfortable sharing some of them with you. Maybe that will help."

He watched a little of the tension leave her body. "Okay. I just know that all this" — she waved her hand around the cabin of the plane — "doesn't come cheap."

"You're right, but here's the reason we can do it, my partners and me. We've been friends for a long time. Went into the SEALs together, although we ended up on different teams. Got out at the same time. Had a big celebratory dinner and decided to test our luck as civilians by buying Powerball lottery tickets."

"Lottery? Powerball? I'm guessing you won?"

He nodded. "The big prize. A little over a billion dollars."

Blaze thought her jaw would hit the floor. "Did you say a billion?"

"I did." He realized he was still holding her hand and gave it a little squeeze. "So you can see why we can be, shall I say, flexible in our fees. And picky about our clients."

"And you bought the plane."

"We did. We didn't want an office in the usual sense. We knew that most of the clients we'd get would not want to be in a place where they could be overheard. Here we can control access and contain things."

"And the name, Galaxy?"

Blaze found himself grinning. "Because the sky's the limit." Then he turned serious. "So you see, we have the resources to dig into your problem and the flexibility to charge whatever we want to."

"I won't let you do this for free," she insisted. "My books sell very well. I have the funds to pay you."

"I wouldn't agree to it, anyway. Payment of any kind is what legitimizes a contract. But let's see what we're getting into first." He rose from the couch. "I'm going to tell Saint to take us back to the hangar." He looked at his watch. "It's close to seven o'clock. Could I interest you in dinner?"

"Thank you, but I'm going back to the hospital. Studies have shown that most patients in a hospital die at night and often on the weekends. I'm praying that my sister recovers, but I don't want her to be there alone."

"Totally understand. Let me just get Saint turned around. I'll be right back."

"You done already?" Saint turned his head when Blaze entered the cockpit.

"We are." He dropped into the co-pilot seat.

"Is that a good thing or a bad? You writing her off or signing her up?"

"It's complicated. At first blush, this doesn't seem like a Galaxy case, but the more she talked, the more pissed-off I got at the way she's been treated."

"Yeah? You taking up for the downtrodden?"

Blaze snorted. "That hardly describes her. She's feisty and angry and rightfully so. I think she's been screwed over by people more powerful than she even realizes. Digging them out will be a challenge."

Saint chuckled. "You always did have a Sir Galahad complex."

"Maybe." Blaze winked, but then sobered. "I'm telling you, Saint, something smells here to high heaven. The police don't write up a one-page report on a hit and run and leave out practically all the details unless something is cooking. No one saw anything, can't even identify what kind of car it is and they basically want to make it all go away. I listened to everything she said and the whole thing shrieks of cover-up."

"So it's a go."

"It is. Let's land this thing so I can get hold of everyone else and brief them. This is all that's on our plate right now, so I want to get the others involved for as long as we can."

"Got it."

Peyton hadn't moved from her position, sitting erect in her seat and holding her wineglass. Blaze dropped to the couch again and leaned forward.

"We'll be making our descent shortly. You going back to the hospital from here?"

"I am."

"Okay. I'll say prayers for your sister."

A tiny smile curved her lips. "Thank you."

"We'll find out the truth," he promised, knowing suddenly that he wasn't going to rest until he did. "Would you like a refill on the wine?"

She shook her head. "One will have to do it for me. I want to be alert when I get to the hospital."

"I can only imagine the emotional stress you're under. In the SEALs, it was tough enough watching your friend severely injured or dying, but your sister? That's a killer."

"And something you never expect to do," She rubbed her thumb against the stem of the empty wineglass. "My sister was a wonderful woman. Although we each went our own way as we got older, we always stayed close. We both had interests in what you'd call the arts. I became a writer and Brianne became a respected commercial photographer. She did stuff for brochures and magazines. The last year or so, she was branching out into landscapes and wanted to do a coffee table book."

"Two smart, talented women," Blaze observed.

"Even though we lived pretty far apart, we were still close. And we always managed a girls' weekend, just the two of us, once a year."

"Sounds like you two are friends as well as sisters."

"We were. Are," she corrected herself. "She's still with us and will be, whatever it takes."

He understood that kind of fierce connection. Although he was an only child, his Galaxy partners had been his friends since they were teenagers. Closer than some people were with blood relatives. He definitely could relate to what she was feeling.

"How long were she and Dane married?"

"Six years. They were beginning to think about children."

That saddened him, for a life to be cut short for what seemed like no reason.

"We can't bring him back, but we can certainly get some answers, for you and your sister both."

At that moment, the plane began to bank. Blaze made sure Peyton had fastened her seat belt before clicking his into place.

Peyton glanced out the window. "I guess we're on approach."

"We are. I'll be getting to work on this as soon as we land." He wanted to say something that would ease the strain running through her, but he knew only answers to her questions would do that.

"Thank you."

When they landed and the stairs had opened, he helped Peyton descend then walked with her to where her car was parked. He couldn't seem to keep his eyes off the sway of her nicely rounded ass or the way her thick ponytail swished as she moved. When they reached her car, she turned and held out her hand to him. Her palm was soft against his and he wondered if her skin was soft all over. Worse yet, electricity sparked between them and nearly burned a hole in his hand.

Jesus holy hell, Hamilton. This is a fucking client. Without the fucking part.

In his entire life, he had never felt his discipline compromised the way it seemed to be with Peyton West. He was stunned at the intense connection between them, something he'd never had with another woman. And what could he do about it? She was a client. He'd damn well better figure out what the hell was going on, and fast.

But he noticed that she reacted to the contact, too, something flaring in her eyes and a tiny gasp escaping her lips. Apparently, she also had major control, because outside that infinitesimal reaction, he'd never have known the contact had affected her.

He'd better keep his shit together.

"I don't want to scare you," he said, "but has it occurred to you that whoever is behind all of this—not just the accident but the coverup—could have it in mind to eliminate you and your sister, also?"

Every bit of blood drained from her already pale face.

"You mean..." Her voice trailed off.

"I mean that Dane knew something that got him killed. What if whoever this is thinks your sister knows it, too? What if the hit and run was meant to kill both of them? And what if whoever this is gets nervous about you raking this all up and looking for answers?"

"I hadn't thought of that." She nibbled on her lower lip.

The sight of it made Blaze's balls ache. *Fucking shit.* Was he sixteen years old? And this was a damn client.

"I think we should discuss some kind of protection for you."

She looked up at him. "I wish I had my gun with me."

His eyes nearly bugged out of his head. That was among the top ten things he hadn't expected to hear from her. "You carry a gun?"

Her lips curved in the first genuine smile of the day. "I live in Texas. I think it's a requirement."

Blaze thought for a moment. "Texas has reciprocity with Florida. If you let me check you out on the gun range and your score's respectable, we'll fix you up."

"Really?"

"My preference would be to have protection of some kind with you and your sister at all times, but—"

She turned even paler at his words. "You think someone would come after us in the hospital?"

"I do," he acknowledged. "You're with her there most of the time, and basically unprotected. It'd be easy enough for someone to slip into the hospital, find your room number and take care of business."

"How soon can we do the gun range?"

"Late tomorrow afternoon sound good to you? I can pick you up at the hospital."

She chewed on her lip again and Blaze ground his teeth, searching for his self-control.

"Yes. That would be good. Can you text me when you're on the way?"

He nodded. "Maybe around four? I want to meet with my partners during the day and see what kind of research we can get done."

"What about Brianne? Is she safe? Will whoever this is try to finish the job with her?"

"Until I can make better arrangements, I'll ask my brother to have hospital security make regular checks on the room."

"Thank you." She blew out a breath. "Thank you so much. Is this a usual part of your services?"

He laughed. "Nothing is usual in our business. Anything goes when it's in the best interests of the client."

"Well, thank you again for taking this on."

"We'll get to the root of this. I promise you."

"Thank you." Relief washed over her face. "I didn't want to ask you, but—"

"But we're all human. I understand. And I'll definitely give you a call in the morning."

They walked back to the hangar in silence. Peyton looked drained, as if she'd used the last bit of her energy and was trying to recharge her batteries before heading to the hospital. Blaze could only imagine the emotional stress she was dealing with. He didn't like to make things personal. It could clutter up one's thinking when working an op.

"I'll be jumping on this right away," he assured her again as he walked her to her car.

"I can't tell you what a relief it is to have you believe something is wrong here. Someone who doesn't keep trying to convince me that I'm nuts and to leave it all alone."

"Oh, there's definitely something out of whack here, but that's the kind of stuff we thrive on. We'll get to the truth, I promise you. See you tomorrow afternoon."

He was still standing there, staring after the retreating vehicle, when Saint joined him.

"Plane all set in the hangar?" Blaze asked.

"It is. How did it go with the client?"

"I took the case. It's a fucking mess."

Saint laughed. "Just the kind you all like."

"Yeah, yeah, yeah." He rubbed the back of his neck as if working out the stiffness of the muscles.

What he really wanted to do was strip off all of Peyton West's clothes and lick every inch of her. What the fuck was wrong with him? For a man whose discipline was legendary, he was having a fucking hard time sending that message to his body. He needed a cold shower. Maybe two, so he could work. And get his *client* out of his head.

"Listen." Saint rubbed his chin. "It's been a wild and hairy couple of days. I'm thinking of heading to the boat and disconnecting for a while, unless you have objections."

Saint lived in a marina on Hillsborough Bay on a sport yacht he'd outfitted with every possible luxury. Whenever he had time off, he disappeared to somewhere, but always came back in great shape, mentally and physically. Blaze was so tempted to quiz him about where he'd gone, but he respected the man's privacy too much. Unless, of course, it became a problem, but that wasn't on the horizon.

"No objections. I'm heading home to dig into this."

"Peyton West seems a very troubled woman."

Blaze shoved his hands into his pockets and stared off down the driveway where Peyton's car had driven off.

"Troubled doesn't describe it. She's got a nasty situation and everyone's giving her shit. And she's scared to death for her sister. Worried whoever is behind the coverup of the hit and run will want to take her out, too. I smell money, power and politics at work here."

"Always a combustible combination," Saint agreed. "You sure you want to get into this?"

Blaze's smile was grim. "Damn straight. Okay, take off and air it out. I'm planning to call the others as soon as I get home."

"If you need another meeting, call me."

"And you'd come back when you finally have a couple of days off?"

Saint looked at him, something flickering in his eyes.

"You guys saved my ass when everyone else wrote me off. Hell, yes, I'd come back. This is my world, too."

For a moment Blaze was overcome with emotion. The bond that tied all of them together wasn't something he could explain to anyone, but he was damn glad of it.

"Okay, then. Keep your phone close at hand, just in case."

Blaze and Saint shook hands and Saint headed to his vehicle. Blaze, just because it was who he was, double-checked the lock on the hangar. Then he pulled up the app on his cell phone and made sure the security cameras covering all the key spots were active and the feed was working. Finally, satisfied that everything was secure, he climbed into his vehicle and headed home.

As he pulled out onto the roadway, he hit the preset number for Nolan. He was prepared to leave a message for the very busy doctor, so was surprised when his brother answered the call.

"I'm guessing this call is to tell me you met with Peyton West."

"It is. You were right. She's got a shit ton of trouble. I smell a load of money and influence pulling the strings here."

"Me, too," Nolan agreed. "That's why I gave her your number. You know how I avoid mixing into your business. Too risky and complicated for me, and truthfully, I'm not even sure what all you guys do."

Blaze chuckled. "A little bit of this, a little bit of that."

"Yeah, yeah, yeah. Anyway, I figured I'd give it a shot. She's not a flake, not neurotic and not a pain in the ass."

"Excellent qualifications." Blaze took the entrance ramp to the interstate, glad to see there wasn't an overload of traffic at the moment. He was anxious to get home. "And I agree with you."

"So you took her on?"

"I did. I'm on my way home to start my research."

"Thanks for this."

Silence hummed across the connection for a moment. "I hope you can help her. I'm not sure her sister is ever going to come out of this."

"Oh?" Blaze frowned. Nolan wasn't usually this negative about a prognosis.

"When the car hit her, she was slammed into the pavement pretty hard. Her head hit the concrete and created swelling of the brain as well as a subdural hematoma. We treated both, but with the brain, everything is so unpredictable."

At once an image hit Blaze of the look of pain and fear on Peyton West's face when she'd talked about her sister.

Damn!

"We'll all cross our fingers, but we'll also work our asses off to at least give her answers. And maybe," he growled, "a little bit of revenge."

"I knew I was right to do this."

I should ask Nolan to keep an eye on her.

But as soon as the thought hit, he discarded it. His brother was a very busy, very in-demand doctor at the hospital. He didn't have time to babysit someone. Blaze would just have to hope Peyton West was very careful until he could take her to the range tomorrow and check her out with a firearm. *And figure out how else to protect her and her sister.*

The next minute, he gave a figurative shake of his head. No, he couldn't leave anything to chance. Not if the people behind the cover-up were as powerful as he believed.

"Listen, can you do me a favor? Have the hospital check on them regularly?"

"You think whoever is behind this would try to get to them here?

"I don't know, but I don't want to take chances until I can make arrangements."

"Sure. I'll take care of it. Okay, gotta run. Thanks for doing this."

Blaze disconnected the call. Peyton's pain had been so visible on her face that it would have been impossible to say no. He'd get answers for her one way or another.

The next thing he did was call his partners to let them know they had a client and give them a brief rundown. They all agreed to meet at his place the next morning around ten. Viper volunteered to start digging into the brother-in-law right away, since he had no big plans for the night.

Once he was home, settled at the desk in his den with a cold beer and a bowl of chips, Blaze opened his laptop and went to work. The first thing he did was search for information on his client. She'd given him a business card and told him that whatever he wanted to know, he could find on her web site. He typed in *Peyton West*, his eyes widening when her web site came up. *Damn!* She was an author all right, and a highly successful one. Half her books had Best Seller banners attached to them and snippets of reviews praised her stories.

The woman in the photo looked a lot different from the one who'd shown up at the plane. In the photo she was all smiles, her glossy chestnut hair tumbling around her shoulders, a teasing look in her eyes. No lines of strain on her face or obvious tension in her body.

He spent more than an hour reading everything he could find. It wasn't too late to cancel the contract if he found any warning signs, but there were none. Instead he felt a sadness for this woman who seemed so happy with a life now torn by incredible tragedy.

Then he dug into Kendrick & Associates, the law firm where Dane was an associate. And a high-value one, if the media coverage of him was to be believed.

Four hours and a large pizza later, he sat staring at his computer screen. Although nothing that he'd read jumped out at him, he still got that funny little tingle wriggling down his spine that there was something dead wrong here.

On the surface, Dane Hollister looked just like what the web sites said — bright attorney, ten years out of law school and a shining star at the firm where he worked. Peter Kendrick, the managing partner, said glowing things about him. The firm apparently had a national reputation as litigators. Clients came not just from all over the country but from outside the United States to have the firm represent them. That meant that they also had to be specialists in international law.

From what he could find, it appeared that Dane worked most closely with Peter Kendrick, representing some of the firm's wealthiest corporate clients. Businesses were always being sued, so he imagined there were big bucks in it. Even he was impressed with some of the client names which were listed in a profile, including the head of an international corporation, a political power broker and the chair of a media conglomerate. Dane Hollister traveled in some elite company. Had he uncovered secrets that a client would do anything not to have exposed? Murder had been committed for a lot less.

Blaze's instincts were shouting that there was something there, and he knew he'd find it. Maybe not tonight, but tomorrow he'd sit down with the others, brainstorm and take it from there. Computer research was only a small part of identifying a problem.

Figuring he'd reached a dead end for the evening, Blaze shut down the computer. What he needed now was a hot shower and a drink. Or maybe a cold shower would suit him better. Except when he'd been focused on his research, he hadn't been able to get the image of Peyton West out of his brain. That sure didn't say much about a guy who was famous for his self control.

He stripped off his clothes and tossed them into the hamper, then headed into the bathroom where he cranked on the shower. One of the perks of spending bucks on his home was all the goodies he could include in it. His walk-in shower took up a quarter of the big bathroom, with multiple rain shower heads and a built-in bench being just the tip of the iceberg.

When he had the water set as hot as he wanted, he stepped into it, poured liquid soap into his palm and began lathering his body. As he moved his palm over his skin, he had a sudden flash of Peyton West soaping his body, her soft hand stroking him, brushing smoothly over his balls.

The image of her, the sun highlighting her rich chestnut hair, the way her slacks followed the sweet curve of her ass and the soft drape of her sweater on her breasts made him want to run his hands over every inch of her body. He could just imagine how rosy those nipples would be, soft in his mouth at first then harder as he sucked on them. Maybe closed his teeth down on them.

What would it be like to slip his dick inside her, stretching inner walls he knew would be soft and wet, her opening tight around him? Did he want to fuck her when he was on top so he could look directly into her eyes? Or from the back, with her on her knees, legs spread wide, both openings so tempting he wouldn't know which one to take first. Then wake up with her spooned against him so he could slip inside her and slowly work them both to orgasm.

Shit!

What the fuck was the matter with him? It wasn't as if he didn't have personal discipline. *But holy god.*

He had reached his groin area and his hand collided with his dick standing at full attention, painfully swollen. He tightened his grip on it and began to rub it with slow, lazy strokes. As he did, he imagined Peyton's fingers there instead, firm but gentle, wrapped around his hardness. Maybe she'd drop to her knees in front of him and wrap her lips around the throbbing head. Swirl her tongue over it as the pace of her strokes increased. He could visualize the spray of the shower cascading drops over her naked body, her nipples erect and rosy.

Leaning against the shower wall, the image so vivid in his brain, he pumped faster and faster. Then, with an intense shudder that raced through his body, he came, spurting all over his fingers. The viscous liquid covered his hand and dripped to the tile on the floor. He stroked and squeezed again and again until he'd emptied himself of every bit of cum.

When the last spasm faded away, his legs were so weak that he slid to the floor. His hands were shaking and his heart pounding as if he'd just had off-the-charts sex with the woman firmly implanted in his brain. He leaned against the shower wall, letting the water pour over him like rainfall. He had no idea how long he sat there, his cock now at rest and lying in his palm. Unfortunately, need still thrummed through his body.

All he could think was, *What the fuck?*

Chapter Four

Peter Kendrick handed a rocks glass filled with bourbon to the man sitting in one of the deep leather armchairs.

"I have a major problem that I need your help with."

Warren Sulzberger drew his eyebrows together in a heavy scowl. It was obvious to Peter that the man was not happy to be here. Well, not any happier than Kendrick was at the situation that had made this happen. He was only glad that his wife was no longer here to see the mess her son had made.

Having to reach out to Sulzberger again really chapped Kendrick's ass. If he were an astronomer, he'd say his life was in retrograde, moving backward from the good place it had been in for so long. He needed Sulzberger's help to reverse the course.

His friend had made no secret when he arrived that he was pissed and unhappy about leaving his big estate in Miami and coming to Tampa again. He only bowed to Peter's demands because he was one of the few men who could pressure him. Peter Kendrick knew where all Sulzberger's bodies were buried—had even helped bury some of the worst—so the man could hardly refuse.

As if the current situation isn't enough, he thought. His mind went back again to the night his son had called him, desperate, then rushed to the house. He could still hear the words that spilled from Owen's mouth, words that had chilled Peter's blood. His attitude wasn't helped by the fact that his son also reeked of liquor.

'*You've got to fix this*,' Owen had repeated over and over, eyes wild, shirt wrinkled. On his way to being sober, he had been petrified at the reality of what he'd done.

Fix it. Kendrick couldn't forget the words that kept repeating in his brain. *Fix it*. Right. Like it was nothing. And now here he was, with more fixing to do. How on earth had he raised such an idiot? He knew that if this wasn't cleaned up, if Owen's involvement in this whole mess wasn't erased, the fallout would hit everyone, including the firm.

He swallowed the bitter taste in his mouth, raging inside that his son had been beyond stupid. Getting in trouble with the so-called Tampa Mafia, an action that had been the catalyst for all of this, was about as dumb as a person could get. He'd told that to Owen, during a nasty conversation when some unwanted photos had shown up. At least, that was what he'd thought until Owen had shown up at his door at one-thirty in the morning stinking drunk and terrified out of his mind at what he'd done. An act beyond stupidity.

"Another one?" Sulzberger's glare would have frozen ice. "Now what? I thought everything was taken care of. That's what you said. Once and done, you told me."

"So did I. This could have been a blowup of epic proportions if you hadn't fixed it," he told him. "Even more than it has been. And please know I appreciate your quick work with handling everyone involved in the situation. We'd be in deep shit if you hadn't been willing to give us all that help. I just hope they all continue to keep their mouths shut. It's more important now than ever."

"They will. I promise you. Fear or greed will see to that. But what's happened now? How much worse can it get? What can you possibly need from me now?"

Kendrick took a slow sip of his own glass of the aged bourbon and stared at the man. Although they had known each other for years and been close friends, that friendship had frayed when Sulzberger had gotten himself into an unholy mess. Peter had maneuvered him out of it. The man's reluctance to be here now was obvious, but Kendrick didn't care. He had a big problem and this man still owed him a huge favor. It was time to pay up.

"Things have taken a turn for the worse. They're bad enough that only your connections can help us. Connections, by the way, that I want to remind you again only exist because I dug you out of a deep hole."

"And I've paid it back."

"Not yet." Kendrick shook his head. "Not until we fix this."

"Fucker," Sulzberger muttered. "We buried everything. Wiped away all traces. Took care of reports and witnesses. What the hell happened now?"

The man might have left Congress in disgrace, but thanks to Peter and his connections in both Congress and the private sector, he had been allowed to do it quietly. His landing in the civilian world had been padded by the enormous amounts of money that had brought him trouble in the first place. Even those peripherally involved in what he'd referred to as The Situation had given him money he'd willingly accepted to stay silent where they were concerned. Cash could take care of everything, no matter how evil it was. That lesson had guided him his entire life.

He'd built a new powerful niche for himself in the lobbying business, shamelessly taking advantage of the dirt on people he had accumulated—he knew where a lot of the bodies were buried. He pushed pressure points where and when he needed them. Kendrick had worked with the man to navigate many of those deals that were somewhat on the shady side. Now he needed payback.

"I appreciate everything you did for me when I was the victim of political jealousy," he went on. "I was—"

"Ha!" Kendrick barked an interruption. "Political jealousy? Victim? Is that what you call it?"

"That's what it was to me. Regardless, the situation is about to get worse. Did he think getting drunk and running two people down would make his problem disappear? What does his wife have to say about all this? She can't be too happy."

"Owen refuses to involve her in this." Kendrick wanted to bite his nails. "I tried to make him see that she's already involved just by being married to him."

"And he didn't understand that?"

"When she and Owen married, I was delighted. The perfect wife for the perfect politician. That's when I began to lay the groundwork for everything. I never dreamed he would fall into a hole like this and threaten everything I've worked so hard for."

"Hollister's wife surviving the accident has created a dilemma." Sulzberger shook his head then took another sip. "If she regains consciousness, we have no idea what she'll remember. More importantly, she was the one who took the pictures that started this ball rolling in the first place. If she starts telling people about Hayden Kellerman and Owen's connection, we're fucked."

"It's not as if I had any control over that," Kendrick snapped.

"Let me think about that. You stay away from it. If something were to happen to her, they'd be looking at everyone and anyone who even said hello to her. And from what you tell me, even dead she could be a problem. Her sister is determined to find answers and isn't about to let go. If Brianne Hollister dies, I'm damn sure she'll ramp up her efforts to find answers. She'll keep pushing and pushing until something cracks. You're damn lucky that the three firms she approached owed you and called you to see if you had objections to them taking the case."

"And thank god they did."

Sulzberger's lips pressed together in a thin line. "But unfortunately, it didn't end there. Which is why I'm sitting here with you. Because there's another problem. Right?"

"That's correct." Kendrick massaged his throbbing temple with his fingertips. "I thought we'd killed any investigation, but now I learned, just yesterday, she's hired some people we know nothing about who have an office in a plane, for god's sake."

"How the hell did you even find out about it?"

"By accident. I thought I should put in an appearance at the hospital to check on Brianne

Hollister. I was just outside her room when I heard her doctor talking to her sister, who spends a lot of time there when she's not trying to make trouble for us."

"What did you hear that's got your panties in such a twist?"

"I heard the doctor telling the sister about his brother and an agency of sorts he owns with some others, all former military. Said this was right up their alley."

Sulzberger shrugged. "Sounds like just some rogue thrill seekers looking to make a quick buck."

"No." Kendrick shook his head. "The doctor mentioned a couple of things they'd handled. These people are the blackest of black ops and the stealthiest of anyone else she could find."

"If so, this could be an even bigger disaster, Peter."

"You think I don't know that?"

Kendrick forced himself to breathe evenly. This whole situation wasn't good for his blood pressure. If he hadn't already spent months, even years, laying the groundwork for his son's career in politics, he would have dropped him off someplace where no one could contact him. But now he had no choice. The campaign to create a political presence for Owen was about to kick off. He'd been grooming his son for this since the day he could talk.

God damn it.

If only there was an easy and acceptable way to kill the whole political career train right now.

Somehow, he should have figured out what was going on with Owen and the gambling and found a way to stop it before it all blew up. He'd known something was wrong. His son had been edgy and uneasy, but he'd chalked it up at first to pressure from the workload. He'd given him cases to handle that played to his strengths and thought that would keep him busy enough to stay out of trouble. The last thing he'd expected was for any of the shit with the Tampa Mafia to escalate out of control and hit the firm, where anyone here could find out about it.

Even then, he thought he'd had a lid on it until Dane Hollister had stumbled over it and he'd nearly had a stroke. Thank god at least Hollister had come to Peter about it first. He'd denied the whole thing, then chewed Owen's ass to shreds.

But what a fucking mess. Hollister had backed off a little, but Peter knew he wasn't through digging into it. Then Owen had decided to 'fix' it his own way and made a bigger mess.

Kendrick took another swallow of his drink.

"So now we have the sister-in-law who, like some avenging angel, is hell-bent on finding the driver. It's a good thing I've been keeping tabs on her. I managed to make sure the traffic cops are out of the way and she couldn't hire anyone to help her. But now she's found these people I never heard of and no one I reach out to knows about them, either. I can't find out shit. Whoever they are and whatever they do, they keep a very low profile and that makes me very nervous. We have to fix this, Warren."

Sulzberger snorted. "What do you expect me to do? Get rid of the sister? You don't think that would make even more noise? I know I'm stating the obvious here, but your son made a fucking big mess. If I fix this, how are you going to control him going forward?"

Kendrick ground his teeth. Sulzberger was right, only it had never entered his mind that Owen would think murder was the answer.

"He's my problem and I'm handling it. I am more concerned right now with the people Peyton West managed to hire. I haven't been able to find a single thing about them except their name. Not even a phone number. Nothing. It's making me nervous." Kendrick drained his glass and rose to refill it at the bar against the wall. "You have the kind of connections that can get that information. I want to know everything there is, right down to how they brush their teeth. Then I want to know how to neutralize them."

"Neutralize them?" Sulzberger snorted. "You don't want much, do you? Why don't you do it yourself? You've got people who can check them out."

"I've already tried and hit a wall. Listen, you're the sneakiest bastard I know. You have much better resources for that than I do. Plus, you have people who can do it without leaving a trail or getting their attention. I want to know what the fuck kind of people don't have an office and fly around in a plane that costs millions of dollars?"

Sulzberger was silent for a long time before he spoke again.

"What happens when you get your information?"

"I'll use it appropriately." Kendrick knocked backed a healthy swallow of the bourbon.

"Peter, if you make a bigger mess out of this, we'll both be in trouble." Sulzberger rubbed his jaw. "You can't kill off everyone who knows what a wild card your son is."

"No, but I can steer them in another direction. Or throw up misdirection, if I just know exactly who they are and how they operate. We're meeting with the team next week to start implementing the program we created."

Sulzberger's laugh had a sarcastic tone to it.

"You weren't able to keep Owen from getting in trouble over his head and trying to kill his way out of it, and you want him to become governor?"

"He'll be fine." Kendrick wanted to grit his teeth. "I just have to get him elected to the office. Then I'll be pulling all the strings and managing the work."

"And you're sure this is going to work?"

"I'm betting heavily on it. First the governor's office, then the Senate, then, if it all shakes out, the White House." His smile had a touch of evil to it. "And a chance for you to finally get your revenge, if you help me with this."

Sulzberger was quiet for a long time.

"If someone besides the sister decides to start pushing," he said at last, "we may have trouble with the police report of the accident."

Kendrick scowled. "What kind of trouble? They entered it in the computer, right? And put in what we told them to?"

"Yes, but it's very sketchy. If the sister makes too much noise, someone we don't have control over could call them on it. Maybe send someone else to investigate. See if there's someone who was there who actually did see what happened." He paused. "Someone who didn't get paid off."

"I thought you said that was all handled."

"I was assured it was. Our men even went back the next day and took care of the payoffs, along with a few well-chosen threats." Sulzberger shrugged. "But if push comes to shove, someone could cave."

"Then we'd better make sure they don't."

"By 'we' I assume you mean me."

"You're the man who can pull the strings," Kendrick pointed out. "And with an expert touch, I might add."

"Is that what you call it?" Sulzberger's laugh held little humor. "You can kill the flattery. I'm in. I owe you, otherwise I'd insist we ditch your whole plan."

"We'd better keep a close eye on everything, especially that damn sister. I'm not about to let her blow this whole thing. It's bad enough my idiot son can't control his impulses." He rubbed his jaw. "When Owen reaches the ultimate goal I have set for him, he'll be in the best position for you to take your revenge." His lips curled in a smile that hinted of irony. "Although the money you've made and the influence you've built should be enough revenge."

"For some. Not for me. The money will never be enough. Those holier-than-thou bastards would have done the same thing I did, given the chance. And what kills me is that many of them did."

"They just never got caught," Kendrick reminded him.

Anger tightened the muscles on Sulzberger's face for a brief moment before he smoothed it out. "You're right. A final nail in the coffin would give me pleasure. However, we have to get there first. Can you assure me that controlling Owen from here on out will not be a problem?"

Now Kendrick had to swallow his own anger — only it was directed at his son, not the man across from him.

"I'll take care of it. Count on it."

Sulzberger nodded. "Then we have a deal. I'll dig into the people the sister has found and get back to you."

Kendrick walked over to where the other man was seated and they clinked glasses.

"To success," he said.

Sulzberger nodded. "To success."

For a long time after Warren Sulzberger left, Peter Kendrick sat in his den, slowly sipping the rest of the bourbon in his glass and letting his thoughts chase themselves around in his brain. He could still recall the defining moment that had changed the other man's life.

Sulzberger had grown up in a family that thrived on politics. His father and two brothers had all gone into it, either as elected officials or behind the scenes. He'd been groomed at an early age to run for Congress, much as he, Peter, was grooming Owen to make a run for governor. Successfully elected, he'd served four terms in the Senate, eventually being appointed to the prestigious Armed Services Committee. In that position, he had been able to swing very lucrative contracts to several of his supporters, earning himself a fat bonus each time.

But some of those friends had a dark side—very dark, like the arms manufacturer supporting a rebel group in Africa. It was to his advantage to keep the rebels supplied with his armaments and make sure they continued to operate. When he learned that a top-secret mission was planned to take down the key rebel leaders, the arms dealer had paid him a fat fucking fee for sharing the information. The rebels had proceeded to decimate the SEAL team. Only two members had survived.

It was a scandal of epic proportions, quickly covered up by the politicians with a combination of payoffs and threats. But Warren Sulzberger had been forced to quietly resign from his seat in the Senate. Two senior senators had forced the issue, threatening to ruin him if he didn't take this way out. That would have precluded what came next for him. As often happened to people who succeeded on the wrong side of the line, he'd opened a very successful lobbying firm. Over the years he'd done many favors for other senators. Now it was time for them to repay that by voting for bills favorable to his clients.

His firm continued to grow, both in its treasury and its sphere of influence, a situation that would have been ruined if he hadn't simply resigned. The word had begun to circulate below the surface that if a person wanted anything done, and not just on The Hill, Warren Sulzberger was the man. But whoever needed it had better be prepared to pay for it.

Kendrick had never wanted a place in politics for himself. He, like Sulzberger now, liked to work behind the scenes, pulling strings. The hunger for power that he controlled consumed him. His son had been groomed from an early age to be the political face of the family and to feed that hunger. The fact that he had shit for brains and little impulse control wasn't going to derail the train that Peter Kendrick had set in motion.

The first thing was to get whatever information Sulzberger would dig up on whoever Peyton West had hired. The next thing would be to get rid of everyone — even the sister, if he had to. But that one would require some delicate arrangements, and he wasn't there yet.

He drained the glass and set it down on the bar.

Owen needed to clean up his act. Associating with the wrong people was bad enough. Being with them at the wrong place at the wrong time, when Dane Hollister could catch sight of him, could create a disaster of epic proportions. One more stupid, idiotic thing his son had done. Erasing all evidence of his son's stupidity was going to take a Herculean effort on

Kendrick's part. But he didn't have a choice. Owen Kendrick was going to sit in the White House or Peter was going to die trying. And that second option was just not acceptable.

* * * *

Peyton hadn't eaten much all day. The situation had pretty much robbed her of her appetite. Still, she knew she had to eat at least to survive. She decided to feed her sugar craving and picked up a half dozen donuts and coffee on her way back to the hospital. As she drove, she thought over her meeting with Scott 'Blaze' Hamilton. He was not at all what she'd expected. When Nolan Hamilton had told her that his brother was a SEAL, a decorated combat veteran with sixteen years of service, the tall, sexy man who'd greeted her wasn't at all what she'd expected. And despite his take-charge attitude, he'd been courteous, even gentle with her as he coaxed her story out of her.

The elegance of the plane had stunned her. When Nolan had said they held their meetings in a plane, she hadn't known what she'd expected, but it hadn't been this. The elegance of Galaxy's plane put many elegant mansions she'd seen to shame. Of course, if they'd won millions in the lottery, price was no object, she guessed. But more than anything, she got the feeling that whatever the men of Galaxy set out to do, they'd get it done.

When she pulled into the huge hospital parking garage, she found herself looking out of both sides of the car as she hunted for a space. She considered herself lucky that one opened up on the third level right by an elevator. For the first time, she was nervous waiting for the elevator to arrive and the doors to open.

Damn Blaze Hamilton for making me edgy.

Yet she knew he was only doing his job. She might not have hired him to protect her, but she knew he was concerned for her safety. She probably should be, too. Whoever had done this couldn't be happy about leaving Brianne alive. When the elevator doors opened, she hurried down the wide hallway to her sister's room, paying attention to the people around her.

Nobody's going to kill you in the hospital.

It sounded ridiculous when she thought it, but then so did someone running down Dane and Brianne. She'd make sure to be diligent.

When she entered her sister's room, a nurse was standing beside the bed, checking her vitals. Peyton was relieved to see it was the same one who'd been taking care of Brianne almost every day on this shift. Her sister was just as still as she'd been for days, her body unmoving beneath the sheet and thin blanket, the outline broken by the casts on her leg and her arm. Peyton's heart ached at the sight. The woman did not deserve this. She was a good person, smart, loving. A wonderful sister, and she'd been a great wife. Of course, Dane had been a terrific husband, and together they'd made a fabulous couple.

She swallowed a sigh, set the coffee and donuts down on the tray table and stood on the other side of the bed.

"How is she?" *Well, that was a stupid question,* she told herself. *You know how she is.*

The nurse's smile was kind. "About the same, but her vitals are good. That's a positive sign."

Brianne reached down to take her sister's hand in her own and gave it a gentle squeeze. It felt so cold to her.

"Is she warm enough?" she asked the nurse.

"I was planning to get her another blanket. When you don't move around, it's hard to maintain a body temperature."

"But—it's no worse than it was, right?"

"Right. It's about the same." She finished what she was doing and typed notes into the computer on the rolling stand, then pushed the stand toward the door. "They X-rayed her arm and her leg today. The doctor says they're healing nicely."

Peyton swallowed hard. "I just hope she wakes up so she can use them."

The nurse smiled. "I have faith. I've seen worse situations than this turn around. And the way you sit with her, holding her hand and talking to her?"

"Thank you. It's just so hard seeing her like this."

"I know, but you being here is the best thing for her."

"Good. That gives me hope."

Peyton bent over the bed and brushed a kiss on her sister's forehead. The one thing she wasn't looking forward to was the moment when Brianne woke up and she had to tell her that Dane was dead.

First things first.

Then she plucked a donut from the box, grabbed the coffee and sat in the chair next to the bed. Snatches from her meeting that afternoon kept playing in her head like scenes from a movie. She could not erase the image of Blaze Hamilton, and it had nothing to do with his ability to help her.

She could still feel the warmth of his palm when he'd shaken her hand at the end of their meeting. Sense the raw energy radiating from his body. She'd bet her next royalty check he was a medal-winner in bed, too, more than living up to his name. Not that she was ever going to find out. She was aware that she appealed to men and she never lacked for dates if and when she wanted them. But she had no illusions about who and what she was. She was sure the women that Blaze Hamilton spent his hours with belonged on magazine covers.

Maybe not. Maybe that kind of woman doesn't appeal to him. Maybe he likes them a little less glamorous, more down to earth.

But just as hot in bed.

Out of nowhere an image of the man naked, lying on the sheets, blasted into her brain. There wasn't an ounce of fat on his bones. Every corded muscle, every inch of tan skin was visible, along with a cock that would take honors in any competition. His lips were curved in a hungry smile and need flared in his golden whiskey eyes. Heat surged through her body and every pulse point throbbed with need.

Holy mother of god!

She was never this undisciplined. Her trademark was unbroken self-control at all times. That was partially the reason she was able to concentrate on writing when she was into creating a novel. She could use her laser-like focus to shut everything else out. Why wasn't she doing it now?

No, her brain was elsewhere, focused on a man who was sex personified. And here she was, sitting next to her sister's hospital bed, with aching nipples and a throbbing pulse at her core. What kind of person was she, for her mind to wander like that and her body to send her messages when her life was centered around her sister and finding who had driven the car? Why on earth was she even having these thoughts, anyway? She made a concerted effort to banish the unwelcome thoughts from her brain. No such luck. She needed to focus on what was important, not what her traitorous hormones were trying to distract her with.

Enough, she told herself. She had a brain and she should use it. Focus on her missions. She took a sip from the coffee she was holding, hoping the now lukewarm liquid would counteract the heat threatening to consume her. Then she lifted a donut from the box, took a small bite and stared at Brianne's still form. That was what she should be focusing on, that and whoever the asshole was who had run into her and Dane with a car.

She wished she knew more about Dane and his practice. The answer had to be there somewhere. She'd done her research on the firm he was with. His clients. The cases he'd worked on. Nothing seemed out of place, at least that she could find. They were considered top litigators. Very powerful. Were they trustworthy? Did they have clients who didn't bear a lot of scrutiny? She couldn't imagine Dane jumping into murky waters, not after knowing him all this time. She needed a lot more information before she could come to any conclusions, though.

And that's what you have Galaxy for, so let them do their job and you do yours.

She finished the donut, discovered she was still hungry and reached for another one. As she took a bite, a memory flashed through her brain, a scene where she and Brianne were sitting in her apartment in Texas with a box of a dozen donuts between them, gorging on the sugary goodness. For a moment her throat tightened and she couldn't swallow. She forced it down with some coffee and took a deep breath. She had to get hold of herself.

Positive thoughts, she told herself. *Positive energy. That's what's needed here.*

"I met some people today." She leaned forward in her chair, closer to her sister's comatose body. "Well, one person. A man." She smiled in spite of herself. "His office is in a plane that I think cost more money than you or I will ever see. And he's really great looking."

Okay, that wasn't good. The image of Blaze burst into her brain and once again her hormones sprang to life.

"But that's beside the point," she went on, and forced herself to mean it. She couldn't believe she was having these thoughts in this situation. What kind of sister did that make her? "I have a good feeling about him. He's going to find out who did this and we're going to make them pay, in many painful ways. But it sure would help if you remember anything at all."

Come on, Brianne. Wake up. Tell me if you saw anything. Help me find this asshole.

"Sounds like a good plan to me."

Peyton jumped, barely avoiding spilling her coffee.

"Here." Male hands grabbed paper napkins from the tray table and blotted her fingers where drops of coffee had splashed.

"Thank you. I'm good." Peyton set the now half-empty cup next to the donut box and rose from the chair to face Nolan Hamilton.

She could see the resemblance between the brothers, but where Blaze was all raw energy and power, Nolan's image was quieter, more refined, his power more mental than physical, although he did look as if he could hold his own in any fight. And they both had that air of quiet, earned confidence that made her feel safe in their hands.

"Sit." He motioned to the chair. "You don't need to stand to talk to me. Besides, you look exhausted. And that's a fact, not a criticism. Go on. Sit down."

She dropped gratefully back into the chair.

"Thank you for giving me your brother's phone number." She gave Nolan a tired smile. "For the first time since everything happened, I have the feeling someone is going to get me some answers."

"Oh, no doubt there. If anyone can find them, it's Galaxy." He studied her face. "You should go get some sleep, Peyton. Your sister is doing as well as can be expected. Maybe even a little better. Her condition is not deteriorating, so I am cautiously optimistic. But you won't be any good to anyone if you collapse from exhaustion."

"I'm just so afraid to leave her." She reached through the bedrails to close her fingers over Brianne's uninjured hand. "I have this awful feeling that if I'm not here, she'll just slip away."

Nolan took one of her hands in both of his. "She made it through this afternoon, right? I just checked her chart and her vitals look okay. I think a few hours of sleep in a bed instead of a chair will do both of you some good."

Peyton was pretty sure he was right. This afternoon's meeting had been pretty draining. On top of the hours she'd been sitting beside this bed, her body was poised on the verge of collapse. She gave Brianne's hand one more soft and gentle squeeze, then pushed to her feet.

"You'll call me if there's any change at all? Even the smallest one?"

"Word of honor. Now get out of here." He picked up the box from the tray table and smiled as he handed it to her. "And be sure to take your donuts with you."

She managed a tired smile as she gathered her things and made her way out of the room. Nolan Hamilton walked beside her down the corridor to the elevator.

"Sleep," he reminded her, "or you won't be any good to anyone."

"Got it. And, Nolan? Thank you very much. For everything."

"Of course."

Every muscle was tense as she made her way to her car in the parking lot then drove to the hotel. At this hour, traffic was thin, so she could spot a vehicle if it was following her. She thought, anyway. But nothing in her rearview or sideview mirrors gave her pause. She was glad when she reached the hotel. With Blaze's words echoing in her head, she opted out of the parking garage and turned her car over to valet parking.

She had to admit, when at last she climbed into bed in her hotel room, that she actually was tired. Mental exhaustion created even greater physical exhaustion. God, she hoped Brianne would wake up soon. Would Galaxy really be able to find the people who had destroyed two lives and make them pay for it?

Usually, when she took the time to sleep, she thought of her sister lying so still in the hospital. Tonight, though, as she closed her eyes, the image in her head was of a tall, lean man with thick black hair, a muscular body and a very masculine face with a very surprising dimple.

Chapter Five

"Okay. See you at four."

Blaze disconnected his call to Peyton and stuck his phone back in his pocket before getting a refill on his coffee. She had sounded okay, or as okay as she could be under the circumstances. He didn't know if he was glad she'd gone back to the hotel last night or not. She was more vulnerable there. More exposed. On the other hand, at least she'd gotten what passed for a good night's sleep. He'd have to think how to handle it if she did that more often.

"She okay?"

Matt 'Viper' Roman leaned against the counter in Blaze's kitchen and took a swallow of coffee from the mug he was holding.

"As okay as she can be under the circumstances. At least she's on the alert now, which helps."

Blaze had called each of his partners the previous evening, giving them a rundown on Peyton West and her situation and outlining what he wanted them to do.

Viper had been the only one with no plans and so had agreed to do some research before they arrived this morning.

Viper frowned. "You really think someone would attack those two women in the hospital?"

Blaze snorted. "How many times have we heard about that very thing happening? She says she's got a carry permit, so I'm taking her to the range this afternoon. If she passes muster, I'll fix her up with a handgun."

"A gun?" Viper grinned. "She sounds like quite the woman."

"She's a client." *Yeah, right.* "I'm making sure she's protected."

"Uh-huh."

"Stuff it." He'd do well to remember the client part of the business, too. "I asked Nolan to have hospital security keep an eye on them in the meanwhile. We need to discuss what's best when everyone gets here."

"Any special reason why we're taking on this particular case? It's not our usual type of activity."

Blaze shrugged. "Maybe I thought we needed a break from a black ops mission into a country not to be named or rescuing a kidnap victim or tracking a stolen shipment of arms."

Viper chuckled. "Nice try. I checked out Peyton West online last night. The fact that this client happens to be a knockout wouldn't have anything to do with it, would it?"

"Not at all. Her story hit me just the right way and I knew we could help her. We can get in the weeds of this kind of stuff where other people can't."

"If you say so."

"I do." Blaze nodded. "Meanwhile, since you were having a hot date with your laptop last night, you said you'd dig into the brother-in-law. Besides looking up our client, did you get it done?"

"Yeah, but truth be told, I didn't find anything the least bit hinky." Viper shrugged. "No shady legal dealings. No client with a grudge. Might as well have had a label on his chest that said Mr. Squeaky Clean."

Now he shook his head.

"This guy is the poster child for Mr. Wonderful," Viper continued. "Top of his class in law school. Worked his way up the food chain in the law firm and is considered a shining star in litigation. Actually, a shark in the making. I couldn't find any threads to pull. Maybe he ruffled some feathers at the law firm."

Blaze snorted. "He'd have to do some pretty bad ruffling, I'd think. From everything I read, they love him. There were even a couple of articles about a few big cases that had been won because of him."

"So maybe whoever was on the other side of a lawsuit was looking for revenge."

"Possible, but mostly they aren't really the kind of people who would run someone down in the street."

"Okay." Viper nodded. "We'll take a look, anyway. But first, tell me more about our client. What's she like as a person, besides being a hot chick and a published author, I mean."

Blaze thought for a moment. If he described how he really saw her, Viper would be all over him. And was she really hot? Well, if the boner he'd had thinking about her was any indication, yeah. Damn hot. Not to mention his little hand job in the shower.

"Smart," he said at last. "And desperate. Angry, too. And tied up in knots over this whole thing. Can't say I blame her."

Viper lifted an eyebrow. "Took you a while to come up with that description. Anything I should know?"

"Not at all." Blaze shook his head. "No. Definitely not."

Viper studied him for a moment. "Okay. Whatever. You said she tried looking into this herself?"

"Uh-huh." He refilled his own mug. "Got nowhere with the cops, and three other firms turned her down. Something smells here."

"Money and influence. The odor they leave is very sharp. Someone has a very heavy hand in this. You don't think the law firm is involved?"

"Not sure." Blaze shrugged. "They don't practice criminal law, so they aren't likely to have shady characters of whatever social status on their client list."

"There are other types of undesirable people they could represent," Viper pointed out. "They're litigators. Maybe a lawsuit went south. Or maybe they rigged something and this Dane tumbled to it. The only way we'll find out is to go over everything regarding the firm with a fine-tooth comb. And also get a first-hand look at the people there." He looked at his watch. "Rocket and Eagle will be along shortly. They might be dragging ass a bit today."

Blaze grinned. "A little R and R last night will do that to you."

Viper shrugged. "Why not? We work hard for it."

"Yes, we do. Okay, meanwhile, you and I can get started."

They set up in the dining room and opened their laptops.

"Let's split it up." Viper clicked a couple of keys. "You want the firm or the guy?"

"I'll take the firm. Let's get to it."

Thirty minutes later, the other two members of their team arrived. Rocket and Eagle filled their coffee mugs and joined them at the table with their own laptops.

"Peyton West gave me her copy of the police report," Blaze told everyone. "She said they weren't too happy about handing it over. I scanned it and moved it to our private cloud storage. Take a minute to open it and take a look."

"This is bullshit." Rocket clicked a few keys then stared at his computer screen. "There's nothing here. Not even a description of the car. 'Brown' covers half the cars in the universe."

Blaze nodded. "Exactly. When she tried to find out more, the cops stonewalled her."

Eagle made a rude noise. "We all know, although we don't like to acknowledge it, that not every cop is as standup we'd like. Bad apples are few and far between, but they happen. Money talks."

"I promise you that's what happened here."

"I want to know more about our client," Rocket told him. "Your info was pretty sketchy."

He'd done that deliberately, not wanting them to develop any preconceived notions about her.

"Type Peyton West in the search bar and you'll find whatever you want. Viper already checked her out last night. Then I'll catch you up to date."

At one o'clock, they ordered food from a local deli. When it came, they took a break to discuss whatever they'd found.

"Nobody's that squeaky clean," Rocket said, taking a sip of his soda. "Everyone slips sometime. It's human nature."

"That's what I say," Eagle agreed. "It's almost too good to be true."

"And maybe she's just what she seems." Blaze bit down on his temper. They were just doing the job. Vetting a client was ingrained in them. "Every once in a while, someone comes along who is."

The others stared at him.

Rocket spoke first. "So that's how it is."

"What? That's not how anything is. I met her, I spent a lot of time with her, I checked her out. She's all good."

"Okay. Fine." Viper held up his hands. "Back to Dane Hollister. Our dead man. They killed him for something, and being the poster child for good behavior isn't it."

Rocket took a bite of sandwich, chewed and swallowed, a thoughtful expression on his face. "What if it isn't him?" he drawled in his slow voice. "What if it has to do with someone or something at the law firm that he happened on by accident?"

"We need to dig as deep into as we can go," Blaze agreed. "Lawyers are very good at hiding things."

"I'll do it," Eagle told him.

Rocket leaned back in his chair. "We need to look into the sister. It's possible Peyton West has no idea what her sister's been doing from the time she left for college until now. All she saw was what they let her see on her visits."

"She's not dumb." Blaze ground his teeth. He didn't want to think that Brianne Hollister might have been able to pull the wool over her sister's eyes.

"I didn't say that," Rocket told him. "But sometimes we only see what we want to see. At least let me make sure that's a dead end. Let me get out my virtual shovel and start digging."

The other three divided up the rest of the chores and set up to work.

"One thing before we get started," Blaze told them. "Once we get this information, we're going to need to interact with these people in person, somehow, some way. You can only find out so much from reading. We've done it before, gone into someone else's territory. We just have to figure out who's going to do what."

Viper nodded. "Agreed."

"I want to bring up one more thing." Blaze shifted in his chair. "Our client needs protection. She's been pushing the buttons of people who've shown they'll do whatever it takes to keep their secrets. If I'm satisfied with what she shows me at the range, I'll see that she's armed, but I'd rather have eyes on her, and her sister."

Rocket nodded. "I agree. If Peyton West isn't with her sister at any time, it means Brianne Hollister is a sitting target. The hospital security can only do so much."

"We don't just want to stick an armed guard at the door. For one thing, the hospital might give us a hard time, and for another, I'd really like to draw out whoever might be looking to kill her."

"What do you have in mind?"

"Oh, wait." Viper snapped his fingers. "We did that job for the head of internal medicine at the hospital. Last year, remember? He was so grateful he said if we ever needed anything, to let him know. How about if I go see him and find out what kind of arrangement we can work out?"

Blaze nodded. "Sounds good. Thanks."

Viper wandered into the living room with his cell phone, away from the conversation.

Blaze woke up his laptop. "We need to figure out who's pulling the strings here. Much as I hate the idea, someone has paid off a lot of people. Cops. Emergency techs. Employees at the restaurant. That has to be the answer, but we also know that's not easy to do. It has to be someone with enough power to scare the shit out of them if they even think about changing their stories."

"Shit, Blaze." Viper ran his fingers through his hair. "That could be anyone. Why don't we just pull up the whole damn phone book?"

"I hear you, but I don't think it's that big a problem. What people with power was Dane closest to? The managing partner of his law firm. Then there are the guy's friends. His connections. Someone who owes him a favor that he could call in. It takes a lot of money and power to scrub a scene like that."

"Okay." Eagle stretched his hands and cracked his knuckles. "I'll start with that guy. See every place his name has popped up and with who."

"He has a son with the firm," Rocket added. "Maybe he's at the bottom of this. I'll dig into him as soon as I finish with the sister."

Viper came back into the room, shoving his phone in his pocket. "I spoke to Dr. Hendry. He has some ideas how we can work the security thing. Meanwhile he's having hospital security give some extra attention to that ward. Blaze, what do you want me to focus on?"

"I think the social activities of the Hollisters. We're already into the law firm, but this could have its origins in some social situation."

"I'm on it."

Blaze looked around at everyone. "Okay. Let's get to work."

* * * *

Peyton was still tired, having slept fitfully, her dreams constantly disturbed by erotic images of the man she'd met the day before. How was it that Blaze Hamilton was the sudden star of unexpected erotic dreams? Each time she dozed off again, there he was, big as life, filling her dreams, his smile sending flashes of heat through her.

She finally decided to give up any attempt at sleep and got out of bed. For a while she tried working on the edits for her latest book, but her brain just didn't want to connect with it. With a sigh, she sent texts to both her publisher and agent, explaining the details of her family emergency and telling them her head was just not in it until she could resolve the situation. Within minutes she had a phone call from her agent and a text from her publisher telling her to take care of family first. They'd just move the release date back and to let them know if there was anything they could do. She felt very blessed to have people like that in her life.

Closing her laptop, she headed to the shower. She'd just get to the hospital earlier than usual, bringing coffee and snacks full of sugar and fat. She hadn't wanted to take the time for a real meal in a week, but she didn't have time to worry now about what she was doing to her body.

* * * *

As she always did when she arrived, she reached for Brianne's hand and gave it a gentle squeeze. She hoped each time there'd be a response, but so far nothing. She brushed Brianne's hair back from her face and rearranged the worn pink plush elephant lying next to her. Petal had been with her sister since her emergency appendectomy years ago. It had gone everywhere with her — college, work, into her marriage. The only time Peyton had been in the Hollister house was the day after she'd arrived, when she'd gone to retrieve Petal, hoping it would somehow reach her sister. She'd found it sitting on her dresser and had to swallow back a hysterical laugh as she wondered how Dane had liked having a threesome with the stuffed elephant.

Giving Brianne's hand one more light squeeze, she dropped into the chair beside the bed, opened her coffee, bit off and chewed a mouthful of blueberry muffin and began her usual monologue to a silent Brianne. She liked to think that reminding her sister of their childhood, their parents — taken from them much too early — old boyfriends, Brianne and Dane's wedding, would help to reawaken her brain. She'd been doing it in bits and pieces, but today she pulled everything she could think of out of her head.

The morning moved along and she never stopped talking. Her voice grew hoarse, but her sister never moved, never responded, never opened her eyes. From time to time, she glanced at the picture she'd found at Brianne's house, a double frame with pictures of her sister and Dane. She'd hoped maybe somehow it could send silent signals, even as she realized how foolish that was. There was so much love shining from them that she had to work hard not to burst into tears.

Peyton finished her third bottle of water since lunch and threw the empty into the wastebasket. She sat back in the chair, trying to force herself to relax. Anguish was her constant companion. How long could a human being remain in a coma before reaching the point of no return? She'd spent the first two days at the hospital researching everything she could find online. She'd learned comas could last from days to years and there was no way to predict them. Some articles said there was some evidence that people could hear and understand words spoken to them — one of the reasons she talked until her voice was hoarse.

She'd also read somewhere that a person could transfer anxiety to a patient. She had no idea if that was true, but she wasn't taking any chances.

She wanted to rail against the situation, to curse loudly and beat the wall with her fists. How the hell had this happened? Dane and Brianne hadn't lived a wild life or hung out with off-the-wall people. They hadn't gotten involved in things they shouldn't and had lived a really good life. They'd even been talking about having a baby.

Peter Kendrick and his son had both been at the funeral, appropriately solicitous and saddened. At that time, they'd given her their cards in case they could be of any help. He'd repeated it the first time she'd called him. By the second call, he'd sounded more reserved.

The last conversation she'd had with him had been far from satisfactory. At first, he'd been just as considerate and comforting as he'd been when he'd called her about the disaster, as well as in their first conversation. But when she'd started to probe for any additional information that could help her, maybe something to do with a lawsuit Dane was working on, his tone of voice had hardened and he'd shut her down. He'd reminded her they were all grieving the loss of her brother-in-law, and more so because it looked like whoever did it might never be located. Told her the police had done what they could. If the police couldn't find anything, then sadly and unfortunately, it meant the person responsible had become invisible. She needed to focus all her energies on her sister's recovery.

It hadn't taken her long to realize she'd reached a dead end with the man. He wanted this over and done with, whether because he knew something or he just didn't want the firm involved any more than it already was.

Which of course only made her more suspicious.

She'd met plenty of people like Peter Kendrick in her life. Wealthy, powerful, privileged. Rules didn't apply to them, and if they were in the legal profession, they could bend them to their own advantage. What she'd managed to find about the firm told her little to nothing. And of course, client lists were private, so she couldn't learn anything that way.

But she had a feeling. She'd been an author for fifteen years, a pretty successful one at that, and had developed a good sense of intuition. In preparing her books, she'd conducted a lot of interviews, so she'd learned to read people pretty well. She didn't know for sure if Peter Kendrick was hiding something that involved him, but she knew he wanted her to go away. Maybe he was just worried about blowback on the firm, but whatever it was, he definitely was trying to get her off the tack she was taking.

She kept thinking this had to involve one of Dane's clients, but how could she find out?

That's what you hired Galaxy for, remember?

And she'd do well to keep that in mind. She opened yet another bottle of water, took a deep swallow and leaned forward.

"Hey, Brianne. Let me tell you about this guy I met yesterday. I had to find someone who could get at the truth about the accident and your sexy Dr. Hamilton turned me on to his brother. Believe it or not, he runs some kind of civilian black ops operation." She chuckled. "It was like being in an episode of a television show. They don't even have an office. Their office is on a plane that I think was designed for gazillionaires." She paused. "Oh, wait. They *are* gazillionaires. They won the Powerball lottery. Anyway, so far, I've only met Dr. Hamilton's brother. He's taking the lead on this. I think you'd really like him. His real name is Scott, but his nickname is Blaze. They all use their military code names."

She took a sip of coffee. "I have to say, his suits him. He's definitely one hot guy."

She studied her sister. Did her eyelids just move? Maybe a teeny bit? Was she trying to smile? God, she was going to drive herself crazy.

Just keep talking.

"What's that? What's he like? Oh, well. Incredible. Big. Athletic. Lots of muscles. Carries himself with that military bearing that turns women on. But smart, too." She leaned in a little closer. "And very, very sexy."

"So my patients tell me." The deep voice came from behind her, breaking into her little speech.

"Oh, my god. Dr. Hamilton." How embarrassing. She felt heat creep all the way up her body and was sure her face was bright red.

He winked. "That's okay. I assume that's my brother you were talking about."

Peyton took a deep breath and managed to settle herself.

"You never know. I might have been talking about you." Could she be any more embarrassed?

His laugh was warm and friendly. "That's okay. I'm used to second place in the beefcake sweepstakes after women meet Scott. Uh, that is, Blaze."

"I think you're both winners." *There.* Maybe that took her foot out of her mouth.

"I was glad to hear you talking to your sister." Nolan Hamilton eased smoothly into a new conversation. "Nothing's been proven as to the value of it, but a lot of medical people, including me, think it has an effect. That the voice of a family member or close friend can reach the patient's subconscious."

"I'd like to think so. This is just so devastating." She looked up at Nolan. "I hope your brother can find out what's behind all this."

"He will. I haven't a doubt. Blaze specializes in doing the impossible. That's why he and his friends were such outstanding SEALs."

"Thanks for putting me in touch with him."

He nodded. "I knew if anyone could get answers, it was Galaxy. Well, I'm just going to do a quick check of Brianne here, then I'll leave you to your conversation."

Peyton watched Nolan Hamilton check Brianne's vitals and test her reactions, lifting her eyelids and checking her pupils, then finally examining her uninjured arm and leg.

"Did the nurse tell you we X-rayed her arm and leg and they're healing nicely?"

"She did. What do you think about—everything else?" She tried to keep the anxiety out of her voice.

"I think she's no worse, and that in itself could be a good sign. Her vitals are good, her arm and leg are healing properly."

"But she's not any closer to waking up, right?"

"It's really hard to say. There's no hard and fast rule about comatose patients. Brianne sustained a head injury when she hit the pavement and it caused swelling in the brain. We're giving her medication intravenously to hydrate and nourish her. As long as she's in this state, her brain can continue to heal. Next week we'll do another scan to see how much the swelling has gone down."

"Last week you said she was improving," she reminded him.

He nodded. "That's right. And I believe she's continuing in that direction, but there is just no hurrying the brain."

Peyton swallowed back the retort that wanted to pop out. "I know you're doing all you can for her," she assured him, "and I really appreciate it. It's just so…hard."

"Don't I know it. Well. I understand Blaze is taking you out for a little target practice today."

"Yes. He's picking me up around four." She managed a grin. "I think I shocked him when I told him I had a carry permit."

"If you did, that's a bonus for you. Hardly anything ever shocks him."

"Thank you again for putting me in touch with him."

"Like I said in the beginning, if anyone can help you, it's the men of Galaxy." He glanced at his watch. "Sorry to run, but I need to check on some of my patients. If you need anything, the nurses are here to help you."

"I guess so is the hospital security guard who makes a circuit on the floor every so often."

Nolan laughed. "My brother's way of unobtrusive protection." Then his face lost all humor. "But better safe than sorry. I'd be very upset if someone tried something in my hospital. We pride ourselves on running a secure place for our patients and their visitors."

"I'd say that there's probably nothing to worry about, but after what happened to Dane and Brianne, I don't believe anything anymore."

"Blaze and his friends will take good care of you. That's a guarantee."

Peyton had to believe that. It was her only chance. Hers and Brianne's.

About a quarter to four, her phone buzzed with a text from Blaze.

On my way. Making some arrangements regarding your sister. All is good. See you shortly.

Arrangements? What kind? Had he learned something that made whatever this was a necessity? She was tempted to text him back and ask him but decided to wait until he got there. She leaned back in her chair and closed her eyes, intent on pulling herself together before he got there. She was stunned when an image of Blaze popped into her brain, especially since he was naked.

Naked?

What the hell?

But she kept her eyes closed, enjoying the vision, at least for a few moments. He was just as muscular as the clothes had hinted at, not an inch of spare flesh on him. His chest was dusted with hair as dark as that on his head, barely covering the flat male nipples that peeked out. And there, between his strong thighs, in a nest of ebony hair, was truly the most magnificent cock she had ever seen.

Not, she told herself, that she had seen all that many. She was choosy about her relationships. One-night stands didn't appeal to her and the men she'd been involved with had been just okay. Sometimes she wondered if her writer's mind had glorified a possible lover too much and no flesh and blood man could live up to her dreams.

That was before she'd met Blaze.

Damn!

How was it that in less than two days, she'd become so attracted to this man? Oh, well, besides the mouthwatering body, the electric presence and the sharp brain, he had also treated her with the utmost respect. She wrote about men like this but hadn't ever met one. She hoped she could keep herself together and not do something stupid.

She had no idea how much time had passed until she heard a knock at the door and turned to see Blaze standing in the opening. Her breath caught at the sight of him, his hardened, muscular body clothed in a tight T-shirt and jeans that outlined his legs. She had to force herself not to glance at his fly and imagine what was behind it.

Holy shit!

She was pretty sure her brain had never taken a side trip like that when she'd looked at other men. She felt as if she'd swallowed some kind of pill when they'd met yesterday that had turned her into someone she didn't know.

"What's the latest word on your sister?"

Peyton sighed. "Still the same. Your brother was in here a while ago and said she's doing as well as can be expected."

"My partners said to tell you they're all thinking good, positive thoughts."

She managed a smile. "Please thank them for me."

He nodded at the bed. "What's with the stuffed animal?"

"I grabbed it from her house." She told him the history of Petal and how she hoped it would make a difference.

"So." He studied her. "Ready to show me what a sharpshooter you are?"

"I think I might surprise you."

"Let's go and find out."

She leaned over the bed, kissed her fingertips and touched her sister's cheek.

"Pleasant dreams," she whispered. "Wake up soon." Then she turned to Blaze. "I'm ready."

Before they could leave the room, a nurse and an orderly walked in.

Peyton looked from one to the other. "What's going on?"

The nurse pulled a sheet of paper from her pocket and handed it to Peyton. "Dr. Hamilton's having her moved to the room at the end of the corridor. I think because it's quieter."

Quieter? Peyton frowned. She hadn't noticed all that much noise.

Blaze took her arm to nudge her out of the way.

"It's all good. I know about it. Peyton, let's get out of their way."

"But—"

"Come on. I'll explain."

If Blaze hadn't been standing there with her, she'd have protested the whole thing, doctor's orders or not. But then at the end of the corridor, near Brianne's new room, was a small waiting area with a couch, coffee table and two chairs. A man in hospital scrubs was seated on the couch, holding a tablet, but somehow she didn't think he was reading from it.

Blaze steered her over to him.

"Peyton West, meet Chuck Wagner."

When the man stood, she realized he was lankier than Blaze but just as tall. *Do they grow giants somewhere?*

"Pleasure to meet you, Peyton."

He shook her hand, and when he turned slightly, she noticed the hem of his top catching on something at the small of his back. *A gun? Here in the hospital?*

"Chuck and his brother, Alan, do contract work for us sometimes," Blaze told her. "He'll be guarding Brianne. We didn't want him sitting in her room. Invades her privacy, for one thing. For another, it gives him no warning if someone who looks out of place comes down the hall."

Peyton looked from one man to the other, a chill suddenly trickling down her spine.

"You think whoever this is would try to kill her here?"

"I think that to do what they did and also use all that power to try to squash it shows me they're desperate and might try anything. We're not even sure if your sister knows anything, but they might not want to take a chance."

The increasingly familiar taste of fear invaded her mouth. She swallowed hard to force it back. The idea that someone would be bold enough to attempt to kill Brianne here in the hospital scared the hell out of her.

Chuck Wagner had reseated himself with his tablet and nodded to Blaze.

"Good to go. Don't worry."

Blaze nodded. "Thanks. Alan's taking the alternate shift with you, right?"

Chuck nodded. "We're set."

"Call if the least little thing seems out of place."

"Don't worry. I will."

Peyton hurried to keep up with Blaze as he strode down the hall.

"Now I'm afraid to leave her."

"She'll be fine," he assured her. "Chuck is the best. Although he wasn't on my team, he was in my platoon. I know for a fact he's an expert both with handguns and rifles and knows six ways to kill a man with his hands."

Peyton shuddered. "I don't know whether to be afraid or grateful."

Blaze chuckled. "Definitely grateful. I'd want him guarding any member of my family."

"I trust your judgment, then." She stepped into the elevator. "I assume Nolan was instrumental in letting you arrange this?"

"He was. He wants Brianne Hollister protected as much as you do. But Viper also pulled a few strings with the director of the hospital. We helped him outwit a little jam last year and he was only too glad to repay the favor."

Peyton could only begin to imagine what that favor consisted of.

"Good. That's very good. Relieves my mind a lot, or as much as it can. Thank you."

She breathed a little easier as they rode down in the elevator. At least she could be assured that while she was gone this afternoon, her sister wouldn't be unprotected.

God. How did we get into this nightmare, anyway?

Chapter Six

Peyton and Blaze said little to each other as they left the hospital and drove to the same location where she'd boarded the plane.

"Are we flying somewhere?" She glanced over at him. "I thought we were going to a gun range. Don't tell me there aren't any locally, because I wouldn't believe it."

"No." He shook his head. "It's local all right. When we set up Galaxy, we knew we'd need to keep in practice. We wanted to avoid public ranges, indoor and out, so we set up our own."

Of course they did, she thought. *When you have all the money in the world, you can even build your own little city if you want.* Truth be told, however, she was just as glad they wouldn't be out in the public eye, under all that scrutiny. Someone could be watching them. Watching *her*. And that might not be as farfetched as it sounded. Two weeks ago, she would have considered it a great plot point. Now everything was suspect and everyone could be spying for *them*, whoever *they* turned out to be.

Blaze drove to the second hangar and parked by the entrance. At the moment, they were the only ones there. He unlocked the door and ushered her inside. At one of the bays, he set out an array of handguns for her to choose from. She had to be careful because she had small hands and she needed a gun she could grip well, finally choosing the Glock Subcompact Slimline.

Peyton looked around. This hangar really was outfitted as a soundproofed gun range, with multiple shooting bays, motorized targets and a storage closet that held a large supply of bullets.

"Impressive," she told him. "Very impressive."

"We try to make sure we practice in here at least once a week," Blaze told her as he took things from the supply area. "We have to always be at the top of our game. We also work out every day if we're not involved with a client."

She hadn't practiced in quite a while, busy as she'd been meeting a deadline with her publisher, so she was a little rusty at first. And slower than usual, taking more time to sight the target. She waited for Blaze to make some kind of comment, but he was patient with her, showing her how to adjust her grip until it all felt comfortable again. She was acutely aware of him standing behind her, of the heat emanating from his body where it lightly touched hers. Of his hands molded around hers while she tested the guns. And his stance, back far enough to give her room but so *there* she was conscious of it every second. She had to force herself to stop thinking about his presence, if that was possible, and concentrate on the target.

He had stacked small boxes of bullets for her on the bay's counter and she could actually feel him watching her each time she loaded the clip, then waiting patiently while she emptied it into the target. However, by the time they'd finished the session, she could tell he was surprised.

"You only missed one in the center circle." His tone had a touch of amazement as he pushed the button so the target slid forward to where they stood.

Her shots were so clustered she had shredded the paper.

Peyton laughed. "I try to practice as much as I can. I mean, why have a gun if you can't use it properly, right?"

"I agree. But I'm curious. What got you into firearms?"

"A book I was writing. My hero had to be an expert with a handgun. Since I'm a fanatic about my research, I bought a gun, with lots of advice, and took an intensive course so I could get my concealed carry license." She grinned. "Now my heroines are sometimes well-trained and find themselves in situations where they need to be good."

He raised an eyebrow. "Your bio says you write romance. I don't exactly read it myself, but doesn't it put a damper on things if the woman is carrying a gun?"

Peyton smiled in spite of herself. "Technically I write what's called romantic suspense. My tag line is alpha heroes and strong women. For a macho guy like you, that means thrillers with a healthy dose of romance and very hot sex."

As soon as she said the words, she snapped her mouth shut. Heat worked its way up her neck and into her cheeks and she busied herself taking the gun apart and checking everything.

Blaze laughed, the deep sound of it wrapping around her and easing some of her tension.

"Macho guys like me? Should I be flattered or insulted?"

"I'd think you'd be flattered."

Oh, lord. She just kept opening her mouth wider to get her foot further inside it.

"Is that a fact. So you do research for your books. Does that include the hot sex part, too?"

Peyton tried to swallow, but her mouth was too dry. She kept her eyes focused on the gun and just shrugged her shoulders. "Not necessarily. I can read a lot about it. For research."

"Yeah? What's the fun in that?"

He touched her arm and she nearly dropped the Glock.

"Oh, sorry." *Great. Very professional.*

He took the gun gently from her hands and set it on the counter of the bay, then turned her so she faced him. For a long moment, neither of them moved. His hands tightened on her and her pulse ratcheted up. She should take a step back. *Now. Right now.* But she couldn't make herself do it.

Blaze opened his mouth, closed it, then cleared his throat.

"I have a confession to make, but first, here's something for you to know about me. I was a SEAL for sixteen years. I received probably the most rigorous military training there is, calling for incredible discipline. The missions we conducted were tough and required every bit of skill and discipline we'd been taught. They were high voltage and often very secret. I never got involved with anyone because I didn't want to distract myself, so all my so-called relationships were very casual."

"That's okay. You don't need to say anything else. I understand. I hope you don't think I was—"

"Stop."

His gaze locked with hers and his hands were warm on her shoulders, his touch burning through her.

"I'm telling you this because it's the first time in all these years that a woman has gotten under my defenses. And I mean, before I could blink. That's not who I am. I shouldn't even be saying this to you, it's completely unprofessional and my partners will probably kill me. I was out of line with my comment, or at least the implication."

"Wait. Please wait." She held up her hand. For a moment she felt as if she couldn't breathe. "What are you saying? You're attracted to me? Is that what you're telling me?"

She expected him to look away, but his gaze never wavered and something flared in his eyes. Peyton wondered if she was still back at the hospital, dozing in the chair, and this was some kind of dream.

"Yeah. That. You really should fire us. Or me. My partners can handle this."

"Your partners." She wet her suddenly dry lips. "Uh-huh. But you said that whoever makes the connection takes the lead on the case. That you would be the one I worked with. I hired you, specifically. Now you want to quit? Is... Is that what you want?"

"Hell, no. Peyton, you've got a dangerous situation here that we haven't even begun to uncover, and I want to get answers for you. I want the truth as much as you do. Believe me. That's why—"

He stopped and just stared at her.

"Why what, Blaze?" What on earth was going on here? Whatever it was, she didn't want him to walk away from this.

"Oh, hell."

He cupped her face in his large, warm hands, his eyes burning with heat, and so slowly she was afraid he'd change his mind. But then his mouth pressed against her, gently but firmly, and heat surged through her body. Her nipples turned to hardened peaks, her sex throbbed as if a bass drum was lodged there and a hunger she'd never experienced before surged through her.

When he nudged her lips apart with the tip of his tongue, she gladly opened her mouth for him and let that tongue sweep inside. Oh, god, he tasted so good, the heady flavor of a real male. It was an explosion of undefined emotion, like nothing she'd ever felt before.

The kiss went on and on, hot and erotic and sexy, until she had no breath left but still could not break away. Blaze's arms banded around her, pressing her body to his. She could feel every ridge of muscle. Every dip and curve, from the solid flatness of his chest and belly to the thick hardness of his cock straining behind the denim of his jeans.

It could have been minutes, an hour, the next day before at last he lifted his head. She didn't know which of them was breathing harder. There was a hunger in his eyes that eclipsed anything she might have expected to see. She wondered if hers reflected the same intensity. And even though the kiss was broken, Blaze still held her tight against his body, his big hands cupping the cheeks of her ass as he pressed against her.

"Jesus," he said at last, his breath still unsteady.

Her smile was shaky. "I agree. What the hell was that?"

Blaze looked as shaken as she felt. "I think it was an earthquake at the top of the Richter scale. Listen, Peyton, I…"

He stopped as if he couldn't find the right words.

She knew exactly how he felt. "Um, well, I…"

He tilted up her chin with the tips of his fingers and studied her face.

"I don't know if I should apologize or celebrate." His laugh was rough and unsteady. "That kiss kicked my ass. Please tell me I wasn't in it all by myself."

"No. You weren't. I thought you could tell." She swallowed. "But how did we get here, Blaze? This isn't like me at all. One minute I'm frantically trying to find out who put my sister in a coma and hiring people whose office is in a plane to do it. The next I'm getting kissed out of my mind, a kiss so hot I think the soles of my feet got singed. Do you know what's going on here?"

"I do." His lips tilted up in a tentative grin. "But you have to promise not to smack me if I tell you."

Peyton let out a sigh. "How can I smack you when I was a willing participant?"

"The first thing I want to tell you is, everything else aside, my focus is on finding out who ran down your sister and brother-in-law and getting justice for you. For them."

"Okay. And the second thing?"

"Whatever that was that just exploded between us? I can't put it back in a bottle, Peyton. And I'm not sure I can keep my hands off you if we do this together. So again, if you want me to step back and let one of the others take lead, I'll understand. I'm not in the habit of taking advantage of women at a bad place in their lives. That's not who I am."

"You don't think I can tell that? I like to think I have good instincts about people. No, Blaze, I think I'm the one who should be embarrassed." She studied his face, looking for some indication of his real thoughts. "This isn't my usual style, either, but I don't think I can turn it off. So unless you want to switch me to one of your partners, we're doing this together." She stopped and drew another breath. "All of it."

Every muscle in his body seemed to relax and relief washed over his face.

"Thank fuck. Really. I thought I had really screwed things up here." He brushed a light kiss over her lips. "How did I get so lucky? Smart, sexy and a crack shot. My partners would kill for this."

Peyton grinned at him. "I'm kind of in a daze myself."

"Meanwhile, let's clean this stuff up and I'll check in with the others. They all had their assignments for today."

"What kind of assignments?"

"Research on all the players. We've all learned through trial and error how to dig deeper and scrounge up every bit of information. We don't start the heavy lifting until we know everything there is to find out about the key players. Just like in the SEALs, research is an important part of every mission."

Peyton cocked her head. "Really? Somehow I didn't see you all hunched over computers. I had images of fierce warriors doing secret things no one else would handle."

Blaze grinned. "Oh, we do that, too. More often than we'd thought we would. And speaking of being hunched over computers, I need to check in again and see where we're at. Let's sit down on that bench where the supplies are and I'll give Viper a shout. We'll both be on speaker so everyone's on the call."

When Viper answered, Blaze put the call on speaker so she could hear.

"Okay, guys, our client is right here with me so watch your language."

Peyton paid careful attention as each of them spoke in turn. She could almost feel the testosterone flowing from the phone, if such a thing was possible. They had dug up more than she expected, but their information also reinforced her belief that she was up against some very powerful people.

Blaze listened without interrupting, paying attention until they were all finished.

"So you're telling me that both traffic detectives are still tied up on an extended assignment? What the hell could that be? It's traffic, right?"

"Nobody would give me specifics. Just said they'd been given a temporary assignment." Eagle's voice had an edge to it. "Could they be more obvious? They might as well have hung out a sign."

"And their supervisor?"

"Said he can't discuss it with people not related to the incident."

"Incident." Blaze snorted. "That's an interesting word to use."

"No kidding." This was Rocket's voice. "I'm following up on Peter Kendrick. On the surface, he looks so clean he squeaks, but I also learned he has a son. A lawyer, just like his dad, and on the list of firm attorneys. He could be just as clean, but maybe not. And as we all know, people will go to any lengths to protect their kids. I'm going to talk to some people and see what I come up with."

"Good. I'm thinking one of us may need to visit the law firm. Can you put together a package with impressive creds and a good story as to why we'd want to hire them?"

"No sweat." Rocket's laugh boomed from the phone. "I'll come up with something really good. Also, I was thinking one of us should connect with Tom Hernandez."

Peyton glanced at Blaze. "He is a part of this team, also? Where does he fit in?"

"He's a longtime friend of mine who put our corporation together and did all the legal work. As we went through the process he became a solid part of the team."

"Good thought."

"Do you want to keep that for yourself?"

Blaze shook his head. "No. He knows all of us now and I have other priorities at the moment."

Peyton looked down at her hands, avoiding Blaze's penetrating gaze.

"Give him a call," Blaze continued. "He's plugged into the legal scene in town pretty deep. Viper's doing a deep dive into the firm and seeing what he can find online, but it would help to have Dan's opinion. And maybe he has some bits and pieces he can share."

"Got it. Thanks. Here's Eagle."

"Hey, Eagle," Blaze acknowledged. "Viper's good enough with research and he has a nose for it, but you're the electronics expert in the group. Can you tap into the CCTV cameras? And is there a way you can find tapes that are three weeks old, or do you have to go to some facility and physically run them? We've got to find that car and identify it. God only knows where it is now, but at least we can figure out who the owner is."

"Lucky for us, Tampa stores all their videos in a cloud for sixty days. I'll let you know how secure it is when I get finished trying to access them. Once I'm in, I'll go through them as fast as I can. I'll head home to do it, because I need a more sophisticated computer, plus my primary one has the appropriate software on it."

"Good enough, but keep in touch. I'll be taking Peyton by the hospital to check on her sister and I'll see if anything's rattled Wagner's cage. First, though, we're going to take another look at the place where the hit-and-run happened. If any of you find anything at all, no matter how insignificant it might be, give me a shout."

"By the way, the other leads you suggested we check out? Nothing there."

"Good. Excellent. Thanks. Keep at it."

"Okay. We'll call if we hit pay dirt anywhere."

Blaze disconnected and put the phone in his pocket. When he rose, he held out his hand to Peyton, wrapping it around hers. Instead of heading toward the exit, though, he stood there for a moment, studying her.

"What?" She frowned. "Is something wrong?"

"I hope not." He blew out a breath. "Listen, Peyton. I just have to get this out there."

Every muscle in her body tightened. *What's wrong?*

"Get what out?"

"If I was out of line before with that kiss, just tell me now. I committed to handling this case for you and that's the priority. I'm damn sure no one else can or will want to cut through the bullshit out there like Galaxy.

Plus somebody's throwing some muscle into this to keep people from doing just that. We want to do this, and I know we can."

She studied his face. "I sense a 'but' in there."

"But I don't want there to be a problem between us. I never come on to clients like that. None of us do. It's an unwritten rule. If you want one of my partners to take over, I'll just step aside. You won't even have to deal with me. Just please tell me everything's okay and that I didn't overstep."

She stared at him for a moment, stunned at how nervous he was about it, then burst out laughing. He stared at her until she finally stopped and caught her breath.

"Sorry. I think that was all the tension catching up with me. No, you weren't out of line. Not even a little. In case you didn't notice, I was as into it as you were. Is it something I usually do? Absolutely not. Is this a normal situation? Again, no. Would I change one thing I did? No once more." She stopped and caught her breath. "This whole business is throwing things out of whack, but I am not one bit sorry about that kiss. I wanted it as much as you did, and you have to know it wasn't one-sided. Not by any means, so don't apologize. If it makes *you* think less of *me*, well, I can't help it."

She halted, silently telling herself it was time to shut up.

Blaze let out a long breath then smiled and stroked his fingers down her cheek.

"This is so off the wall for me," he said. "Maybe I jumped in with both feet, but I'm not walking away from it, and I'm glad you aren't, either." He brushed a light kiss on her mouth. "Damn glad."

She smiled. "Good."

"Okay, then." In the next minute, he was all business again. "Listen, Peyton. Before we hit the hospital, I want to drive by the scene where the disaster happened. Rocket checked it out already, but I want to see for myself. You up for a ride, or you want me to take you back to be with your sister now?"

"No." She shook her head. "I want to go with you. I looked at it as well, but I want to know what you see from your perspective."

"Then let's go see what we can find out."

He held her hand as they walked to his car. For the first time since she'd received that phone call in the middle of the night, Peyton began to think that they would find answers and someone would be made to pay for what happened. As they headed back into the city, she pulled out her cell and called the hospital.

She glanced at Blaze while she hit the speed dial for the number.

"I know it's a waste of time, but I always call for reports when I'm away from Brianne for any length of time. If anything happened, they'd contact me right away."

"Not a waste if it puts your mind at ease. Brianne's situation is so unpredictable. She could wake up any time, right?"

She breathed a sigh of relief when the nurse she spoke with told her there had been no change in Brianne's condition.

"At least she didn't suddenly get worse," she told Blaze when she disconnected the call. "It's the only thing I have to hang on to right now."

"It's that old saying," he told her. "No news is good news. Right?"

"Right. But now I'm ready for something. Anything."

"Let's see if the scene tells us anything new."

They worked their way into South Tampa through the five-thirty traffic and over to Calypso. The parking lot across the street was full—probably, Peyton thought, with cocktail hour hangouts killing time until dinner. She'd been told Calypso's dinner hour didn't really start until seven. Before that it was cocktails in the bar or appetizers in the wine cellar. Probably, she thought, so they could handle the cost of the dinner. She'd looked up Calypso online and nearly passed out at the prices. Dane Hollister must have made a damn good living to be able to afford to take Brianne to places like this.

There was curbside parking across the street from the restaurant and luckily, as Blaze pointed out, this was not a street where one usually found people walking. She could see someone was leaving just as they pulled up. He parked and turned off the engine.

"Let's head up the sidewalk a little way. We can't drive slowly enough to see what I want."

"We'll be the only people walking," she commented.

"I know, but we'll pretend we're looking for an address. Come on."

He was good at this, she realized. He actually acted as if they were searching for a place.

"The car came from that direction." Blaze indicated with his head. "If it was parked in this line, it would have been facing away from Calypso, so whoever was driving would have had to turn around. Let's see where else it could have been."

Peyton realized at once this was not a street that saw a lot of walkers. There was a boutique hotel, a couple of small office buildings and some small, eclectic businesses. Some of them had parking spaces at the side.

"Whoever it was could have been waiting here." Blaze pointed at one of them. "Or here. Or the next one. You can see the entrance to Calypso from any of them, the way the street takes a little jog."

"So it was just a matter of watching until they came out. But…"

They stopped, waiting for the car that wanted to pull out into the street.

"Let's wait until we get back in the car," he told her. "We're the only ones walking. Here we are."

Once they were in the car, he cranked the engine so the air conditioning would come on, but he didn't pull away from the curb.

"How did whoever it was know…"

"They had to know…"

They both spoke at the same time, looked at each other and grinned.

"You first," she said.

"This wasn't a random thing. Calypso is not a place that you just drop into and hope they have a table free. You have to make reservations, so whoever did this had access to Dane's calendar."

"So…someone from his office?" Peyton frowned. "I didn't get that vibe when I was there, but then I wasn't looking for it. I focused only on Kendrick. I wasn't thinking of anything else."

"We need to make a list of possibles. People who would know their schedules. The places they liked to go. Who would be in a position to know about that reservation no matter how far in advance it was made?" He snapped his fingers. "What happened to your sister's belongings after the accident? Her purse?"

Peyton frowned. "I think they're in a drawer in her room. The nurse apologized that they'd had to cut off her clothes to treat her, but I didn't care. The clothes were the least important things. I didn't think about anything else. Why?"

"She has to have a cell phone. These days, everyone who breathes has one. And what does everyone have on that piece of equipment besides phone numbers?"

Peyton scrunched her forehead. "Many things. I'm not sure what you're looking for."

"A calendar, Peyton. Notes. Photos. Every time they even think of doing something they put it in their phones. They take pictures of the oddest things. People keep their entire lives on their cell phones." He snapped his fingers. "And even if the phone is destroyed, everything gets stored in the cloud. The all-knowing cloud."

"If you have sign-in information and passwords," she reminded him.

"First, we have to find the phones, Dane's as well as Brianne's. Then we'll worry about passwords. What happened to Dane's stuff?"

"The clothes were destroyed. If he had anything else, your guess is as good as mine. I don't know what happened to his car. Didn't think to ask. I assumed it was leased by the firm and they took care of it. Sorry, it just wasn't high on my list of priorities."

"Understandable."

"His parents might have taken anything salvageable, but they never said a word to me. The body was still at the medical examiner's when I got into town. From there it went right down to the funeral home. I'm sorry, Blaze, I just wasn't thinking straight at the time. And it never occurred to me that we might need whatever he might have had with him."

"And why would you? There was no reason to think it was anything but what it looked like."

He reached over and took her hand as if it was the most natural thing in the world. The contact soothed her jangled nerves and she wound her fingers through his.

"Where did your sister keep her camera equipment? Did she have a studio somewhere?"

"She had a place set up at the house. Since most of her work was for advertising and promotional pieces, she didn't need a studio."

"We need to find those pictures she took," he pointed out, "and see if there's a way to identify the people in them."

"Of course," she snapped. "We should check Brianne's stuff at the hospital first. We're going there right now anyway, right?"

"Yes. After that, I'll hit their house and see what I can find."

"I want to go with you," she insisted.

"I thought you'd want to sit with Brianne."

"I do, but this is just as important. Maybe more so. I want to get to the bottom of this, Blaze."

"Okay, but first let's stop at Calypso and see if we can pry any info out of their staff, like how far ahead their reservation was made and what time it was for. All we know is it was late in the evening. When we get Brianne's phone, if we can open it, we might find any notations she made about it."

They drove around the block, and when they were even with the restaurant, Blaze turned in to the parking lot across the street.

"How late are you open?" Blaze asked the attendant who came out of the little shack.

Peyton noticed it wasn't the same man who had been here when Brianne and Dane were run down, the one she'd tried to question without success.

"Calypso closes at eleven during the week and twelve-thirty on the weekend. Someone is here usually until a half hour after that. The restaurant has a tiny parking lot so most of their customers park over here." He handed the parking ticket to Blaze.

Peyton cleared her throat. "Are you here all the time?"

"Right now, I am. I usually only work Sunday through Wednesday, but the weekend guy got another job, so I'm stuck with all the nights until they hire someone else."

It was obvious to Peyton he was anything but happy about the situation.

"That's too bad," Blaze sympathized. "You happen to know any reason he left?"

The attendant, who Peyton judged to be about twenty-five, shrugged. "Maybe he got tired of people pestering him with questions about that accident."

"Oh?"

Peyton had to bite her tongue to keep from saying anything. Better to let Blaze keep it going.

"Yeah. I guess everyone was driving him nuts. He was just here one day and gone the next."

"Oh. Okay. Well, thanks. Hope you get some help soon. Let's go, honey. And let's be very careful crossing the street."

Peyton swallowed a grin at 'honey' but let him take her hand in his. She was stunned at the spike of electricity that raced up her arm, and the memory of their kiss flashed in her brain.

Get it together, girl.

"Be careful of the traffic," Blaze reminded her.

As if it wasn't engraved on her brain. As two cars zipped past them, she couldn't help trying to imagine what had happened that night. Nausea bubbled up in her throat as she visualized the carnage of the scene. *God!* What if Brianne never came out of her coma?

Don't think that way. Be positive.

Then they were inside Calypso's. There were several people in front of them, so they had to wait to speak to the hostess.

"Can I help you?" She smiled at them when it was their turn, her professional personality in place, her dress slacks and ruffled shirt looking as if they'd just come from the store. "What name is the reservation under?"

"We actually don't have one," Blaze began, "but — "

"Oh, I'm so sorry. We don't take walk-ins. We're always booked away ahead, but if you'd like to pick a date now?"

"We're actually looking for a piece of information." Blaze looked at the reservation book in front of her. "Do you by any chance keep those books after the date has passed?"

Her perfect forehead wrinkled in a tiny frown. "Excuse me?"

"Well, for example, will you keep that reservation list after tonight or throw it away?"

She stared at him as if he had two heads. "Um, each book holds the reservations for a month. Once the book is full, the manager keeps it for thirty days in case we need information before throwing it away. Why are you asking?"

"Whew." Blaze looked at Peyton. "Maybe we'll win our bet."

"Bet?" The hostess quirked a perfectly shaped eyebrow. "About Calypso?"

"Yeah. We have a bet with friends of ours that they didn't celebrate their anniversary here. I told the husband I thought he was too cheap." He winked at her. "They insist they had dinner at Calypso, but I think my pinchpenny friend took his wife someplace else." He leaned in a little. "And I just love to get his goat."

"I don't know if I can give out that information." She fiddled with the pages in front of her nervously. "And people are lining up behind you."

"We'll wait. In fact, how about if I buy my lovely wife a drink while you take care of customers? Then you can give me a look at the book for five minutes." He rested one hand on the podium where the book was and only Peyton saw his fingers flex once.

The hostess covered whatever it was with her own hand and chewed her lip, casting a nervous glance over his shoulder.

"Oh, well. I guess I could do this. Just don't tell my boss. What's your friend's name and what date were you looking at? I can check it for you as soon as I seat these people."

Blaze gave her the information as soon as she returned to the podium and waited while she flipped through the pages of the book.

"It's here," she told him, studying a particular page and giving them the date. "They had a nine-thirty reservation. We were jammed that night, so it was the earliest we could fit them in, even though they called in three weeks in advance." Her lips curved in a tiny smile. "People book for Friday and Saturday weeks in advance. Sometimes months."

"I know it's a popular place." Blaze gave her his devastating grin. "Well, damn. Thanks a lot for your help, even though it's going to cost me big bucks." He took Peyton's hand again and guided her toward the door.

"I'm glad she didn't recognize the name," Peyton told him as they crossed the street.

"I'd hate to say anything bad about her, after she did us a favor, but I'm not sure our hostess pays attention to things like that."

"She did smile when you referred to me as your lovely wife," she teased.

"You *are* lovely. Don't forget it."

She didn't know quite what to say to that, so she just stood silently while Blaze handed the parking attendant their ticket and paid the tab.

"You guys didn't stay for dinner?" the kid asked.

"No. Got a call and had to leave." He took his keys from the kid and hustled Peyton to the car. "Let's get out of here. We have stuff to do. Our next stop, however, is the hospital so you can lay eyes on your sister."

"Thank you," she breathed. She didn't expect any change, but she could always hope.

Chapter Seven

Chuck Wagner looked up from his tablet as Peyton and Blaze came down the hallway from the elevator and stood to greet them.

"Quiet on all sides," he told them in a low voice.

"No unusual traffic?" Blaze asked.

"None. Your brother must have put the word out, because before anyone went into the room, they stopped and showed me their ID badges." He grinned and tapped his tablet until he brought up a program. Then he turned it so Blaze and Peyton could see it.

Peyton's eyes widened as she stared at the screen.

"You tapped into the hospital's employee database?"

Wagner shrugged. "Gotta make sure the pictures on the badges match the ones in the system. Right?"

She looked at Blaze. "Whatever you charge me, it's worth every penny."

"I'll remember that," he teased. The he sobered. "Let's check on your sister and take a look at her things."

Brianne looked to be in exactly the same position as when they'd left her.

What did I think, that she was going to get up and dance?

She took a moment to stand beside her sister's bed, reached for a hand and gave it a gentle squeeze.

"We're going to find out who did this," she promised. "Then we'll make them pay in spades." She paused. "I found a really great guy who's helping me. He and his partners will get answers. I know it."

She moved over to a wall that had a built-in closet, drawers and a mirror, and pulled out one of the drawers. Brianne's things were folded in neat piles, although there wasn't much. A cardigan sweater that apparently she hadn't been wearing that night, since it was still in one piece. Bloodstained shoes that she ought to throw away. A folded scarf. *And yes! There!* Beneath the sweater was her sister's purse. She held it up for Blaze to see then opened it, and smiled when she pulled out a cell phone.

"I knew she'd have it with her." She tapped it and the screen image popped up.

"Do you have any idea what her password might be?" Blaze asked.

Peyton shook her head. "I'm hoping it's something as easy as her date of birth or the date of her wedding. She was big on numbers."

"Wait until we get in the car to do it."

"Okay."

"I still want to go to their house. If Dane was suspicious of anyone, or had a confrontation or whatever, there might be something to give us a clue.

Do you think he might have written it down and put it someplace in the house?"

"Anything is possible. Researching my books, I learned never to say never and that anything can end up being a clue."

"Then let's get out of here. I'll see about opening the phone in the car."

After touching base with Chuck Wagner again, they took the elevator down to the lobby.

"Hold on a second," Blaze told her as they headed into the parking garage.

"What for? I want to see if I can open this phone."

"I agree. But first I think we should take your car to the hotel and have them valet park it. I don't intend for you to go off by yourself for anything, so we'll only need the one car."

She stopped as they entered the first floor of the garage. "Just leave it with the valet?"

"Unless you don't want to pay the extra expense. I just think it's safer if we leave it where it's not easily accessible."

Her eyes widened. "You think they'd try to damage my car?"

"Maybe with you in it." He held her back again. "You've been banging on enough doors and shaking enough trees to put a lot of people on notice," he pointed out to her. "Anyone who would commit the kind of crime that nearly killed your sister will do anything to stop you from finding out who they are. So yes, I think they would sabotage your car in some way. Lie in wait until the next time you use it."

"I'm used to writing about these things, not living them." She blew out a breath. "Okay. Then let's get my car and you can follow me to the hotel."

His extreme caution actually made her nervous. He insisted she get into his car and let him drive her to hers. Then he checked hers all over before she climbed in.

"I'll be right on your tail," he reminded her.

And I have my gun, she reminded herself, hardly able to believe she was even thinking it. Before they'd left the range, between the hot kiss and true confessions, Blaze had made sure her gun was loaded and given her a box of bullets.

'Let's pray you don't have to use this, but better to be prepared.'

Now she realized it gave her a feeling of security. Somewhere this had moved from checking out people who might want to cover up a scandal to realizing it was a lot more than that. They just had to find out what. She had to admit, she felt a lot better when her car was in the hands of valet parking and she was riding with Blaze.

So much had changed since she'd first climbed into this car earlier today. Had that been just a few hours ago? It was hard to believe. Their entire relationship had changed, making her acutely aware of his presence, the scent of the after shave he used, the flex of muscles in his arms as he drove. Her own body was giving its automatic responses. Only the urgency of the situation gave her the strength to pull in the frayed edges of her control.

And if one kiss did that to her, what would a full-body contact be like?

"Peyton?" His deep, rough voice pierced the fog around her brain.

"Yes?"

"You okay? I asked for your sister's address so I can plug it into the GPS."

"Oh, sorry. Here it is." *Focus*, she told herself. She was on a mission and couldn't lose sight of it.

Once she'd given him the information, she pulled Peyton's cell phone from her purse, turned it on and began looking for different passwords that would get her past the locked screen. She tried birthdays, wedding dates, even college graduations, but nothing seemed to work.

"Try numerical versions of names," Blaze told her. "Or places that were special to them. People who were special. Others…"

"I know what it is." She grinned as an idea hit her. "You know that stuffed animal you saw that I put in bed next to her? Petal?"

"Yeah. You think that's it? I mean, people have used things stranger than that."

"I won't know until I try it."

She converted the letters to corresponding numbers and there it was. She laughed as the home screen came into view, a photo of Petal. *Of course.*

"Check her calendar first," Blaze told her. "See if there are any other events surrounding that dinner that might raise a flag."

Peyton scrolled through everything for the three weeks leading up to the dinner. Her sister certainly had a busy life. She found many photography appointments for portrait sittings plus some notes that she was sure referred to her newer venture. She frowned at a note attached to one item that just said, *Tell Dane.*

"There's one tiny little weird thing here. I'm checking her notes now to see if she expanded on it."

Brianne certainly kept her life recorded in her notes, Peyton thought, as she scrolled through them. She stopped when she came to one that said, *Gandy Bridge. Beach. Tell Dane.* It had been taken just before dark, and most of the image was filled with boats on the water.

What was so special about that spot that she needed to remind herself to tell Dane? As little as she knew about the area, she did know the Gandy Bridge ran from Hillsborough County to Pinellas County. Brianne had driven across it a couple of times when Peyton was in town, taking her to some place on the other side of the bay. It was bordered on one side by a public beach and a scattering of businesses, mostly restaurants or maritime places. Maybe Brianne had found one she wanted Dane to take her to for dinner or Sunday brunch.

She didn't even remember what was on the other side. Was Brianne looking at sites for waterscapes?

Peyton opened the Photos app and scrolled through to see if her sister had taken any pictures. Sure enough, there were several taken from various spots where she'd pulled over, including those across from the beach side. They showed a combination of commercial properties and a large apartment complex. There were people in some of them, but so small she could hardly make them out, and the pictures would only enlarge a certain percentage.

"Find anything?" Blaze's voice broke into her thoughts.

"I'm not sure. After we go through the house, could we go someplace and look at all this together? There are pictures here of people that I'm not sure why she took."

"Casual ones she might have been hired to take?" Blaze suggested.

"No. That's not what these look like. It feels like something not good caught her attention and she wanted to ask Dane about it. That's why the note, I think."

"That's what I had in mind. My instincts tell me there's something in there that will at least give us a hint, and they haven't been wrong yet. Let's go through their house, then we'll go back to my place. Viper is still there, doing a deep dive on the Internet. We'll pick up some dinner on the way. That work for you?"

"Yes. Of course. Whatever you think we should do."

She opened the mail app next and immediately dozens of emails popped up.

"Holy shit! Everyone in the world must have been trying to reach her. I need to go through these."

"Later," Blaze told her. "You should check her messages, too. There just might be something in there that's a clue to what this is all about."

"God. I hope so."

"But first, the house."

Brianne and Dane lived in South Tampa, in a large two-story house surrounded by mature landscaping. The stucco was painted an off-white and the trim a dark red. Peyton had always thought how rich it looked. She and her sister never discussed finances, but when they pulled into the driveway and Blaze let out a slow whistle, she knew her impression had been right.

"Your brother-in-law must be pulling in some hefty fees," he told her as they climbed out of the car. "Houses like this in this neighborhood go for the high six figures."

"I have no idea what he made. I know the house is gorgeous, the neighborhood is high-end and they live a good life. Brianne said he's a top junior litigator, but when the three of us were together he never threw his weight around or pulled the ego act. He's always been just the really nice guy who loved my sister and treated her like royalty."

"We may be barking up the wrong tree, but something made someone run them down and we're going to find it. Got the key?"

She pulled it out of her pocket and unlocked the front door.

"Wait. Let me get the alarm."

He touched her arm. "Uh, Peyton?"

"Hold on just a sec." She moved away from him.

"Peyton, the alarm didn't go off."

She stopped still two feet from the alarm panel on the wall, stunned to realize he was right. And suddenly afraid.

"Why? When I left here with the Hollisters, I definitely remember resetting it. I knew the place would be empty."

"Let me check it. What's the code?" He punched it in as she recited it to him. Nothing happened, so he tried it again. When he turned to her, his face was set in a dead serious expression.

"What? What is it?"

"I'd have to take the panel off the wall to make sure, but I think someone used an EMP to kill it."

She wrinkled her forehead. "A what?"

"Electromagnetic pulse unit. One press of a button and it kills all power to the unit." He flipped a switch on the wall and a ceiling light in the foyer came on. "Okay, so they didn't fry the electricity for the whole house, just the alarm. They knew the place was empty and that the few seconds it took to reach the alarm wouldn't be a problem."

"Holy mother." A cold shiver raced down her spine. "What kind of people are these?"

"That's what we're trying to find out," he told her. "Do you know who their security service is? They should be notified."

"And a new system put in to replace this one."

Blaze shook his head. "Uh. We'll do that. No offense, but whatever they install will be nothing compared to what we use. We need to keep *everyone* out."

That same chill began working its way through her system.

"Are you sure?"

"Trust me. And this is part of why you hired us." He took out his phone and dialed. "Viper? Yeah. Call Frank and tell him we need his Super X system installed and they need to get on it tonight." He gave him the address. "We'll be here a while, so have him get his ass in gear."

Peyton stared at him. "They're doing it now?"

"Yes. They'll give me a call when they get here so I can open the door for them." He grinned. "Otherwise I might shoot them by mistake."

She swallowed a little gasp.

"Just kidding." He shook his head. "Sorry. Bad humor. Listen, do you have the number of the security company the house is hooked up to? You really should call them and let them know what's happened. They may even have been trying to call."

"No. I'm sure it's here somewhere. I didn't even think about it, to tell you the truth. I bet it's on Brianne's phone. I'll look. I wonder why, if the system is shut off, they didn't call to check? Isn't that what they do?"

"Yes. My guess is that whoever set off the alarm called the security company pretending to be Dane, as soon as it sounded, and cancelled the service."

The sick feeling in the pit of her stomach began working its way through her system.

"God, Blaze."

"Don't think about it now. We're getting it taken care of."

"I wanted to ask you." She wet her lips. "If no one's in the house, do we really even need a system?"

He cupped her chin in a warm palm and stroked it with his thumb. And just like that heat streaked through her, waking up her hormones and stoking her pulse that suddenly thundered in her very hot sex. What was the matter with her? This was serious business here, and all those disobedient hormones kept doing was whispering *fuck him* in her ear. She didn't know whether to be angry with herself or embarrassed. She had to stop herself from squeezing her thighs together against the demanding hunger.

She was so involved in her traitorous sex drive that she didn't realize at first that Blaze was speaking to her.

"Excuse me? I think my mind wandered for a minute."

And how embarrassing is that? she asked herself.

He smiled, humor flashing in his eyes.

"It's okay. I was getting kind of distracted myself." He brushed his fingers against her cheek, a brief, light caress. Then the serious look was back. "Okay, back to business. I was saying, I don't want to add to your stress, but if whoever broke in before didn't find what they were looking for, they may come back. I want to know if they do. And maybe catch them in the act."

The sick feeling seeped through her again.

"How will you do that?"

"Silent alarm. It will hit Frank's control center and be sent to all of our cell phones."

"God. I can hardly believe this is happening." She rubbed her forehead as if she could straighten out the jumbled thoughts in her brain. "Who is doing this, Blaze? And why? For god's sake, why?"

He moved close to her, his presence wrapping around her like a cloud of warm air. When he cradled her face in his palms, those traitorous hormones leaped up and began to tango through her veins.

"Tonight," he told her in a slow voice. "God knows this is hardly the time for it, and you can fire my ass if you want. I can't believe I'm even saying this, but if I don't get inside you pretty soon, my cock might explode. Tonight, when we've done all this, we're going to see if this is a fire or just a flare of heat. Count on it."

Peyton was stunned, except after the incendiary kiss they'd shared earlier, she didn't know why. What could she say? She was riding the same wave of intense sexual desire he was. So what did that make her? Her sister was lying in a coma and she was suddenly in the grip of strong sexual heat, thinking about Blaze Hamilton standing before her nude.

"I don't know… Is this… Are we…What is this?"

"We're going to find out." He brushed the lightest kiss over her lips. "You can count on that. Tonight. Now, come on. Let's get moving. I'm surprised his parents didn't go through here while they were in town. Surely there had to be things of his they wanted."

Peyton shrugged. "I was with them and they just seemed to want his clothes for the funeral. They could hardly even talk about it, much less go through his things here. Trust me, I know how they felt. Besides, they said it wasn't right. They'd wait until Brianne…woke up…and go through it all together."

"Peyton." Blaze turned her to face him and took both her hands in his. "You'll be able to do this? Search everything with me?"

Could she? Did she even have a choice? There were too many questions without any answers. She took in a deep breath and let it out slowly.

"I'll be fine. I have to be."

"Okay, where do you want to start?"

She looked around. "The den is just down this little hallway here. Dane used it more than Brianne, but maybe we'll find things from both of them."

She'd always loved the rich oak paneling in the room, the built-in bookshelves, the heavy oak desk where Dane worked on cases when he had to bring them home. She and Peyton had sipped on the rich Kentucky bourbon in the liquor cabinet and curled up in the big leather armchairs when they'd been alone in the house. Emotion clogged her throat and she had to work hard to keep back the tears.

"You okay?" Blaze was right in front of her, one big hand cupping her chin and tilting her face up to him.

"I hope so." She let out a shuddering breath. "I have to be. I can't stop until we get to the bottom of this."

"You all right with going through the desk?"

"Let's do it." But as soon as they approached the desk, she stopped and frowned. "It's not here."

"What's not here?"

"His computer. He carried a laptop with him, but he had the computer from electronics heaven here on his desk. Said he preferred to do a lot of research at home where no one who didn't belong could walk in and see what he was doing."

"Where's his laptop?"

She shrugged. "Beats me. It could have been in the car. A couple of times when we all went out, he had it with him and locked it in the trunk while we were inside whatever restaurant we were at."

"We need to find that car." He pulled out his cell and hit a number. "Yeah, Eagle? Whatever you're doing, put it aside and find out what happened to Dane Hollister's car. Call the lot where he'd parked it that night. They wouldn't have let it stay there indefinitely, so start there. Use every contact you've got. And when you find it, search every inch of it. We're looking for his cell and his laptop. Yeah, yeah, I know. Yeah. Okay, whatever it takes. And keep me in the loop."

"How will he even know where to look?" Peyton couldn't imagine that it was just sitting in the open somewhere. And it wasn't still at the restaurant parking lot. Either they'd gotten rid of it or whoever ran them over had.

"Eagle knows all the tricks. He'll find it, whatever happened to it. Did the police mention it at all?"

She shook her head. "And I'm sorry, I didn't think to ask."

"It's okay. Your focus was completely on your sister. We'll find it, sitting in some impound lot somewhere."

During the next hour, they went through everything in the room, even taking the drawers from the desk to see if there was anything hidden behind or beneath them. They had turned on the lights against the growing dark when Blaze's cell rang. When he hung up, he looked at Peyton.

"The security guys are here. Come outside with me. I want you to meet them."

To Peyton's eyes, Frank Weller could have been cut from the same mold as Blaze. Tall, lean, muscular, all business. He did smile when he shook her hand.

"Viper explained the situation. We'll get you fixed up." He looked at Blaze. "The usual?"

Blaze nodded. "Exactly."

"We've got quite a few hours here, then. You gonna hang around all that time?"

Blaze shook his head. "How about meeting us here about nine tomorrow morning and walking us through it."

"No problem. Nice to meet you, Miss West. We'll make sure you don't have any more problems, at least with your house security."

"Is he a former SEAL, too?" she whispered to Blaze as they walked back into the house.

"They're the best."

"Don't we have to tell him what we want?"

Blaze chuckled. "We've done this enough times that Frank knows exactly what I want. And Viper gave him the rundown, like he said. Let's get back to work."

They headed back into the den and resumed their search. Finally, Peyton straightened up from going through the cupboards beneath the bookshelves and rubbed her forehead.

"This is going to sound very stupid," she began, "but it's too neat."

Blaze lifted an eyebrow. "Neat? I just thought maybe the guy was a freak about it. You know, with all the folders and paper aligned, the books symmetrical. That kind of stuff."

She shook her head.

"Dane wasn't a slob, by any means, but he wasn't obsessed about stuff like that. Any papers he was working on were always stacked just a little off kilter on his desk. And the books never looked like that. He and Brianne were both readers and were always pulling books out then putting them back. This looks like someone used a level and a measuring tape to put everything in its place."

"But to someone who didn't know him, would it appear that he was? Just from a casual look?"

She shrugged. "I don't know. I guess. Yeah, maybe. Why?"

"Because someone's gone to a lot of trouble to put everything back the way they *think* it was. I'd say they took the desk apart and searched every draw and cubbyhole, putting the papers back with concentrated precision. Same with everything else. They wanted to make sure no one would think anyone had been in here."

"Then what were we supposed to think about the missing PC?" She glanced around the room.

"Maybe that he'd taken it in to be repaired or something."

She snapped her fingers. "Let's check Brianne's work area. This house has a sunroom, believe it or not, and she just loved it in there. Said it was so light and airy."

The sunroom was tucked in next to the living room. Since it was now dark, the first thing she did was flip on the lights. She immediately noticed all the dead and dying plants

"Oh, no." She wanted to cry. Brianne had loved those plants. Why hadn't she thought of them and figured out a schedule to water them?

Because all I could focus on was my sister herself. I didn't care about stupid plants.

Well, she'd come back tomorrow, if she could, and see what could be salvaged and what had to be thrown out.

"This is a shame."

For a moment she had forgotten that Blaze was behind her.

"You have no idea. Brianne loved these plants. She loved this room." She waved at the two walls of floor-to-ceiling windows. "On nice days it was flooded with sunlight, so bright and cheery you had to feel good just sitting in here."

Blaze pointed to a desk set up where the walls met, angled into the corner.

"I'm gathering this is where she worked?"

"Uh-huh." Peyton frowned. "She said all the sunlight made her feel happy. And on stormy days she'd light the fireplace on that opposite wall. Said it made the room cozy." She swallowed back tears. No time to cry now. They had work to do. "Her computer's missing, too."

"Desktop or laptop?"

"Laptop. She said it was much easier for her. Besides, she could take it with her if she wanted and have everything she needed. So maybe there were computers in that car." Then she shook her head. "No, if they were going out for a late dinner, neither of them would have computers with them. They had very definite lines between business and personal."

"Someone was damn sure one or both of them had some kind of information that couldn't see the light of day." Blaze rubbed his jaw as he took in every bit of the sunroom. "This room's put together, but a little more casual than the den."

"Because Brianne was a more relaxed person. Not that Dane was uptight," she hurried to correct herself. "She just didn't care as much about coloring inside the lines."

They went through everything in the sunroom, then, to make sure they didn't miss anything, checked out the rest of the house. At the end, however, they didn't find anything that set off alarm bells. Nor did they find Dane's cell phone.

"It was just a wild chance, anyway." Peyton smoothed a stray hair back from her face. "My guess is it would have been with him in the car. He never went anywhere without it. God only knows where it is now. Probably in the trash. The car, too."

Blaze started to answer her when his cell rang.

"Hey, Viper. How goes it? Yeah? Uh-huh. Uh-huh. Okay, well, keep at it. There's a link somewhere. Okay. I'll be there in about forty-five."

"Did he find out anything?" Peyton tried to keep the anxiety out of her voice.

"Not yet, although he said he's dug up a ton of information about the law firm where Dane worked. They're apparently one of the top in the Southeast, with a client list that reads like a regional Who's Who. He's still at my townhouse working, which by the way, kudos to him, because he's not a desk kind of guy. But when he gets his teeth into something, he never lets go."

"So he had some results?"

"Not a lot, but enough to keep digging. He wants to go over what he's turned up. He's pretty sure the link is with the law firm, but he says he needs a fresh set of eyes on it. We just have to figure it out. And maybe

Eagle will call with a report on Dane's car. Let's lock up this house and get out of here."

"I want to show you the pictures in Brianne's phone, too, along with a note she made that I don't understand. Maybe you can figure it out."

"I'll do my best."

He stopped her at the door, cradled her face in his palms and lowered his mouth to hers. The kiss was a sizzling combination of heat and passion and tenderness, and unlike any other kiss she'd ever had. When he slipped his tongue between her lips, she welcomed it gladly, sliding her own over it and gently scraping it with her teeth. They stood that way until she was sure neither of them could breathe. She sensed his reluctance when he lifted his head at last.

"We have some unfinished business here." His voice was rough with hunger.

"Do we?"

"Yes." Heat flashed in his eyes. "You know it, too."

She just nodded, mesmerized by the hunger in his gaze.

"But we have other business first," he went on. "Just wanted to let you know I haven't forgotten what that kiss tasted like. Come on. Let's go."

She was surprised that he took her hand and held on to it as they walked out of the house, considering Frank and his crew were all over the place. It made her feel safe and secure, something she desperately needed right now.

She waited while Blaze handed the house key over to Frank and confirmed that nine in the morning would be a good time to hook up and walk through the new system.

"They'll be working all night," Peyton whispered as they walked to the car.

"Nothing new for them. Really. It's all good." They made a quick stop at a takeout barbecue place before finally heading to Bayshore Boulevard and Blaze's townhouse. They parked in the garage and she followed him inside, wondering as she looked around what she'd expected. It certainly wasn't this.

Polished parquet covered the floors and sleek yet comfortable-looking furniture filled the rooms. The kitchen was efficient and high tech, and in the living room a floor-to-ceiling window wall gave an unobstructed view of Hillsborough Bay. With darkness lowering its curtain over the city, she could see the lights of downtown sparkling and flashing. As much as she'd loved staying at Brianne's, Peyton thought she could sit in this room forever and never want to leave. *What a great place to write a book.*

Better watch it, girl.

She needed to keep telling herself that no matter the chemistry between them, when this was over, it was over. Whatever was happening between them — or didn't — couldn't last. They might as well live on two separate planets, as different as their lifestyles were. How on earth did this all pop up, anyway, when she was in the middle of such a critical situation?

To keep her mind from straying any more, she took out Brianne's cell phone and opened the Message app.

"Holy crap." She stared at the number of messages that popped up.

"What?"

"There's a ton of messages and voice mails here, not to mention the emails. It'll take me forever to go through them."

"Not to worry. I have a program to sort them. Then we can peg the important ones."

Of course he does. Is there anything these men can't do?

Blaze's townhouse was a reflection of the man himself, not one wasted inch, everything designed for maximum utility. The open floor plan gave the feeling of well-utilized space, with the dining room between the kitchen and the living room. The furniture had sleek lines but was designed for comfort. A floor-to-ceiling window wall looked out at the view of Hillsborough Bay. Across the stretch of water, the lights of downtown sparkled in the night. It could have been a picture from a magazine.

And there, seated at the dining room table, was another Blaze clone focused on a laptop in front of him, studying the screen. He looked from one of them to the other, eyes slightly narrowed as if assessing the situation. Could he sense the electricity between her and Blaze? Would he make an issue of it? What if he did?

I've already made a mess of things. Damn it!

"Let me make the introductions here. Peyton West, meet Matt 'Viper' Roman. Peyton's our client. Better treat her with kid gloves."

Viper looked at her and winked. His dirty blond hair was a little shaggy, but other than that, he had the same lethally quiet air of power and containment that she'd felt the first moment she'd laid eyes on Blaze. Whatever was going on, these men would handle it and keep her safe.

He held out his hand. "Nice to meet you, Miss West."

"Peyton. Please."

"Okay, Peyton. And I'm Viper." He stood and shook her hand. "I can promise you Galaxy will get to the bottom of this mess."

"An appropriate name for people to help me," she told him, "since my life's been in retrograde since I got the call about Brianne. Everything's moving backward and I can't seem to stop it. No forward motion in anything."

"I'm sure we can reverse that motion." Then he grinned and switched his gaze to Blaze. "Providing, of course, you feed me."

Blaze laughed. "It's in the kitchen. I'll dish it up right now. Then you can fill us in on what you found. After that, I want you to unload the messages from her sister's phone so we can sort them and see if there's anything we need to save. After that you need to download some specific pictures from the same phone and see if you can do a facial recognition match." He glanced at Peyton. "My software for that isn't too bad, but it's standard. Viper's got one that's much better."

"Good. I'm all for that."

Chapter Eight

Peyton watched as Viper sat back in his chair and stretched his neck from side to side. She had to will herself to sit quietly and not ask him if he'd found anything.

Then he smiled at her. "I've got a match."

"Really?" She leaned forward. "You actually found one?"

She'd been skeptical at first, until she discovered that the program Galaxy used was more sophisticated and cast a wider net than anything the police used.

"That's incredible! How did…"

"We had someone design it for us," Blaze told her.

Her lips curved in a tired smile. "Of course you did. I won't even ask you for the details because I know I won't understand them. It's not important. I just want to find out what you discovered."

"Okay. Come sit here next to me so I can show you."

She moved to the other side of the table and took the empty chair next to him. Blaze pulled one up on the other side. Viper clicked his mouse and the screen filled with one of the pictures he'd downloaded from Brianne's phone. It was one of those taken on Gandy Boulevard, obviously, from the lighting, taken just before dark. Where had Brianne been going by herself at that hour? Or had she been coming from someplace and been inspired by the images? Peyton knew she was really getting into her landscape photography.

This first picture showed a building by the water with *Seaside Marine* painted on it. Even at what was obviously a late hour, there were several cars in the parking lot. Four men stood next to one of the cars and it was easy to see from their body language that this wasn't a friendly meeting. Three of them stood in a posture very threatening to the fourth.

"The question," Viper told her, "was why did your sister care so much about pictures of these guys? You said she was getting into landscape photography, but that doesn't include people."

"Right. And she took several of them. And made a note to tell Dane. So why?"

"Because two of these men work for Hayden Kellerman, president of Bistro Hotels."

Peyton frowned. "Is that what came up on their identifications?"

"But more importantly, referred to as the head of the Tampa Mafia."

Her eyebrows shot up to her hairline. "The what?"

"You heard me. The Tampa Mafia."

"Sounds like something out of a movie. It's real? I thought the Feds got rid of it ages ago."

"Not so." Viper shook his head. "Although it's morphed a lot from the days when Santo Trafficante ruled it from Ybor City with an iron fist. Besides loan sharking, murder, extortion and corruption of public officials for their own benefit, it now includes gambling, drug smuggling and sex trafficking. It might not be discussed as widely as it used to be, but according to what I found, it's well-known in the right places. The reach of this particular group extends throughout South Florida and into the Caribbean. Even to parts of Europe."

"How on earth does something like this connect to Brianne and Dane?" She rubbed her forehead. "This is giving me a headache."

"I have no idea," he told her, "but you can bet we'll be digging into it with a deep shovel. Today they hide behind rich, respectable businesses and that may have been the connection to the firm. They may have wanted representation in a lawsuit, and that firm is one of the best in the Southeast."

"My god!" She rubbed her face. "But that still doesn't tell me what made my sister stop and take their pictures. How did she even know who they were?"

"I think it's the very unhappy guy that caught her attention. His name is Owen Kendrick. He's the son of Dane's boss."

She stared at the picture. "Are you kidding me? I know she's met Owen and his wife, but she couldn't have any idea who these other guys were."

"No," Blaze agreed, "but I'd say your sister was a very smart lady and her intuition told her something was wrong. That's why she wrote a note to herself to tell Dane and show him the pictures."

"But then what?"

"Any number of things," Blaze said. "Dane could have told Peter Kendrick and showed the pictures to him. Asked him why Kellerman's thugs were hassling

Owen. Maybe Owen had a gambling problem that no one knew about. Kellerman's deep into high-stakes gambling, and he's noted for sucking people into debt that he can then manipulate to do things for him. Or he could have gone to Owen first and asked him what the hell it was about. My guess is that somehow Kellerman's got his hooks into Owen Kendrick. If he told him where he got the pictures, Owen could have panicked. Maybe he thought Dane or Brianne would tell people about it."

Peyton shook her head. "Dane would have gone to Peter if he couldn't get anywhere with Owen. His concern would have been for the firm and what effect, if any, this would have on it. That and nothing else."

"But what if Owen thought he could control Dane's reaction, except he was worried about Brianne? Worried she'd say something to someone."

"You think that's what this is all about?"

Viper nodded. "I think there's a good chance this is a big part of it. However, I suggest we need to find out more about the kind of person Owen Kendrick is. About the firm itself and if that's where the connection to the Tampa Mafia is. Like Blaze said, it's possible they wanted to hire the law firm and there was a problem. All of that. Anything. I don't know, but we damn sure need to dig deep."

"You're checking into Peter Kendrick's personal connections, too, right?"

Viper gave another nod. "There's some stuff I dug up that smells a little bad, but I don't want to say anything until I know for sure."

"Don't let us stop you. Add this to your list of things to find. Any connection whatsoever could give us a thread to pull. And sooner is always better than later."

"Your personal motto, right?" Viper teased.

"Damn fucking straight. It's what kept the Team together, except for…" He stopped and shook his head.

"Except for what?" Peyton asked.

"I'd rather not say. Maybe another time. Right now, you've got enough heavy stuff to deal with."

Peyton rubbed her forehead, doing her best to ignore the tiny headache brewing.

"Do you think it was one of these people who called the security company and had the service discontinued? After they fried it with the EMP?"

Blaze shrugged. "I'd say that's the most likely answer. But there are other players in the game, and we have to check every one of them."

"I can hardly take it all in. It just seems so far out of anything my sister and brother-in-law would be involved in."

"And they were probably innocent bystanders." Blaze rubbed her neck. "Tomorrow we'll go through everything we found about the law firm as well as some of Peter Kendrick's connections. I think you've had enough for tonight."

"I agree."

She closed her eyes and leaned back in the chair, soothed by the touch of his hands.

"And I think that's my cue to leave." Viper shut down his laptop, unplugged the cord and shoved everything into a messenger bag. "Blaze, we all going to meet in the morning?"

'Yeah. We'll pool all the info and go from there. Hopefully Eagle will have been able to pull an image off the CCTV cameras. I also want to see if you can get a line on what happened to Dane Hollister's car. And high on the list is digging out the connection between Peter Kendrick and the so-called Tampa Mafia."

"I think we need to go for a little flight to nowhere," Viper suggested.

Blaze nodded. "I agree. You'll make the arrangements?"

"Consider it done."

"What does that mean?" Peyton wanted to know.

"It means," Blaze explained, "that we're going to load ourselves and all the computers onto the plane and have a meeting where no one can see us or overhear us. And plan our next steps."

Peyton leaned back and looked up at Blaze. "You think even meeting here isn't safe?"

"I'm not taking any chances. With the kind of stuff we're just beginning to dig up, I don't want to take risks of any kind."

"Remember," Viper said, "Saint took off for a couple of days."

Blaze gave another nod. "But he also knows that when we have a client, he can be called back at any time. That's what he gets the big bucks for."

"Then I'll let him know."

"Okay. Then yes, we need to wrap it up for the day."

Viper hiked the bag's strap over his head. He looked from Blaze to Peyton and back again, as if he had a question he wanted to ask but thought he should keep his mouth shut. Blaze didn't say a word, either. Finally, Viper headed toward the door, but stopped before opening it and looked at Blaze again. Peyton sensed some sort of secret message passing between them. When Viper spoke, she knew she was right.

"Hope you know what you're doing, buddy boy. Remember the rules."

"I'm fine. Everything's under control. My brain hasn't stopped working."

"Just make sure," he said in a voice so soft Peyton had to strain to hear it, "it's your big brain and not your little one."

"Nothing's going to be a problem. Take my word for it."

Viper studied him in silence for a moment. "Okay. I trust your judgment. Don't screw that up." He raised his voice. "Goodnight, Peyton."

"Goodnight, Viper. See you tomorrow."

"I can't wait," he joked.

Then he was gone.

She looked at Blaze when he walked back into the room.

"I'm guessing you're breaking some kind of unwritten rule."

Peyton hadn't realized how tired she was, or how tense her muscles still were, until after Viper left and Blaze locked up for the night.

When he turned off the last of the lights except the nightlight in the kitchen and the lamps in the bedroom, she grinned.

"I take it I'm spending the night?"

He stopped, studying her face. "Is that a problem? I thought—"

"Just yanking your chain," she told him, curving her lips in a smile. "No problem at all. But I could definitely use a shower."

"Right this way."

He took her hand in his large one. It had the double effect of sending flashes of heat through her system as well as making her feel secure. He led her up the stairs, through a large bedroom and into a bathroom that had her drooling the minute she stepped into it. Big didn't begin to describe it. Against one wall was a clawfoot tub with all the fancy gadgets. A vanity ran along one wall and opposite the tub was a glassed-in shower that Peyton thought was big enough to hold a dance.

"Soap in the little niche in the middle. Sorry I don't have shampoo. I don't want anyone I bring here to think they can get comfortable, so no hair dryer either." Blaze pointed to the wall closest to the shower and grinned. "But I do have heated towel bars."

She knew it was unreasonable for a little thrill of satisfaction to run through her at his statement, but there it was. She smiled at him.

"I can rough it. I can do anything as long as I can step into that shower. After everything we've discovered so far, I need a shower in the worst way."

He pulled loose her ponytail holder, letting her hair cascade to her shoulders, and ran his fingers through it.

"We'll just make do." He touched his lips to hers for a quick moment. "Want me to set this all up for you, or..."

"Or?"

"I could, uh, help you with your shower."

Peyton looked up at him, reading in his eyes the same things she was feeling.

"I think I could use some help. Besides..." She licked her lower lip and was rewarded with the tightening of his entire body.

"Besides?"

"I thought maybe you'd like a shower, too."

He studied her face, as if he could look through her eyes, deep inside her, and read what was going on in her mind.

"Just to be clear. We do this, I don't think there's any going back. I should probably keep my mouth shut, but I've never had a woman hit me this way. It's all in or nothing."

"I'd never settle for nothing," she whispered.

"Good. That's good."

He unbuttoned her shirt with slow movements of his fingers, all the while keeping his gaze locked to hers. He tugged the tails from her slacks and brushed the fabric off her shoulders and down her arms. He dropped his gaze to the swell of her breasts, sucking in a breath before swiping his tongue across both mounds. Just that brief touch made her tremble and her legs feel unsteady.

"I'm not going to rush this." His voice had deepened and now had a rough edge to it. "Just so you know."

He molded his hands around her breasts, squeezing the plump flesh with a gentle movement. When he reached behind her and unfastened her bra, she let her arms fall to her sides so he could tug her bra straps down and toss the garment to the side. She had to clutch his forearms to steady herself as he lowered his head to suck one nipple, then the other. Little nips with his teeth, tugs with his lips, swirls with his tongue. Deep inside the wet heat of her sex, a craving set up that thundered through her with the force of a drum.

What the hell? So she hadn't had sex for a while. She'd always been able to do without it when she wanted to. As long as she had her hand and her toys, she didn't need anyone else.

She thought.

Just Blaze's light touch on her body had set every pulse thrumming and a need, a craving, racing wildly through her body. She wanted him inside her. His cock. His fingers. His tongue. His...

Holy Jesus, Peyton. Slow it down.

But she didn't seem able to. While he was tonguing each nipple and scraping the tips with his teeth, she tugged his soft-collar shirt from his jeans. Pulling it free of his waistband, she shoved it upward until he released his hold on her long enough to get the shirt over his head and toss it to the side.

Oh, god, his chest.

Peyton smoothed her hands over it, feeling the tickle of the rough chest hair and the pucker of the flat nipples. She was sure she could do this endlessly, if not for the fact she could hardly wait for the two of them to get naked. She didn't ever remember being this turned on by a man, this hungry, no, *ravenous* for his touch.

She unfastened his jeans, her knuckles coming into contact with an erection that made her suck in her breath.

Holy shit!

She pushed both his jeans and his boxer briefs down past his hips and wrapped her fingers around his cock, squeezing and stroking at the same time.

"Easy there." The rough edge of his voice let her know he was just as affected by what was happening as she was. "Let's not get to the end before we've barely got past the beginning."

She looked up at him, seeing a muscle twitch in his jaw even as hunger burned in his eyes. And she couldn't help it. She gave that rigid shaft another squeeze. Then she released it, lowering her hand and letting the tips of her fingers drift over his balls. She wasn't by any means a passive partner when it came to sex, but with Blaze she was driven by such a high degree of hunger and need that she didn't even know where it came from. She hadn't even known the man for twenty-four hours, and look at her.

She didn't care. He wanted her and she wanted him and blazing between them was the 'something special' she'd heard other women talk about but had never felt.

"Let's get in the shower and slow this down a little."

As if.

But Peyton took a deep breath and tried to settle herself. She skinned out of her jeans and bikinis while Blaze kicked his own jeans and boxer briefs aside. He opened the shower door and, as he reached in to turn on the water, adjusting the rain shower heads, she took a moment to study his lean, muscular body. *Yum*, she thought. All she wanted to do was run her hands over every delicious inch of him.

Well, no, that wasn't exactly *all* she wanted to do.

He turned his head, gave her a flash of that devastating grin and held out his hand. "It's ready. Come on in. The water's fine."

She stepped into the big glass enclosure, letting out a sigh of satisfaction as the gentle kiss of the warm rain shower skimmed over her body. Blaze closed the door and adjusted the spray so that it flowed easily over her. Cradling her head in his palms, he lowered his mouth to hers, the pressure just firm enough to send little showers of sparks cascading through her. Just that simple contact was so erotic that every bit of her body responded, nipples hardening to an almost painful point, her sex throbbing with desperate need.

Then he lifted his lips from her, gently swiped his tongue over them and grabbed a dispenser from the built-in tiny alcove. He squeezed a heavy dose of the shower wash into his palm and backed her up to the wall.

"Just relax," he coaxed. "Let me make you feel good."

She had to admit that making her feel good was exactly what he did. His hands, lathered with the soap, coasted over her body, squeezing her shoulders and sliding down her arms. His touch was featherlight and made every inch of her skin sizzle. She wanted him to go faster, but she also wanted him to slow down so she could enjoy every second to its maximum.

Blaze moved her so she leaned against the wall, glad for the support, because her legs were already weak and shaky. Closing her eyes, she let herself fall into the soothing movement of his hands. His fingers danced over her collarbone and down through the valley between her breasts. He traced light circles around them before capturing the tips and gently squeezing them. A light pinch, but flame shot straight through her body to her sex, which was already throbbing with an insistent demand for satisfaction.

He was equally gentle as he moved his hands down over the slight curve of her belly until he reached the top of her mound. She had expected him to be somewhat rough, to have a heavy hand, but instead his caress was tantalizingly light. Teasing. The sensation was hot and so very sexy. It made her weak at the knees and hungry for more.

When he slid his hand away, she moaned a protest.

"More, please."

"Like this?" His voice was right at her ear, the feather of his breath tickling her. He slid one finger between her folds and found her clit, scraping it with his fingernail.

Peyton sucked in a breath and tried to clench her thighs around his hand, but he moved it away.

"Yes. Like that. Do it again."

He nudged her thighs apart and eased his hand back and forth through her wet slit. Wet, she knew, from more than the shower water. Pressing his mouth to hers, he slid his tongue inside while immersing his finger in her warmth. He added another and she moaned. When he began moving those fingers in a slow, smooth, in-and-out movement, she had to clutch his upper arms to steady herself because she wasn't sure her shaky legs would support her.

She tried to push herself down on his fingers and urge him to go faster and deeper, but he seemed determined to keep things at the slow pace he'd set, knowing it was tormenting her. He was taking her slowly up that erotic slope, drawing her close to the top but not letting her get there yet.

He never varied the rhythm of his strokes and the steady friction of them created a tension deep inside her, the genesis of an orgasm. It began to spread through her body, a rhythmic thrumming that surged into the core of her sex. When she clamped down on him and tried to ride those flexible, talented fingers, he laughed in her ear, a low, deep sound that only ramped up the desire bursting inside her.

Without moving his hand or interrupting the rhythm, he slid his lips over her cheek and along her jaw until he reached her earlobe, which he nibbled on with tiny bites. Her inner muscles clenched over his fingers and she tried again to ride them. But as soon as she did, he eased his fingers from her body, eliciting a cry of protest from her.

"Ssh, ssh, shh." He breathed it into her ear. "We have a long way to go."

I'm going to kill him. That is if I don't explode first.

He turned her unprotesting body so she faced the tiled wall and placed her hands over her head, palms against the tiles. In the next moment, she felt those strong hands kneading the tense muscles of her shoulders and her upper arms. She was sure she could stand here and let him do this forever if her body wasn't sending her other urgent messages.

When she hummed her satisfaction, he swept her hair to one side, placed an open-mouthed kiss on her neck then gave it a gentle bite. A shiver raced over her that had nothing to do with the water.

"Feel good?"

He nibbled his way across her shoulders then ran the tip of one finger down her spine. Before she could organize her brain enough to answer him, he slipped that finger gently between the cheeks of her ass and glided it over the puckered opening.

She was sure her groan of pleasure was the answer he was looking for.

But then, just as easily, he slid the finger lower and stroked her inner thighs, first one, then the other. She tried to push back at him, signaling just where she wanted him to move his hand, but again he laughed softly and bit her earlobe.

God!

What was happening here? She was never turned on this fast. Never. Oh, she liked to think of herself as responsive, but holy damn! She'd met this man less than two days ago and she was ready to climb up his body and impale herself on his very impressive cock.

Without warning, he turned her to face him again, cradled her face in his hands and took her mouth in a kiss so voracious it stole every bit of her breath. His tongue swept inside, dueling with hers, tasting every inch of her mouth. When she closed her teeth gently over his tongue, his moan vibrated through her body. With obvious reluctance, he pulled his head back.

"Jesus! You are…incredible."

"You, too," she whispered.

He adjusted the shower head so it sprayed directly on her, washing away the soap he'd lathered all over her body. *Isn't he going to finish what he started?* She could hardly stand up, she was so ready to explode.

Without saying another word, he nudged her legs apart and slid his fingers into her again.

Oh, thank god!

She closed her eyes, ready to give herself over to what was building.

"Look at me, Peyton," he growled. "Open your eyes."

When she did, she saw a hunger burning in his that matched her own. Whatever he saw in hers, he increased the rhythm and pressure of his strokes. *More. Harder. Faster.* He curled his fingers at just the right angle to increase her need. She dug her fingers into his arms, holding on for dear life as the orgasm raced up from inside her and exploded with incredible force.

Her inner walls clamped down on his fingers inside her at the pressure of his thumb on her clit, and she rode them with a fierce fury as she spasmed again and again. He kept up the steady movement until the last tremor subsided and she collapsed against him, unable to stand by herself anymore.

"Easy," he whispered. "I've got you."

He held her tightly against his big, hard body, one arm banded around her, his other hand stroking her gently as the last of the orgasm faded away.

Peyton looked up at him, every bone in her body feeling like liquid. He cupped her jaw and pressed soft kisses to her mouth.

"We're not even close to being finished." He grinned. "I hope you know that."

"I think I might need a minute to catch my breath." Her laugh sounded thready even to her own ears. "And I didn't get to take care of you."

"Oh, well." His grin was lecherous. "Don't even think we're done here. But I don't want you to waste your energy soaping my body. I have other uses for it."

He opened the shower door, lifted her out and grabbed a towel from one of the heated racks. When he had wrapped her in it securely, he sat her on a padded bench in front of the vanity. She had never felt so coddled in her life.

"Just give me a minute. Don't go anywhere."

Peyton's laugh was unsteady. "Don't worry. I couldn't move if I tried."

What the fuck am I doing?

It ran through Blaze's brain in a never-ending cycle as he soaped his body and rinsed off. He should have turned the case down. His brain had kept telling him that the moment he met Peyton West. It had kept shrieking it louder and louder during the plane ride and had nearly done him in when they'd said goodbye after the meeting. And when he'd seen her today, he'd known he was going to do something he hoped he didn't regret. He certainly couldn't discuss it with his partners, although the way Viper had looked at him tonight, he was sure it wasn't as hidden as he thought.

One thing he knew for sure. Touching her body everywhere, bringing her to orgasm with his hand, beat anything he could remember since he was sixteen. She was so soft yet firm in the right places. And responsive. *Holy fucking shit!* He'd been determined that their shower together would be all about her, but now he was left with a boner that could poke a hole in the wall.

And that thought made him rinse off quickly, turn off the shower and step out. Peyton was sitting on the bench where he'd placed her, still wrapped in the big towel, but she'd pulled a smaller one from a rack and was drying her hair.

"Sorry about the lack of a dryer," he told her again.

"No problem. I'm good at improvising."

She looked at him and grinned, and every part of his body turned warm. He hung up his towel, lifted her to her feet and yanked hers away from her body. Just looking at her fresh from the shower, a slumberous look in her eyes from the orgasm that had raced through her body, her nipples rosy, made him want to take her right here on the tile floor. Then he told himself no. She was worth so much more than that.

He lifted her in his arms and carried her into his bedroom, pausing only long enough to strip back the covers before placing her on the sheets. And wasn't he just damn glad today was the housekeeper's day and he'd had her change the sheets.

Jesus! She looked so gorgeous in his bed, that rich chestnut hair spread out on the pillow, eyes burning with need. She ran her tongue over her lower lip, making it glisten, and desire shot straight to his balls. He knelt between her legs, bending them at the knees to give him better access, but before he could do anything, she pushed him. He was so startled, he tumbled to his side and lay there looking at her, puzzled.

What the hell?

"Is something wrong?"

"Yes, it is." She pushed herself up and moved so she was straddling his thighs. "You haven't had your turn yet."

"What? Wait." He tried to push her onto her back again. "Babe, I'm so hard and horny right now it wouldn't take much to finish me off. And when I get there, I want to be inside you. Scratch that. I *have* to be inside you."

"Just a little taste," she promised.

Before he could say or do anything else, she wrapped her slim fingers around his aching shaft and slid them softly from root to tip and back again. He sucked in a breath at her touch, gritting his teeth to maintain some thread of control. Her hand on him just felt so fucking good.

But then she swiped her tongue over the head, gently probing the opening with the tip, and he nearly lost it. He had to fist his hands to hold himself together and keep from coming right then and there.

Peyton licked the soft velvety tip even as she stroked up and down again. He was so hard it was almost painful, but he reached for that famous SEAL control, because he wanted her to do this forever.

"What—" He jerked his eyes open when she took her hands away.

"Even I can see you're close to the edge," she told him. "And I want you inside me, too."

"Good," he growled. "Because here I come."

When he had her on her back again, he spread her legs and bent them at the knees. She was wide open to him, every glistening pink inch of her. Lifting her legs and placing them over his shoulders, he held open the lips of her sex and slid his tongue over her heated flesh.

Peyton gasped, sucking in her breath and letting out a tiny moan.

He did it again. Another moan.

Jesus!

She tasted so fucking good.

He thrust his tongue deep inside her, feeling the tremors in the tiny muscles. Then he dragged it back out, teasing her swollen clit as he did so.

"Oh, god."

She arched her body up to his mouth and squeezed her thighs against him, so he did it again and again, sure he'd died and gone to heaven. As he laved her over and over with his tongue, he felt his dick thickening even more. Pressing her open with his thumbs, he gently bit her clit then reached into his nightstand drawer for a condom. His hands were actually trembling as he rolled it on.

He slid into her wet heat with a feeling that he was coming home. Her heated flesh closed around him, gripping his cock as he slid it all the way in. He had to close his eyes and reach for his control, or this would be over in seconds. And he wanted it to last as long as possible.

He studied her face, which was flushed with desire, lips kiss-swollen, long lashes brushing her cheeks. The pulse at the base of her throat beat furiously, matching the beat of his own heart.

"Open your eyes." He heard the hunger in his own voice. "Look at me, Peyton."

She lifted her lids as if they carried a heavy weight on them, and when she did, he saw a hunger in her eyes ferocious enough to match his own. He took her mouth with a need so fierce he wasn't sure it would ever be satisfied. Tangled his tongue with her delicious one. Scraped it lightly with his teeth.

And when her inner walls clenched around him, he began to move. In and out, a slow slide, his cock dragging against the tight channel. Then a deep thrust and another one. Again. And again.

He dipped his head, took one of her taut, rosy nipples between his teeth and bit gently on it, tugging it lightly, before doing the same to the other tip. The little sounds of pleasure she made went straight to his balls. Thank god he could feel how wet and slick she was, because he was damn near getting to the end of his rope.

And still he never took his eyes from hers. He swore he could see flames dancing in that rich green, heat that reached right into his core.

Then the time for going slow was past. He increased his rhythm, thrust and retreat. Peyton tightened her legs around him and dug her heels into the small of his back, pulling them together even more tightly.

"Faster," she urged.

And he obliged, pounding into her harder and faster, again and again, the edge so close he could see it. Feel it.

Then…it was there.

They exploded as one, her muscles clenching his dick, squeezing it hard. They shuddered together as they came again and again.

He had no idea how long it went on until finally, he collapsed forward on his elbows, shaking, his heart beating a million miles an hour. Or was that hers he was feeling? He wasn't sure he could even tell. He brushed stray tendrils of hair from her cheeks and smiled, happy when her mouth curved in an answering smile.

"I might have had better sex sometime in my life," he told her, "but I sure can't remember when." He touched his lips to hers. "I don't have words."

Her tiny smile told him she was trying to play this casual.

"That's okay. Your body did the talking for you. You must get in a lot of practice at this."

For some reason, her words bothered him. They shouldn't have. He was a man who always made it clear to women he wasn't in it for the long haul or a permanent arrangement, and so far, everyone had been happy with that. But for whatever reason, Peyton West didn't fall into that category. She was in one all by herself. He already knew, in a little more than twenty-four hours, that this was different and he didn't want to let her go.

And how stupid was that? They hadn't even been on a date yet. Hadn't done the tell-me-about-yourself thing. Even lived in different cities. Then a thought struck him and nearly sucked the breath out of him. What if she was involved with someone?

No. No, no, no.

He only knew what he'd learned on the Internet and from observation, but if Peyton West was involved with someone else, she wouldn't be here in his bed with him, naked and flushed from hot, sweaty, satisfying sex. So what came next? She was a client with a complex, urgent case, and he always took care of business. They all did.

All. His partners. What the fuck would they think about this?

"Blaze."

"Yeah?" He blinked. Then he kissed her again.

"You looked so deep in thought there." She swallowed. "Listen. In case you're worried, I don't expect anything else from this. I mean, it was great! No, stupendous. No spectacular. But I don't want you to think —"

He kissed her again to stop her from talking.

"I was just wondering how the hell this happened. I know you for just a little more than twenty-four hours and already I don't want to let you go. That's a big first for me."

He waited, not sure he wanted to hear what she'd have to say.

She blew out a breath.

"I should tell you I'm all about no entanglements. I have a career I've worked very hard for and all my focus is on that." Her face tightened. "At least it was until this happened with Dane and Brianne." Then her expression softened. "But just so you don't think you're the only one who's crazy here, I'm having the same feelings you are. How nuts is that?"

He chuckled, the tension around his chest easing.

"I guess that means we're both nuts. And hold that thought."

He eased from her body, pinching the edges of the condom, and headed for the bathroom. In seconds he was back and sliding into bed next to her. He pulled her against him so his body curved around hers, and slipped an arm around her waist, cupping a breast in his palm. He gave it a gentle squeeze, rolling the nipple in his fingers.

They lay there like that for a long moment, so long he began to wonder if she'd changed her mind.

"I'm not sorry about this," she said at last. "Maybe I'm losing my mind, but if that's the case, I don't think I want to find it."

"Ditto." He cleared his throat. "We're going to find out who did this, Peyton. And we're going to see where this goes. We can do them both at the same time. Do you believe that?"

She let out a long sigh. "Yes. I shouldn't, but I do."

He smiled against her hair. "Me, too."

He fell asleep with her naked body curved against his and memories of their hot sex flashing in his dreams.

Chapter Nine

Peter Kendrick looked at his watch. It was the evening and the last thing he wanted to be doing after a long day in court was sitting here in his den with Warren Sulzberger. But the man was doing him a huge favor and he owed him a lot. And if it got Owen off the hook, he wouldn't care if it was three o'clock in the morning.

He glanced at the other man now, who was sitting in one of the large armchairs in the den in his library, sipping single malt Scotch and smoking a cigar. Despite the subject of their meeting, he should have looked relaxed. Instead he looked like someone sitting on an electrified fence. Kendrick was sure that whatever news he had was far from good, and not for the first time wanted nothing better than to beat the shit out of his fully grown but hardly mature son.

"First of all, I cannot tell you enough times what a fucking big mess your son has made. Accept the fact that it's so big it's taking an earthmover to clean it up."

He took a swallow of his drink. "You also didn't think the sister would be a problem, and look at the mess she's stirring up."

"We're handling it."

Sulzberger made a rude noise. "You mean I'm handling it."

"For which I am very grateful. Thank you." He ground out the words. They had still barely scratched the surface of what needed to be done. "By the way, your people obviously did a good job at the Hollister house," Kendrick pointed out, "since there hasn't been any fallout from it."

"Of course they did." Sulzberger glared at him. "My people always do a good job. And we now have both laptops and the desktop computer. Besides, the crew I sent was meticulous about not leaving anything out of place. They left it exactly as they found it."

"Damn, Warren, I'm giving you a compliment and expressing my gratitude." Kendrick smiled, although there was little humor in it. "The fact no one has reported any break-in or anything stolen is more proof, I'd say, that no one is checking on the house. You even took care of the problem with the security system."

"We needed to kill it to gain entry to the house. Couldn't have any alarms going off to the security company. Then we called and canceled the service, which, under the circumstances, no one questioned." Sulzberger took a sip of his drink.

"I'd have asked you to do it sooner, but I couldn't afford to have anyone show up before the funeral and Hollister's parents left town. Too chancy." Kendrick took another swallow of his drink, bigger than the last one. He'd need a gallon of whiskey by the time this clusterfuck was taken care of.

"I agree. You know these people. How long do you think it will take before someone finally does check up on it?"

Kendrick shrugged. "I'd guess, under the circumstances, a long while. The parents are gone, Brianne Hollister is still in a coma and as far as we know the sister is focusing all her time and attention on her."

"Except when she's badgering the police or trying to hire a private investigator." Sulzberger's voice had a nasty edge to it.

Kendrick had to restrain himself from snapping at the man. He couldn't argue the implication that much of this was his fault for not keeping a closer eye on his son in the first placed. "She hasn't been to the house. If she did go and had discovered anything out of sync we'd have heard about it by now."

"I agree." Sulzberger shifted in his chair. "Let's talk about the cars next. You were worried someone would come out of the woodwork and remember Owen's car, and give a description to the police, possibly someone we couldn't get to. You asked me to get rid of it and it's done."

"Good. He's driving a rental for the moment while he decides on a new car. Anybody asking gets told his car is in for service, but we're thinking of buying a new one. It's taken care of."

"Also, I reached out to make sure all the tapes that had the image of the, uh, incident on it have been erased."

Kendrick arched an eyebrow. "You believe?"

"Let me rephrase. I know we have. It's gone from everywhere. Even if someone somehow got a description, without license plates and without a vehicle they have no place to go." Sulzberger's smile held little humor. "Enough money can make anything go away."

"And the car itself?" Kendrick frowned. "What did you do with it?"

"It's in pieces, but of course, that won't necessarily stop someone from looking for it. Worse if that someone knows what the fuck they're doing. If they start digging into every little corner and they don't stop until they get answers."

"How would anyone even know to look for Owen's vehicle? His name hasn't been attached to this at all."

Sulzberger snorted. "Only because we've paid off everyone we had to and twisted a few arms to make sure of it. You should have let them pick up Hollister's car. That at least would have satisfied them for a while. Strangers will wonder about it."

Kendrick rubbed his forehead, trying to ease the beginning of a headache.

"His cell and laptop were in there. I couldn't let them get hold of those. God only knows what was on them."

"You could have had someone just wipe everything," Sulzberger pointed out.

"This is better. So let's have the most important thing you came to tell me, Warren. Enough beating around the bush." Kendrick stared at him. "I appreciate everything you're doing, Warren, but it's late. I have a headache, I feel a crisis brewing and you've been dancing around this issue since you got here. So let's have it."

"It's not going to make you happy." Sulzberger shifted in his chair.

"I didn't expect it would. Enough, already. Who the fuck are these goddamn people who are now sticking their noses into this? And where did she find them?"

He noticed that Sulzberger looked distinctly uneasy as he nodded.

"I just want you to know it took a lot of digging to find out who they are."

Kendrick took a sip of scotch, needing it to hold on to his self-control. This had to be really bad if Sulzberger was avoiding it. "Then you'd better give it to me. What did you find out about them? How bad could they be? She can't possibly have the kind of connections for anyone we'd have to worry about."

"If that were true," Sulzberger pointed out, "you'd have been able to find out who they were without me."

"Yes. I hear you."

Sulzberger rubbed his forehead. "Be prepared. You won't be happy. I'm not. There's a lot on the line for both of us."

Kendrick leaned forward. "What the hell does that mean? What is there about them that I won't like?"

Sulzberger nodded. "Plenty."

Kendrick ground his teeth. "Then for god's sake, you'd better let me have it."

"Remember that unfortunate business that caused my untimely departure from the Senate?"

"Unfortunate business?" Kendrick's laugh was anything but humorous. "Don't you mean a bucket full of shit that we all dug you out of? Selling the information about a SEAL Team mission that got nearly everyone killed? And almost got you sent to prison? *That* unfortunate business?"

"Whatever." Another pull on the cigar.

"Why are you bringing that up now? I thought we'd buried that in the bowels of hell."

"Apparently there are some things you can never get away from. Just as you asked, I managed to learn the identity of the people Peyton West hired. They are very private, high-level, ultra-covert contractors. All Special Forces, all former SEALs, and even an idiot knows what that means. On top of that, they are obnoxiously rich and very picky about the jobs they take."

"And?" Kendrick was losing what little patience he had left. What the fuck was going on here? "Will you get to the fucking point already? Don't tell me the people Peyton West hired have any connection to that other nasty business."

"The leader of that SEAL team, Scott Hamilton, is now a partner in the agency looking into Dane Hollister's death."

Kendrick felt an icy little shiver crawl up his spine. This could be an even bigger disaster.

"Tell me about them."

"They call themselves Galaxy. God knows where they came up with that name. He has three partners and, worse yet, all of them are SEALs, and that means they are trained to execute in ways you and I never even thought of. They can do and find things no one else can. That's what they do."

"For god's sake, Warren." He bit down on his irritation. He had to think of Owen, not the man across from him. He had to do whatever it took to put an end to this mess. He didn't need this curve ball. "These men aren't gods."

Sulzberger snorted. "Maybe, but they think they are. We can't just buy them off or get rid of them some other way. Not these men. Besides, Scott Hamilton, the SEAL Team leader, swore he'd kill me if he ever got his hands on me, and I don't doubt for a minute he'd do just that."

Kendrick had to restrain himself from hurling his glass across the room. Or punching Sulzberger in the jaw. The asshole with the unquenchable thirst for money and power had created a situation that was going to haunt them forever. If he, Kendrick, had been smart, he'd never have helped Sulzberger slide out of that fucking mess way back when and ultimately end up more powerful than he'd been in the Senate. But they'd known each other for years, the man was Owen's godfather and he'd felt an obligation.

Now, however, he feared it was all about to come back to haunt him. All because his son, who he was grooming for political power, didn't appear to have any self-control.

He drew in a deep breath and slowly let it out. "Do you happen to have a suggestion of how we *do* deal with this?"

Sulzberger was silent for a long moment, then took a slow sip of his drink. "Peter, you know I've been doing my best to make this whole situation go away, but I don't know if I can butt heads with Galaxy. I have no leverage over them, not to mention the fact they have a target on my back. I can tell you this is one big fucking mess."

"That you can't make go away."

"Exactly. If I keep poking around in this," Sulzberger continued, "they're sure to find out it's me behind all the digging — then I'm well and truly fucked. I've done what I could for you and now I have to get out of this."

"You have to be kidding me."

"Not even a little. I just wanted you to be prepared, if this all blows up, that it's my ass I'll be covering first. I've given you all the information I've got. I made sure we covered everything over, got the cops and everyone else to back away from this and label it a hit and run accident, driver unknown. That's all I can do. I have to back the hell away from this and protect myself."

"Yeah? How about a way to neutralize them? You're the one with all the shady contacts."

"Shady?" Sulzberger's face darkened. "You didn't mind taking advantage of my so-called shady contacts when it suited you. Besides, from what I could find out, there's no way to neutralize these people."

"Damn it." Kendrick ground his teeth. "You owe me, Warren. I saved every strip of your bacon when you needed. Well, now it's payback time, and I'm not letting you off the hook. This is my son we're talking about."

"A son who you discovered too late had a craving for gambling that he can't control," Sulzberger snapped. "When the Tampa Mafia came to your office demanding representation, you should have turned them down with a little more finesse. Or figured out how to help them. Or at least connected them with another attorney who didn't mind a little dirt on his clients and is just as much a shark in court as you are."

"Yeah, right," Kendrick snorted. "How the hell was I supposed to do that? They cover themselves a lot better than they did seventy years ago, but if you ask the right people, they tell you the truth. These people make billions with their hotel chains, but apparently that's not enough. They use it as a cover for smuggling and distributing dope and for the sex trade."

"Trouble showed up the day they came to your office. These people have revenge perfected as an art."

"As if I had a choice." He sighed. "No way could I represent them. And anyone else running a check on them, like we all do with major clients, would turn up the same garbage I did. I had my nuts in a wringer no matter what I did." He shook his head. "I just didn't realize they would take out their revenge through Owen."

The memory of it all still made him sick to his stomach. The owners of a chain of high-end boutique hotels were being sued for a number of reasons, and for an obnoxious amount of money. They had tried to retain Peter to represent them in a lawsuit, but he had passed. For one thing, he hadn't liked them personally. For another, when he had done some checking, there'd been things that just hadn't added up.

Then a criminal attorney he was friendly with had told him they were referred to behind the curtain as the Tampa Mafia. They were part of elite society because wealthy people got a jolt from hanging out with rich criminals. And besides, they gave millions to charity, money they could certainly afford. Money covered a multitude of sins. But that made him think that the people suing them had a very good case.

He'd learned the hard way they didn't like being turned down. With practiced efficiency that had pegged Owen as a young man with weaknesses, they had seduced him with the lure of high-stakes gambling. When he'd begun to lose, with carefully orchestrated games, the desperation to win again had consumed him. Before long, he'd been in way over his head and the Tampa Mafia had been turning the screws. They'd known Peter was never going to represent them, so they'd taken pleasure in destroying his son. Sending a message, so to speak.

Don't fuck with us.

If only an unforeseen set of circumstances hadn't turned Dane Hollister on to the situation. If only Brianne Hollister hadn't been driving on the Gandy

Bridge that particular day at that particular time. If only his son hadn't gotten drunk that night and decided to do something desperate. If only.

How many times had he repeated those words to himself, each time tasting the bitterness that clogged his throat? It continued to fill him with self-loathing that he hadn't noticed any of the symptoms that would have given him a clue to what was happening. It wasn't the Tampa Mafia who had turned Owen, although they'd certainly had their revenge in doing so. He, Peter, had to accept most of the responsibility, for not paying more attention and catching any of the signals. But there had been no warning, no signs, nothing. It had come out of nowhere and hit him like a runaway train.

Had he been so blind? Had the son he was so proud of, the top student, smart young lawyer, model husband primed for the march to political success, been hiding secrets from him all this time? Secrets he'd been too busy or too blind to see? He had been too immersed in his own life and the firm to notice what was happening in his own family.

His marriage to Diane Winslow, daughter of an influential and wealthy financier, had fit right into Peter's plans for his son's future. Oh, yes, vivacious Diane, who seemed so in love with his son and had seemed just as shocked as he was when this had all threatened to blow up.

He had no idea where his daughter-in-law stood. What did she think now? She and Owen appeared very compatible and happy, so where was she in all this? Was she even aware of what was going on? Had she deliberately made herself absent and unavailable since the disaster or was Owen, always the chivalrous one, deliberately keeping her out of the way?

Jesus! What a shit show this was turning into. He'd asked Owen to bring his wife to the office so he could talk to both of them. Owen, however, was keeping a low profile, doing a lot of work remotely, taking carefully selected client meets, and said she didn't need to be involved in anything.

"Are you listening to me?"

Warren's strident voice broke into his thoughts.

He gave himself a mental shake. "Yes. I'm listening. You don't have to keep reminding me that this is quite a mess we're in."

"Of your son's making."

Kendrick snorted. "Let's not forget your own mess which is swirling in the pot here. Give me everything you've got on these people. I mean everything. If you have to run like a coward, go ahead and do it. I'll figure out a way to get them off Owen's back, but you've got to get all the information. I'm not kidding. Otherwise, forget it."

"I can't have this all come out again," Sulzberger protested. "If people get wind that I'm helping you, or someone decides to spread the rumors from Washington, it will destroy my life."

"But at least you'll still have one." He held up his hand when Sulzberger opened his mouth to object. "Never mind. It won't do any of us any good for all that shit to rise to the surface again. There'd be no keeping a lid on it this time."

"No argument here. So, what's our plan?"

"First, tell me everything you learned about them. Where they came from. How they operate, what they can do, what do I worry about the most. And how, if they keep at it, they could possibly find a dismantled car and identify it."

Sulzberger sighed. "Fine. Let's start with the fact that they won a Powerball lottery of more than a billion dollars and started a dark private contracting company whose only office is in a plane that cost a million bucks. When you swallow that, I'll tell you about their connections, also all former SEALs. All a bunch of fucking do-gooders who aren't afraid of anyone or anything."

"There has to be a way to stop them. Tell me everything and I'll figure it out."

At least he damn well hoped he would. How had everything just gone to hell like this?

The conversation lasted for the better part of two hours. Kendrick wanted every single detail, no matter how tiny. If he was going to have to move forward by himself, he needed every piece of information he could get. Sulzberger gave him all he had and they began to plan. It wouldn't be easy, but they had to get these people off Owen's back.

It would have been better if they could just get rid of them, but it appeared that wasn't a likely option. Not with Sulzberger ready to bail and the men so high profile. He'd have to figure out something else.

* * * *

Blaze knew he should let Peyton sleep. Yesterday had been exhausting for her, both physically and emotionally. Today would be more of the same. Rocket had texted just now that they were a go for a plane meeting. Wheels up at nine o'clock, which was still two hours from now. And Eagle was bringing breakfast. What could be better?

Last night, he'd had the most incredible sex of his life, and that was really saying something. In his thirty-four years, he'd had plenty of sexual activity — his share and probably someone else's, too. Nothing had compared to what had happened with Peyton and he wanted to think they'd barely gotten started.

Wait. What? Barely gotten started? Where had that come from? Blaze Hamilton didn't do any arrangement longer than twenty-four hours. Oh, he might have a repeat performance, like he did with Fran when they were both available, but it was never more than just two people having an evening of no-holds-barred sex.

So what was different here? In less than twenty-four hours, both his dick and his brain were demanding a commitment he knew he should ignore. The problem was, he didn't think he wanted to.

He watched Peyton sleep for a moment, her chest rising and falling with each breath. Her glorious chestnut-colored hair was spread out on the pillow, her body still flushed rosy from the aftereffects of sex. One arm was flung over her head, the other resting next to her. The sheet had slipped down far enough that he could see those mouthwatering breasts with their taut, rosy nipples and just a hint of her belly button. Hungry to see every bit of her, he tugged the covers down her hips and legs and past her feet until her entire body was exposed to his gaze. And what a body it was.

He slid down the bed until he could wrap his fingers gently around one ankle and began to string kisses along the inside of her thigh all the way to her hip. She shifted against the contact and a little moan whispered from her lips.

"Ssh, ssh." He inhaled her scent. "It's all good. I just need a little taste to start my day. That okay?"

Her eyes flew open, the heat in them matching what he felt.

"What…"

He chuckled. "I'll take that as a yes."

She looked down the length of her body to him with slumberous eyes.

"Is it even past dawn? I'm hardly awake yet. But I—"

"You don't have to do a thing," he assured her. "This is all on me."

He coasted his mouth down the other leg, pausing to nip the soft flesh now and then, the sharp little moans coming from her going straight to his hungry dick. He drew a line with his tongue just above her very neatly trimmed pubic hair, stopping for a moment to wonder, as he had the night before, if she kept it trimmed for someone else and if he'd have to kill the bastard.

He couldn't help himself. He had to use the tip of his tongue to trace the seam of the folds of her sex. She moaned again and lifted her hips just a little.

"Feels good. I want more."

"Tastes good, too." He chuckled. "And I plan to taste it a lot."

One more soft lick and he moved up her body to lave the swirl of her belly button. She whimpered, the sound going straight to his cock, causing him to grit his teeth. *This is just for her*, he told himself, even if he did want her lips around his dick.

The skin at her navel was apparently super-sensitive, because as he licked, he twirled his tongue and even nipped with his teeth, and her moans grew a little louder and she began twisting her hips back and forth.

He moved further up her body, trapping her legs beneath him, and reached for her breasts. Her nipples were so taut and firm that he couldn't resist taking a little nip at each of them. He didn't want to leave them, but he wanted one kiss before he got down to serious business. But when he tried to kiss her, she turned her head away.

"I still have overnight breath. Yuk. I taste terrible."

He laughed again softly. "Nothing about you tastes terrible. But, okay, I'll just have to kiss someplace else."

Before she could recognize what he was doing, he scooted back down the bed, lifted her legs and spread them wide enough to kneel between her silky thighs. He stared at her for a moment, aroused by the glistening drops of her juices on her pubic hair. Bending down, he gave them a slow lick, wringing another moan from her.

When she reached for him again, grabbing for his head as she'd done before, he rocked forward, braceleting her wrists with his fingers and dragging her hands over her head. "Lock your fingers together over your head." He heard the command in his voice and hoped it didn't turn her off. But Jesus, this woman! He wanted everything with her.

When she did as he ordered, he smiled and went back to business.

Spreading the lips of her sex wide, he ran his tongue over the slick pink flesh it exposed, tasting her clit before closing his teeth over the little tip. Peyton groaned and thrashed beneath him, but lay there as he directed with her hands clasped above her head. As he continued tormenting the little nub of flesh, he could feel it swell and heat up beneath his mouth.

Using his thumbs to open her wider, he teased at her opening, again with the tip of his tongue, swirling it in tiny circles again and again until her groans grew louder. When he thrust his tongue inside her, she screamed her pleasure, bucking her hips up to him. God, she tasted so good, sweet and flowery and spicy all at the same time.

He fucked her with his tongue again and again, moving one hand enough that he could capture her clit with two fingers. When he pinched it, she screamed and came in a sudden rush, riding his tongue, her hips moving to increase the intensity of the friction. Her inner muscles were still flexing when he abruptly pulled back, sat up and reached into the nightstand drawer for a condom.

"Yes!" She panted, eyes wide and glazed with passion.

He pulled her arms down, flipped her over and dragged her to her knees. He could hardly wait to fuck her like this. When he ran the tip of one finger through the cleft in her buttocks, her body tensed. He stopped, holding perfectly still. If this gave her no pleasure, he'd do it differently.

"Don't like this? Peyton, you don't have to do anything you don't want to."

"I-I don't know if I like it or not. I've never done it this way before."

Holy shit!

"Any special reason?" He kept his voice calm and even.

"Yes." She swallowed so hard he could hear her. "To me that's the most intimate act you can do. Even more than…than what you were just doing. I've never been with anyone I wanted to open myself up to that way."

Blaze was so stunned that for a moment he couldn't think of what to say. The women he bedded were into anything, and that meant absolutely everything, without batting an eyelash. He drew in a deep breath, steadying himself.

"We're not going to do anything you don't want to." He reached for every bit of control he had. "That's not how I roll."

"I don't... I want..."

He curved his body over her and whispered in her ear, "But this is almost as good."

He slid his finger into her sex, finding it still soaked and quivering with the last tremors of her orgasm. *Yes!* He could hardly wait.

He rested his hands on her hips and placed a soft kiss on each cheek of her ass.

"Deep breath, Peyton. Here we go. I can't wait any longer."

He nudged her opening with the tip of his shaft, drew in another breath and drove into her with one swift thrust.

Oh, Jesus!

He had to stop a minute and take a breath. If he'd thought things might not be as intense as they'd been last night, he was definitely wrong. If anything, his feelings were stronger, which just blew his mind. And he had no idea where they were going with this, but he definitely was all in.

Squeezing her hips, he began the steady in and out movement, thrust and retreat, thrust and retreat, slow and steady at first but then faster and faster. She was slick and wet and tight as hell, her inner walls gripping him like a vise as she moved with him and creating a delicious friction. On and on it went. He could tell she was close again and he reached for his last frayed thread of control so he didn't let go ahead of her.

And then there it was, an orgasm of what he'd later think of as cataclysmic proportions. They crested together and exploded, her sex squeezing him hard as he spasmed inside her. There was nothing but himself and this woman and this epic orgasm.

And then...

Then they were finished, Peyton collapsing beneath him as if her limbs had turned to water, her breathing heavy, body slick with sweat. Blaze could identify with that because he felt the same way, in spades. His body was spent from the most intense orgasm he'd ever had. Oh, wait. Except for the one last night. *Holy fuck!* His heart was pounding so hard it echoed in his ears and his lungs were begging for more air. He'd never in his life had a woman affect him this way and he wasn't quite sure what to do with it. One thing he knew for sure. He wasn't walking away from this. He hoped he could convince Peyton to do the same.

Bracing himself on his forearms, he placed a string of gentle kisses the length of her spine, then slid from her body and eased off the bed to dispose of the condom. When he returned, she was still lying there, exactly as he'd left her, gorgeous hair spread out across her shoulders, her naked body flushed from the heat of passion. He sat beside her on the bed and ran his finger gently down her spine, bringing out delicious shivers.

"I'd love to crawl back in here with you, but we need to be at the hangar before nine. If we shower together, do you think we can keep our hands off each other?"

She rolled over to look at him and laughed.

"It would be a much harder exercise in discipline if we hadn't just expended all our energy."

He brushed a kiss over her lips. "You're right on that one. Okay, then. Let's get to it."

Chapter Ten

The sun was barely up when Blaze woke her. Peyton could hardly believe he'd woken her so early. She rarely had morning sex, usually because she wouldn't stay over at someone's place or have them stay over at hers. She couldn't believe how exhilarated she was, a feeling that carried her all through their meeting with Frank and the run-through of the new security system in the house. The security man had even changed all the locks and handed a new set of keys to each of them.

"If someone tries to get in again, they'll get nailed," he assured them.

Now, still zinging from their early morning sex, she climbed the stairs to the plane ahead of Blaze. She was still astounded at the effect he had on her...that they had on each other. He overwhelmed her, yet at the same time made her feel incredibly special. He didn't swallow her, as others had tried to do. If she worried about anything, it was that she'd never get enough of him.

And today she needed to put that aside for the business at hand.

As she moved into the cabin of the plane, she got her first look at the other two partners. Standing in the area where she and Blaze had sat was a man even taller than Blaze. His hair was dark like Blaze's, almost midnight black, but where Blaze's hair stopped at the nape of his neck, his was long enough that he tied it back with a leather thong.

"Peyton, meet John 'Rocket' Hardin. Rocket, say hello to our client."

"Pleasure to welcome you aboard, Miss West."

Rocket's hand was warm, his grip firm, and she felt the incredible strength behind it. She got the feeling at once that he, like Blaze, was a man she could trust with her life.

"Please call me Peyton. Thank you so much for taking me on as a client."

"I respect Blaze's judgment, as we all do for each other. And from what we've learned so far, I think Galaxy is just what you need. We'll get this taken care of. Count on it."

"Thank you."

He stepped aside and Blaze nudged her forward to the middle section of the plane. Here everything had been configured to create a conference table setting. Laptop computers sat at three places with notepads covered in writing beside each. Viper looked up from scribbling on one of the pads, rose and held out his hand to her.

"Nice to see you again, Peyton."

She was relieved that he didn't have a knowing look in his eyes like a lot of men would have. When he looked from her to Blaze and back again, the hooded glance told her it had more to do with the information he'd dug up than whatever was going on with Blaze.

"I have some interesting things to share. Blaze, you might want to look at the stuff first."

A knot formed in Peyton's stomach.

"What is it you want to hide from me? I'm a grown woman, Viper. I can take whatever crap it is you've dug up, even if it makes Dane and Brianne look bad. I have to know."

"What? No, no, that's not what I meant." He raked his fingers through his hair. "It's just, some of this stuff is pretty brutal."

"Then I definitely need to know. Somewhere in there is the clue to who killed Dane and put Brianne in a coma. I can handle anything to get that information."

She sensed Blaze behind her, then felt the warmth of his hand on her shoulder.

"She can handle it," he told Viper. "No secrets. Okay?"

Viper nodded. "You've got it."

Blaze eased Peyton into one of the chairs at the table then sat beside her, opening his own laptop.

Just then, the man who she assumed was the fourth partner came up from the compartment in the back of the plane. He was the leanest of the partners, and possibly the shortest, although she judged that they all topped six feet. His hair was light brown but with an interesting white streak that ran from his forehead to the back of his head. He had piercing brown eyes and a hawk nose and he reminded her of something but she couldn't think what.

He held out his hand to Peyton. "Vic Bodine."

"Nice to meet you, Vic."

"Call me Eagle." He grinned. "I'm not sure I answer to Vic anymore."

And that's exactly what he looks like. An eagle, ready to attack. No wonder that was his call sign. She'd love to know how the others had gotten theirs, especially Blaze.

Blaze cleared his throat. "Let's get seated. I'll go check with Saint and see how soon we'll be taking off."

"Saint is right here. Welcome aboard again, Miss West."

Peyton turned to see yet another tall, muscular man standing in the cabin.

"Peyton," she corrected again.

"Everyone, we'll be taking off in five. I'll let you know when we're at cruising altitude." He nodded at everyone and headed to the cockpit.

Peyton settled more comfortably in her chair and looked around the table. She didn't think she'd ever been surrounded by so much testosterone in her life. But rather than make her feel uncomfortable, it gave her a feeling of security, one that she really needed right now. She'd been on edge since she'd gotten the call from Peter Kendrick and nothing that had happened since then had done anything to make her feel better.

Except of course for last night, but that was a whole different ball game, one she needed to put out of her mind while they focused on the business at hand. Not that it was all that easy, sitting next to Blaze and almost seeing the sexual energy crackling from both of them. She'd had a decent number of lovers, some better than others, but none had ever made her feel so exhilarated or charged as Blaze. She had no idea where it was going and right now was not the time to figure it out, but it stunned her to realize how much that connection settled her.

There was something else there, too. They'd touched on it a little, then backed away, *Because we've known each other such a short amount of time.*

Moments later came the roar of the engine, the smooth roll as they taxied to the runway and finally the takeoff as they lifted into the air. Peyton looked out of the window at the blue sky surrounding them dotted with puffs of clouds, so peaceful as opposed to what they were about to discuss. She hoped these men had found some real information and they could finally get some answers.

Saint's voice over the intercom jolted her back to the present.

"Gentlemen and lady, we are at thirty thousand and good to go."

Eagle pushed out of his chair. "Food and coffee first. Otherwise my brain won't work."

He headed for the compartment at the rear of the plane, which Peyton could see even at a distance was partially outfitted as a galley. Rocket followed him, and in what seemed like seconds they returned carrying breakfast sandwiches and pastries, dishes and coffee.

"Better stoke the furnace," Rocket told them. "We may be up here a long time and you'll need to feed your brain."

When everyone was seated again with their choices, they each opened their laptops. Peyton noticed that Blaze had left his closed. She glanced over at him and lifted an eyebrow.

"Mine's just backup. In case. Everyone will send whatever they've got to me. I wanted to be able to listen without distraction." He looked over at Viper. "Okay, you're up first."

"Background before anything else." Viper woke up his screen. "I have information you need to have to set the stage for everything else."

Blaze nodded. "Go."

Viper tapped his keyboard.

"Like I said last night, no matter how people might try to deny its existence, there is indeed such a thing as the Tampa Mafia. They aren't as open about it as they once were and spend a lot of time and money to cloak themselves in respectability. While they are still major players in illegal enterprises, and they control a lot of the gambling, they've become more sophisticated. International money laundering and sex trafficking, major drug distribution and always the age-old murder for hire, only more refined. Not to mention corruption of public employees so they can manipulate laws for their convenience. And these days, especially in the United States, everything is run under the umbrella of a legitimate business enterprise, Bistro Hotels."

"Bistro operates internationally," Peyton said slowly. "I've even stayed in a couple of their facilities when I was traveling to do research. They are all so beautiful and classy. Are you sure the men in that picture work for them?"

"I am." Viper clicked a couple of keys then turned his laptop so she could see the screen.

Peyton studied the man whose picture stared back at her. In his head shot he looked like a polished, uber-wealthy businessman, with his expensively styled hair, his classic face with high cheekbones accented by the carefully trimmed scruff beard. He was dressed in a dark business suit that she was sure cost as much as many people's salaries, a white shirt and a precisely knotted tie that she knew from the pattern was a Hermès. He shrieked money and power, but at the same time, even from the computer photograph, he generated a presence of evil.

"Tell us," Blaze said.

"The Kellerman family has been an integral part of the Tampa Mafia for generations. I put together a diagram so you could see the evolution." Viper turned his laptop so everyone could see. "His grandfather was a capo in the Santo Trafficante empire. Trafficante was one of the most powerful and feared Mafia bosses in this country. Kellerman's family had come here from Sicily, like Trafficante. That, along with his degrees in business and law, made him a prime candidate for entry into the upper echelon of the organization. When Trafficante died in 1972, Kellerman, as the heir apparent, stepped into the leadership role without an argument, even though he was just thirty-five at the time."

He clicked a button on the keyboard.

"He grew the business by creating alliances with crime families as far away as Croatia and Venezuela, as well as expanding throughout the Southeastern United States. Prostitution morphed into the sex slave trade. He forged alliances with drug cartels to expand his distribution network and cemented his relationship with them by importing underage girls from Europe to marry off to the old men who have a fierce, perverted hunger for them. He's also into everything from gambling to murder and whatever will make him money and give him control, just like the Mafia old days."

Peyton swallowed hard and tried to blink away the images that popped into her brain. "And no one has ever managed to stop him?"

"He has more public and elected officials on his payroll than Congress does, I think. Not to mention owning a number of police in key places. He was untouchable."

"You say *was*," Rocket pointed out. "He's not still active?"

"At eighty-four, he's pretty much retired. This picture is actually of his son, Hayden Kellerman, Junior. He's the one who saw the benefit of expanding the hotel chain and using it as a blind for the sex trade, drugs, gambling, even smuggling. Bistro Hotels are among the most popular spots for anyone with money or position. But while you're enjoying the spa treatment, the gourmet food and the six-hundred-thread-count sheets on the beds, on another floor women are being drugged, brutally raped and sold to the highest bidders, either individuals or whorehouses. And card games with a minimum fifty-thousand buy-in are taking place."

For a moment, Peyton thought she might be sick. She wasn't a dummy. She knew all about illegal trades in everything from girls to guns. As a romantic suspense author, she'd certainly done enough research on them. But there was a big difference between reading about it and actually being confronted with the reality. She lifted her coffee cup with shaking hands, hoping she didn't spill the liquid as she took a sip. *How on earth is Peter Kendrick involved in all of this?*

"He also," Viper continued, "has the most efficient squad of killers anyone could ask for. And that's only scratching the surface. Whatever you need, Kellerman and his so-called staff are the ones to see about it. He has shell corporations set up to run the Mafia money through. Deposits it in an offshore account, then hopscotches everything two or three times to a bank where he has a blind trust set up."

Rocket sat back in his chair and let out a soft whistle. "Jesus. How the hell is Kendrick's firm involved with this?"

"That's what I want to know." Peyton looked around the table. "I can't tell you how far removed any of this is from my brother-in-law."

Rocket gave her a hard look. "Are you sure?"

She started to answer him, anger surging through her veins, but Blaze put a hand on her forearm.

"I checked the Hollisters out stem to stern before taking this on," he told the others. "Dane Hollister is so clean he squeaks."

"Those photos." Viper clicked a couple of keys and brought them up on his screen, turning it so everyone could see. "Why are three of Hellerman's thugs having a decidedly unfriendly conversation with Owen Kendrick?"

"And what bad luck had my sister driving by at that moment?" Peyton wanted to know. "I can't believe she knew who these men were."

Blaze tightened the hand he had on her arm. "Don't get upset. She probably didn't. But she recognized Owen and saw some decidedly unpleasant people who were obviously threatening him. She took the pictures to show her husband. And to his misfortune, he went to Peter Kendrick about them."

She ran her hands over her hair, smoothing it back and tightening her ponytail. It was taking every bit of restraint not to scream and beat her fists on the table. How in god's name had this happened? What ungodly twist of fate had put Brianne and Dane in the middle of this evil situation?

"I can't believe that Peter Kendrick himself is the one who ran down my sister and her husband."

Viper nodded. "I agree. I don't believe he would have. Not his style. In all the information I dug up on him, there's no hint of violence of any kind. But if he confronted Kellerman about it, he could easily have had someone do it."

Rocket frowned. "Would he really go to Kellerman? Tell him to stay away from Owen? I mean, knowing the man has a virtual staff of killers and wouldn't hesitate to pull the trigger on either father or son?"

Blaze looked around the table. "We can't know what people will do in times of stress. How many times have we seen the unexpected in all our years as SEALs?"

"That's true," Rocket agreed. "But we need to look at everything before we settle on a conclusion and move forward. Viper. What else have you got?"

"Still looking into Peter Kendrick's private life, checking his friends to see if he has anyone he could tap for something like this."

"I dropped by and had a drink with Tom Hernandez," Rocket told them. "He said if we had anything on Peter Kendrick, he'd be shocked. The man was a star of the legal community and could be nominated for Citizen of the Year. Sits on a number of boards, contributes to charitable causes and doesn't cheat on his wife."

Viper burst out laughing. "So he has nothing in his private life to worry about? We ought to clone him."

"He also said Owen has a reputation as a great up-and-coming litigator. Respected by the local legal and business community. Checks all the boxes, you know?"

"That doesn't eliminate him," Rocket pointed out. "We all know lots of people who look good on paper but are rotten underneath it all."

"True," Blaze agreed. "Don't forget those pictures on Brianne's phone. They're a good indication that he plays a major role here, somehow."

"True. We know how that goes. We need to make sure we don't miss anything." Rocket looked over at Eagle. "Okay, we've got the background. Now let's have the nitty gritty. Were you able to hack into the CCTV cloud and find anything?"

"As a matter of fact, yes. Well," Eagle amended, "sort of."

"What does that mean?"

"First of all, I knew it would still be in the cloud because the company running it contractually has to store it for ninety days. They couldn't wipe it altogether. However, they made it very difficult to find. Someone with a lot of money and-or clout is handling this, Blaze."

"You mean Kendrick?"

"He has the money," Rocket told them, "but I don't think he has that much clout. Doesn't have the ability to provide the pressure needed. Besides, he can't afford to be caught doing anything illegal."

"So he's got someone doing his dirty work for him. Someone he's paying?"

"I think it's more than that, but we'll get to that later. Now. I nearly went blind, first looking for the footage then trying to get a clear picture."

Peyton's pulse skipped a little. "But you did find something? Like maybe the car and who's driving it?"

"At least the car," Rocket told her, "but the driver's a little harder. Here. Let me show you."

Like Viper, he clicked a few keys then turned his laptop so everyone could see the screen.

"I got lucky here, sort of. At the time this happened there was a CCTV camera on the street where Calypso is. It caught the car coming down the street at an accelerated pace at the exact moment Dan and Brianne Holloway crossed to the parking lot."

"But that's great!" Peyton felt the first finger of excitement. "Why didn't you say so when we first sat down?"

"Because there's a problem. Watch and you'll see what I mean. The driver was so hunched over the wheel and the car was going so fast we can't get a clear picture. Just watch, okay?"

Peyton focused hard on the screen. It was just as Eagle said. The car whipped out of the space where it was parked just as Brianne and Dane began to walk from Calypso. It accelerated and hit them just as they were about to step onto the other sidewalk. The sight of the impact made her so nauseated that she thought for a moment she'd lose it sitting right there. The car just plunged right into them, knocking them flat, and sped off. It was a blur, but they could tell it was obviously brown. However, only part of the license plate was caught on camera and just as Eagle said, the driver was turned away and hunched over the wheel.

For a long moment everyone stared at the screen in shocked silence.

"You can't even tell who it is." Peyton was struck by the urge to hit something. "It could be anyone. Maybe someone they didn't even know."

"I'm still trying to clear it up," he explained. "Whoever did this meant business, and we have to find out why. I know you all agree with me that it's a product of the situation with the Kendricks and Hayden Kellerman, so now we have to find out the details."

Blaze cleared his throat. "Okay, next move. We need to find that car. Eagle, were you able to do anything with a partial license plate?"

"I ran it through every piece of software I've got that could pull it up, but everything beyond the first two characters is blurred. It almost looks like the driver made an attempt to cover it over with mud or something."

"So this definitely isn't just some drunk who raced down the street too fast," Rocket pointed out. "Whoever it is may not have done the best job of concealment, but they made a strong effort. This means it definitely was deliberate."

"And not one of Kellerman's thugs," Viper added. "They'd have done a better job covering it up. Or maybe used a stolen license plate. I'd say we're definitely looking at an amateur here."

Everyone was silent for a long moment. Peyton was still trying to process what she'd seen on the laptop screen, along with all the information that had been dumped. She felt as if she'd fallen into an alternate universe. She wrote about things like this. She didn't live them. And although she always tried to breathe reality into her stories, most of it was fiction. This was not. A shiver raced over her skin and she rubbed her arms.

"You okay?" Blaze's voice was low and soft but everyone heard him.

She swallowed hard and reached for the coffee to take a steadying sip, but it was ice cold, so she put it right back down.

"Let me get you a refill." Eagle reached for her cup, giving her a warm smile as he did. "Don't sweat it. We've all been there. Stuff like that never gets easy to see, even when the people are strangers."

"Thank you."

When he set the refilled cup back down in front of her, she gripped it with both hands and swallowed some. Immediately, her jittery nerves began to settle. But the arm that Blaze slid around her, giving her a gentle hug, did even more. She wasn't a needy person, was used to taking care of everything herself, even her emotions. But this was an emotionally challenging situation and she wasn't afraid to lean on him.

Peyton knew after the previous evening that Viper sensed something going on between her and Blaze, and now she figured Eagle and Rocket were wondering about it. Blaze could tell them whatever he wanted and she'd just follow his lead, but she needed him right now. Needed his strength.

"Better?" Eagle asked as he took his seat across from her.

"Much. Thank you. Coffee's always the best medicine."

"Okay." Blaze gave her a final, light squeeze and turned back to the others. "We need to tap into every resource we can to identify that license plate."

"I agree." Eagle looked at everyone in turn. "But it's going to take software more sophisticated than what I have. I'll have to reach out to a contact of mine."

"Then do it," Blaze told him. "If your software won't do it, we need someone's who will, and we don't have any time to screw around. Also, any luck in finding out what happened to Dane's car?"

"Yeah, but it doesn't help. Peter Kendrick 'kindly' offered to return it to the leasing company and his parents were grateful they didn't have to deal with it."

Rocket snorted. "How fucking nice of him."

"That means he's got Dane's cell phone and laptop, so we can kiss those goodbye."

"Yeah, but it's more important to find out about the car that ran down the Hollisters." Eagle pushed out of his chair. "Let me go in the back and give him a call."

Eagle climbed out of his chair and headed back to the galley. Peyton saw him lean against the counter, pull out his phone and hit some buttons.

Peyton glanced at Blaze. "I didn't think you could make cell phone calls at this altitude."

"The phones are tied into the plane's wireless network, which is as powerful as we could get. We can't be without phones, even at thirty thousand feet."

"Good. That's good."

"We need to—" Blaze started.

He was interrupted by the ringing of Rocket's phone.

"I'd better take this," Rocket told them, looking at the screen. "It's Tom Hernandez."

Peyton watched him answer the call. Every muscle in his face tightened and anger flashed in his eyes.

"Fucking shit." He gripped the cell so hard Peyton was afraid he'd break it. "Are you fucking kidding me? Yeah. Yeah. Okay. But I want to know every nugget you dig up the minute you find it. Okay. Thanks."

Everyone watched as he practically slammed the phone down on the table.

"What is it? I know it had to be bad to make you lose it like this."

"What's up?" Eagle asked at last.

"That was Tom Hernandez. Apparently, someone's been asking questions about us. Well, originally about Peyton and who she hired to look into the murder, because that's what it is."

"Me?" Peyton thought for a moment her heart would stop. "What are they looking for?

"What?" Eagle blinked. "What the fuck? How did anyone even connect us?"

Rocket shrugged. "Actually, they've been asking about Peyton. They —"

He stopped when Blaze's phone rang.

Blaze looked at the readout, eyebrows pinched together.

"What's up?" he answered. "What? What do you mean? What did she say? Did she have a name? Uh-huh. Uh-huh. Uh-huh. Okay. No, you did exactly right. An even better reason for you to hang out there. Yeah, I'll be by to pick it up in a while. Don't let it out of your sight."

"What?" Rocket asked.

"That was Chuck Wagner at the hospital. One of the nurses he's gotten to know stopped to see if he needed anything and they got into kind of a Chatty Cathy thing. She said she was on her way to Brianne Hollister's room and commented that the sister's fans must follow her everywhere. Chuck asked why, and she said one of them came to the hospital with a present for Brianne. To show Miss West how much she cared. She was on her way to give it to her."

A chill raced over Peyton as she listened. "God. That's too scary. I hope Chuck stopped her from giving it to Brianne."

"Next best thing. He watched to make sure all she did was set the package on the bed table. Then as soon as she left, he hopped into the room and grabbed it. Stuck it in the bathroom sink to drench it with water, just in case. Then he placed it in a messenger bag he's got with him. I don't think these people would send an explosive device to the hospital. That would garner too much attention. He's sending it to a company Galaxy has used whenever necessary. He'll call me when he has some answers."

"Fuck." Rocket slammed his fist on the table. "Did the nurse happen to get a name? Anything at all?"

Blaze raked his fingers through his hair. "No. She said she asked twice, but the woman seemed too nervous to give it to her. She wasn't too nervous, however, to tell the nurse she hoped Peyton West was turning over every stone to find out who did this, and that she was getting some really good help. Because what happened to her was awful. Just awful. And there hadn't hardly been anything in the news about it. Such a damn shame. Poor Peyton must be heartbroken. I don't like it."

"Neither do I," Eagle added.

Peyton looked from one to the other, nausea welling up in her throat yet again.

"What does this mean?" She hated that her voice sounded so pitiful. She cleared her throat and spoke again. "Tell me exactly what this all means? Why is someone asking about me? About Brianne."

Blaze cleared his throat. "My guess? Whoever made sure the police wouldn't tell you anything and bribed or threatened everyone else involved got feedback you'd hired someone and they're digging to find out who." He glanced sideways at Peyton. "One of the main reasons our office and everything related to this business is right here in this plane."

"And by the way, I have a lot of fans and none of them have *ever* done anything like that. I'm successful but not a superstar."

"There's always a first time," Rocket pointed out.

"That's true, but this is just so strange." A thought popped into her mind and the fear surged back yet again. "What if whoever this is tries to kill her again?"

"I'm going to take care of that right now." Blaze punched a number into his cell. "Yeah, Nolan. Good. I didn't want to have to page you. Listen. You have to move Brianne Hollister, and I mean now. I have good reason to believe whoever killed her husband will try for her in the hospital. What? Yeah. Uh huh. Okay, thanks. Oh, and I'm calling Chuck Wagner to go sit in her room right now and glue himself to her while she's moved. Thanks."

His words sent a chill slithering along Peyton's backbone. Blaze had been worried about it enough to have someone standing guard outside her door twenty-four-seven, but what if some nut actually got into her room?

Peyton gripped Blaze's arm. "Thank you. I mean it. I can't—I—"

God. She sounded like a blithering idiot.

Blaze wound his fingers around her hand and gave it a gentle squeeze.

"We won't let anything happen to her. That's a promise."

Eagle rose and headed toward the cockpit. "I'll tell Saint it's time to head back."

Blaze nodded. "Thanks. Once we get on the ground, we have a lot of work to do. I want to know who's pulling all these strings. Kendrick may have put it in motion, but I don't think he's got the kind of clout to find out what he wants on his own. Plus, he can't afford to show his face to do it, and frankly, I don't think he's dirty enough, if at all, to connect to people who can do this."

"So someone's helping," Rocket agreed. "Someone with a lot of money and a lot of back room power. I'll stop by and see Tom as soon as we land and get everything I can from him. He might even have some ideas of his own."

"And we have to find out who is nosing around Brianne before before—" Blaze stopped.

"Before they actually get to her," Peyton finished for him. "It's okay. You can say it. I'm past the initial shock and fear, and I want to do whatever I can to help."

"We all do," Viper assured her.

She looked around the table at each of them. "I can't thank you enough for taking me on as a client and helping me. I just—" She stopped and hauled in a breath. "I told Blaze and I'll tell you. Whatever you charge, if I don't have it, I'll find a way to get it. Really. Thank you."

"I told you," Blaze said. "Don't worry about it. We're good to go. The important thing is identifying the killer. And figuring out who the fuck is digging around about us and how they knew you hired us, Peyton. And who the hell sent a package." He looked around at the others. "So, everyone, let's make a list of who's doing what so when we land, we get to work."

Chapter Eleven

Peter Kendrick was not a happy man. At least five times a day, he asked himself how things had spiraled so out of control. One minute he had a prestigious law practice where his biggest problem was how much money he could get in a settlement for a client. The next he was trying to keep his son from being arrested for murder. Now he sat on the screened patio of his son's home, each of them holding a glass with ice cubes and fine aged bourbon. It was a tossup which of them needed it most. At this point, he wasn't sure if an entire bottle would help his nerves.

He looked over at his son.

He has good reason to be nervous.

Peter thought it, although he didn't want to say it. Things were edgy enough between them as it was. He'd insisted Owen stay away from the office, which—thank the lord—his son hadn't argued about. And he had a logical excuse. He was distraught about the death of his friend, Dane Hollister, and the fact that Dane's wife was in a coma that so far had been irreversible.

If people mentioned they weren't aware the two couples were friends, Peter had a ready answer. Dane was very particular about not appearing to curry favor. He wanted to earn a partnership on his own, not because he and the senior partner's son were friends, but it was important to keep following directions.

So Owen and Diane were hiding out south of Tampa on Sanibel Island in a vacation home they'd built there. Peter hoped that by the time this was over, the marriage would still be intact, as edgy as Owen was every time he talked to him. But now things had changed, which was why he'd had his son drive to Tampa. This was not a conversation to have on the phone.

"Did you hear what I said? We have a new problem."

"Yeah? What kind of problem?"

"Brianne Hollister's sister is here and she's shaking a lot of trees. We managed to block her for the most part, but she's tenacious. She's not giving up."

"What the fuck can she do?" Owen snapped.

Peter gave his son a look that should have shriveled him.

"She's smart, she's focused and she's not letting this go. And Sulzberger, who pulled all the strings up until now, has opted out."

Owen stared at his father for a long moment, rose from the chair and began pacing, thrusting his fingers through his hair in a nervous gesture. He never came undone like this, but hell and damnation! He'd never been in a situation like this before, either. Peter could see that he was holding on by a thread, one which he'd have to somehow strengthen, especially with Sulzberger deserting him.

"Are you telling me he just told you he's done with this?" There was no hiding the panic in his eyes. "He owes you. A lot. You told me that. What the fuck do we do now? I thought this was all dead and buried. A hit and run by an unknown driver. Lay low a bit and it will all settle down. Now we're in another fucking mess?"

"You should have thought of that before you ran over two people," Kendrick snapped. "If you hadn't gotten stinking drunk and done the most absurd, outrageous thing in the world, we wouldn't be having this discussion at all. I'll never understand what possessed you. No." He shook his head. "Back up. If you hadn't been seduced by high-stakes gambling, if you hadn't fallen into Hayden Kellerman's trap, if you didn't owe him a bundle of money, none of this would have happened. Fate was definitely shitting on you when it sent Brianne Hollister down Gandy Boulevard at the exact moment Kellerman's thugs were threatening you."

"Fucking pictures. I thought I'd convinced Dane it was nothing. How did I know he'd bring the pictures to you after he talked to me? You said he questioned the connection. Thought it should be looked into. That I might be in trouble. If what he knew, or thought he knew, got out, it would ruin my life. You know that."

"He wouldn't have done anything." Kendrick reached for his control. "Didn't you trust me to handle it? I said I'd take care of it, didn't I? Did you forget the political campaign we've been building for you, that I've put so much time and effort into?"

"Ah, yes," Owen sneered. "The beloved politics."

"Don't give me that attitude. You want this as much as I do. Just take a deep breath and listen to me."

"Listen?" Owen raked his fingers through his hair. "Even you can't control the Tampa Mafia. What if Dane didn't like your answers about those pictures? If they got out, they'd have opened the door to a lot of shit. Kellerman would have jumped all over us and they would have created a major scandal for you. The firm. I— We would have lost everything. Everything! My career would have been in the toilet and yours along with it."

"Where would he go with them? He was too smart and too conscious of his position here to rock the boat. He'd have figured it was my problem to handle and left it to me. Of course—and I can't say this enough times—we wouldn't have had a problem at all if you had any kind of discipline. If you hadn't been drawn by the high-stakes card games. Hadn't gotten yourself in debt to that scum."

"But—"

"But nothing. Weren't you smart enough to know what was up? Didn't you think it was funny that they'd invite my son, after I turned down their request to represent them, to an elite card game?" He waved his hand in the air. "What did you think? That they just wanted to be friends? How stupid are you, anyway? I thought you were smarter than that."

Owen just stood there, not saying a word, a muscle in his jaw twitching furiously. Anger and fear warred in his son's eyes.

"And those pictures," he went on. "I could have found an excuse for them. You know me. I can create paper out of thin air."

Kendrick rose and walked to the built-in bar in his den. He poured short drinks into two more rocks glasses and handed one to his son. He sipped his slowly as he gathered his thoughts. Ever since the night Owen had burst in with the devastating news, his life had been in turmoil. His practice was in more danger than if the Tampa Mafia connection had finished wreaking its vengeance on the firm and using Owen to do it. He'd gotten Sulzberger involved and now the SEALs the man had betrayed might pin a target on him. Not to mention, they were not the kind of people he could control.

He took another slow sip to help him force a calm he didn't feel. When he spoke, he chose his words carefully, locking his anger away for the moment.

"Then you had to go and take stupid to a higher level. I'd have thought you were smart enough to know that murder only exacerbates a problem. Someone always has to pay for it. I'll say again, killing Dane and almost killing his wife was the worst thing you could do."

"Enough already," Owen shouted, raking his fingers through his hair. "You don't need to keep repeating yourself."

"Apparently I do, since you still don't want to listen to me." Kendrick shook his head. "It has taken a lot of money and a lot of pressure to wipe any trace of you from that event. You're not so dumb you aren't aware of that. And now we have other problems, which is why I wanted you to drive up to see me. Peyton West has hired men who can't be bought or influenced and who don't give up. Ever. That's why I wanted Diane to come with you."

"I told you and told you. I want to leave Diane out of this." He practically spat the words. "She has nothing to do with this. In fact, she begged to come with me, but I'm keeping her as far away as possible. That's how it is."

"No, that's not an option."

Kendrick was doing his best to hold on to his rapidly fraying temper. What the fuck was with this whole thing about keeping his wife out of it? One of the things he liked about Diane was her pedigree and her classy image. She came from wealth and blended easily into the parts of society that were so important, not just for Owen's legal practice but for the forthcoming political campaign. She needed to be here, showing her support for her husband.

Owen glared at him. "I'm telling you—"

"Forget it." Kendrick snapped the words. "The choice is no longer yours. I want her up here. Warren Sulzberger pulled every string he could to get this thing covered up. Do you have any idea how hard it was to bury the CCTV tapes? Neutralize witnesses? Have the cops bury it? Not to mention getting rid of your damned car. You think it wasn't a big problem? I wanted you gone until we got the worst of the mess cleared up, but now you need to be here before people start asking questions. And the public needs to see your wife standing in solidarity with you in the current situation. Mourning the sad death of one of your colleagues."

"If everything's taken care of, why do you need her?"

"Damn it, Owen." He wanted to smack his son. "Like I told you, the current situation has changed. We have trouble out there I wasn't expecting or prepared for."

Owen stared at him. "I'm asking you, what current situation? You just said you and Sulzberger managed to shut all the doors on Brianne Hollister's sister. That's what he was helping you with. Right?"

"Right. Until he ran into a problem of his own. Now we may be stuck because of it."

"Stuck?" Fear flashed across Owen's face. "What does that mean exactly?"

"Warren made sure none of the top firms would let her hire them to look into what happened. However, someone turned her on to a very special firm who took the case and are working to get her answers."

"Damn it, Dad. How special? Why are they different?"

"These are not your average investigators. They're all former Navy SEALs, the cream of the crop. If anyone can get her the answers she wants, it will be them."

"But you told me there was nothing left for anyone to find," Owen reminded his father.

"Under normal circumstances, yes, except these people aren't normal. They don't understand the meaning of the word 'no'. Trust me. They know how to do this. They'll dig and dig and dig until they get what they're looking for."

"Fuck." Owen resumed pacing. "Just fuck."

"A very appropriate word, because if these men uncover anything, we will all be fucked." He sat down in one of the big armchairs, still holding his drink. "We have to have a plan of action going forward. The first thing we're going to do is go over every single thing that you did that night, including where you got so drunk and who might have seen you."

Owen blew out a breath. "Shit. Can't you buy off the sister or something?"

Peter stared at him. "Are you fucking kidding me? Buy her off? Would anything be a better indicator that she's on the trail of something? I didn't realize I'd raised such an idiot."

Owen wiped his hand over his face then chugged down the rest of his drink and slammed the glass on a small table.

"I'm not an idiot. Just unlucky. You need to help me fix this. Think of what this would do to Diane."

"You should have thought of that before you got involved with Hayden Kellerman. Certainly before you got drunk and got behind the wheel of your car. I have not got one idea what the fuck you were thinking."

"I was thinking that if I got rid of the problem, we could cover everything up."

"Yeah." Kendrick rubbed his forehead. "How well did that work out for you?"

"But I—"

"Just shut up and sit your goddamn ass down so we can make some plans. Whatever it takes to fix this, you'll do exactly as I say. Period. Starting with getting your wife up here. Now."

* * * *

Peyton had seldom been so glad to see the end of a day. From the meeting on the plane that morning to meetings with the partners to studying database search results, she felt as if she'd been run over three times by a truck. Possibly the worst moment came in the early evening, at the meeting with Rocket and their attorney, Tom Hernandez. They had stopped to get a quick bite on the way, but now the food sat like lead in her stomach.

"Just wait until Tom gets everything out before you say anything," Rocket cautioned.

"Why? What am I going to say about it? How bad is it? I don't even know who's after us. Right?"

"Just… Keep your shit together."

Peyton couldn't imagine who or what would make Blaze so angry that Rocket had to warn him before revealing the information.

He looked from Rocket to Tom and back again.

"Well, somebody better tell me. And yes, I promise to behave. How bad could it be?"

Rocket waited a moment then nodded to Tom to give him the information.

"You know," the attorney said, "you aren't exactly the word on the street, which is the way you wanted it. Your names are given out only to specific people who are vetted in advance."

"Yeah, yeah. I know all that. We planned it that way." He made a motion with his hand to speed it up.

"I mention that because it would take someone with powerful connections to be able to ferret out this information. It would take a lot of pressure from a powerful source."

Blaze huffed his impatience. "Let's have it already."

"The person who's been digging up info on who you are is your old enemy Warren Sulzberger."

Blaze stared at the man for a long moment. Peyton could almost feel the cold anger rising inside him, and a look came over his face that she hoped never to see again. She was stunned by his fury.

His eyes were filled with rage. "Are you fucking kidding me? Is this some kind of joke?"

Rocket shook his head. "I wish. But he's got the connections and can apply pressure."

"How did I not know he lives here? How did none of us know? Why didn't this show on our radar when we decided to settle here? I thought he'd disappeared from sight." He was clenching his fists, his whole body rigid with anger. Then, with an abrupt movement, he rose from his chair and began to pace the office.

"He actually lives in Miami," Rocket told him.

"He has a large estate there," Tom added. "He seldom comes up here and my guess was that until all this happened, he had no idea you all had settled here and opened Galaxy."

"You can tell me it's none of my business, and it probably isn't, but who is Warren Sulzberger? Why is this a big deal?"

Blaze made a visible effort to control himself.

"It most certainly is your business, because he's inserted himself into it."

"Sulzberger was a senator from Miami," Tom explained. "He sat on the Armed Forces committee and was a pretty big cheese on the Hill. Had lots of connections."

"So what did he do?"

She thought Blaze would answer her, but he walked over to the window and stood looking out, still seeming to grapple for control.

Rocket cleared his throat. "I can tell you that. He was filling his pockets with big bucks by selling information on military missions in trouble spots around the world."

Peyton's jaw dropped. "You have to be kidding. I mean, I've read about it in suspense novels, but I kind of had the idea that was just made up as a plot point."

"If only." Rocket took a swallow of coffee from the mug in front of him. "One of the last pieces of information he sold for huge dollars was about a mission in Africa conducted by a SEAL Team."

Peyton pushed down the sick feeling rising in her throat.

"Let me guess. Sulzberger sold the details of the mission to whoever the target was."

Rocket nodded. "The whole mission was blown. Everyone was killed except for the team leader and one other SEAL."

"The team leader was Blaze," Tom added, "in case you haven't gotten the drift by now. Only he and Ace Bluestone survived, and Ace lost both legs."

Stunned, Peyton glanced over at Blaze, who was still standing like a mountain of stone, fists clenched, every muscle in his body taut with tension.

"Oh, lord. Blaze, I am so sorry."

One short dip of his head was the only indication he had heard her.

She looked back at him and Rocket.

"I don't remember anything about this in the media, so I guess it was all covered up?"

Rocket snorted in disgust. "No shit. He had many powerful friends both in and out of government who allowed him to resign, citing health reasons, and swept it all under the covers. Then he took all his ill-gotten millions and opened a lobbying firm where he makes even more money. He knows where so many bodies are buried in Congress that he can effectively twist arms."

"But how and why is he involved with this? I promise you neither Dane nor Brianne knew who he is."

Tom heaved a sigh. "That's where it gets crazy. From what I've learned through my sources, he's instrumental in putting a lid on the police investigation into Dane's death and preventing anyone from talking to you or answering your questions."

She was stunned. "But he doesn't even know us."

"That's right," Rocket agreed. "But he is tight friends with Peter Kendrick. Some have said it was Kendrick's connections that helped him wriggle out of Congress pretty much unscathed. Now Kendrick is asking for payback."

Peyton's eyes opened wide. "You think Kendrick is involved in Dane's death?"

"No, but I'd say there's a good chance his son, Owen, is. Those pictures that were on your sister's cell phone of Owen Kendrick and three members of the Tampa Mafia? This is just a guess, but it's possible Dane went to his boss at the firm, Kendrick, to tell him Owen might be in trouble."

"From there," Tom went on, "I'd guess things went from bad to worse. The so-called accident was meant to kill both of them. If Owen was the driver of that car, I'm guessing he told his father. Peter Kendrick probably did all he could to cover this up, but, Peyton, when you started asking questions and pushing for answers, he needed help to push back. He probably called Sulzberger to get them out of this mess."

The room was filled with silence for a long moment. Then Rocket cleared his throat.

"I can't imagine anyone so stupid they'd think running down two people could be swept under the table."

"Powerful people are used to being able to do anything," Tom reminded him. "That means ordinary people often get the shaft."

Peyton sat quietly, taking it all in and doing her best to maintain a calm she didn't feel. All she could think of was Brianne still comatose in her hospital bed and Dane's coffin being lowered into the ground. How utterly lacking in morals and discipline was Owen Kendrick to get involved with the Tampa Mafia, then kill Dane and cripple Brianne to try and keep a lid on it?

"How did you find out all this?" she asked Tom.

His mouth curved in a hint of a grin. "I have as many friends in low places as he does. They like to stay in my good graces."

Everyone was silent for a long moment. Peyton sat in her chair, fingers twisted together as she tried to control her racing pulse and tamp down the fear gripping her.

"Motherfuckingsonofabitch."

The expletive exploded from Blaze's mouth like an arrow shot into the air. He turned and looked at Rocket. "I'll kill him. I will tear every limb from his body, stuff them up his ass and set him on fire."

Peyton just stared at him, not knowing what to say.

"You weren't on that mission, Rocket, but you saw Ace when he was brought in. I'm fucking damn lucky I didn't get hurt worse than I was."

Rocket nodded. "When we got the full report, I was destroyed. Reading it was one of the most difficult things I've ever done."

"How the fuck did Sulzberger even know who to ask about this?" Blaze raked his fingers through his hair.

"Think about it, Blaze." Tom's voice was pitched low and steady. "First of all, Kendrick was definitely tying up any and all loose ends. There are people who know us, know Galaxy—although not a lot—who are part of that hidden segment of society that doesn't broadcast itself. That's the part of the population that provides us with clients. Plus, a man who made millions selling military secrets to the enemy would certainly know who those people are and be able to connect with them. We're just lucky we have better connections than he does."

"I'd like to grab him and tear off every one of his limbs," Blaze repeated.

"No less than he deserves," Rocket agreed. "But first things first. If Sulzberger is involved in this, Peyton and Brianne both need a lot of protection. Especially Brianne, who is in a very vulnerable position."

At that moment, Blaze's cell rang, and he looked at the readout.

"It's the lab. Hey. What did you find?" As he listened, every muscle in his face tightened and a hard look came into his eyes. "Okay. Fine. Email that report to all of us, would you? Thanks for doing it so quickly."

When he disconnected, he looked around the table at everyone. If he'd been angry before, he was enraged now. It was a quiet rage—*the worst kind*, Peyton thought. *Now what?*

"The contents of the box weren't explosives. I guess the person who sent it didn't want to blow up the hospital."

"Then what was in it?" she asked.

"A powder similar to ricin, only instead of killing you, it just makes you sick." His hand tightened into fists. "It can paralyze you."

Peyton didn't know if she was going to be sick, or faint, or both.

"Oh, my god," she whispered.

"Fuck." That was Eagle.

"Double fuck," Rocket added.

"I could kill these fuckers." Blaze's voice was cold as ice.

At least it had cooled his rage, although this might be worse. She watched him pull himself together with obvious effort. Thank god for his SEAL discipline. Her mouth was so dry she had to swallow twice before she could speak.

"You already moved my sister to a different room and have the Wagner brothers hanging around outside. Should we have more than that?"

"Yes." He nodded. "And Rocket's correct. Between this and Sulzberger, the game has just been upped ten notches, so that's no longer good enough. For all we know, he's the one who sent that box. He's a sneaky fucking bastard with all kinds of connections of the scummiest kind. I'm calling Chuck to let him know things have changed, then, Rocket, I'm calling Leo DeLuca."

Rocket's eyes widened, although so briefly Peyton might have imagined it. *Who is Leo DeLuca?*

"Bringing out the big guns, are you?"

"Figuratively and literally."

Peyton wrinkled her forehead. "Who's Leo?"

"When we need extra sharp muscle with a lot of backup, he and his guys are the ones we call. They're also former SEALs. No one gets by them."

"Do you have a whole battalion of them just waiting for you to call?"

Rocket gave a short laugh. "Oh, they aren't waiting for anything. They've got their own agency going. They handle a lot of different assignments."

She wasn't sure she wanted to know what they were, but if they could keep her sister safe, that was good enough for her.

"I'll call Chuck first." Blaze looked at his watch. "Actually, it's Alan's shift right now." He punched some numbers. "Yo. Alan. Change of plans. Grab your stuff and move into Brianne Hollister's room. I'm clearing it with my brother. Nobody goes in unless you or your brother has eyes on them every single minute and checks what they're doing. I'll have Nolan give you a list of medical personnel assigned to her case so you can check their badges. And make sure they all see your weapon. Right. Okay. Call you back."

A tendril of fear crawled up Peyton's spine. She had thought her sister was in danger before, but now it seemed a new player had entered the game who upped the level of danger considerably.

"You really think she's in that much danger?"

Blaze nodded. "Without a doubt. I know this fucking bastard. He won't leave it to chance that she'll regain consciousness and remember anything."

Peyton listened as Blaze called the man named Leo and barked some orders at him. Then he called Nolan and filled him in on everything.

"I don't want to make your hospital a war zone," he said, "but I have to protect that woman. Can you cut red tape for me here without getting into trouble? Yeah? Good. Okay, then." He looked at the other men. "All set. Tom, can you text Leo pictures of Sulzberger and Kendrick? Not that I expect them to show up themselves, but just in case."

"Sure. Give me his number."

"What about Peyton?" Tom asked. "She's the real target now. Even if they eliminate Brianne, they know Peyton won't stop looking until she has answers and proof. That's why she hired us."

"I'd think both Peter Kendrick and Warren Sulzberger have enough brains to know that if they go after Peyton, we'll be after them. Sulzberger went to all the trouble to learn who she hired. Now they've got the details, so they know this isn't just your average security agency. They have to know we'd come after them first thing."

"If Kendrick's desperate enough," Rocket pointed out, "it may be worth the risk. Look at everything he's done to protect his son so far. Cover up for him."

"He should have trained him not to get involved with people like Kellerman in the first place."

Tom shook his head. "I have to say I'm really surprised. Kendrick's firm has a top reputation as litigators and they're highly respected throughout the Southeast. I don't see the connection there, either with Kellerman or originally, with Sulzberger."

"We'll just keep digging until we find it," Rocket assured him.

"Meanwhile, if Brianne Hollister is sufficiently protected, now we need to focus on Peyton."

A muscle twitched in Blaze's cheek. "You don't have to worry about her. She won't be leaving my sight for one second."

Tom and Rocket exchanged a look.

"Well," Tom drawled. "Okay, then."

Rocket nodded. "And you need to take a deep breath. It won't do us any good if you explode and kill this guy and end up in jail. We know where he is now. We can take care of him."

"We'll see. You just get things set up with Leo. He's expecting a callback in ten. I'm headed to the hospital. Then we'll see."

It didn't take an idiot, Peyton thought, to see the man was ready to explode with fury. After she assured herself Brianne was okay and well-protected, maybe she could help Blaze lose a little of the stress before he had a heart attack.

"I'll see that he's okay," she told them in a soft voice. "Blaze, it won't do anyone any good if you stress out before we get to the finish line."

It surprised her when he reached for her hand and gave it a light squeeze.

"I won't. Not until I tear that fucker apart and make him pay."

"Take a breath, Blaze," Rocket urged. "We've got all the bases covered. Viper is still trying to enhance the stills from the CCTV cameras so he can trace the car. He seems to think by this time it's gone to a chop shop and been dismantled, and I think he's probably right. However, we may be able to pick up the trail. He's working hard at it."

"It may be enough," Tom said, "just to get a clear picture of the driver. That's better than the car. You agree, Blaze?"

"Yeah, I do. While I'd like to rip Owen Kendrick, if it is him, to shreds, I think I'd rather see him rot in jail. I still can't figure out how he thought killing two people would solve his problems, especially the way he did it. That only calls more attention to the situation."

"You just take care of Peyton," Rocket told him, "and we'll do the rest."

Peyton could see that Blaze was struggling to keep himself under control. For a man who'd learned strong discipline as a SEAL, it had to be tearing at him that he wanted to go against everything he'd trained for to achieve vengeance. As much as she, too, wanted these men caught and punished, she knew the rest of Galaxy plus Tom Hernandez would handle it properly. Blaze needed to take a deep breath before he went off the deep end.

And she was sure she had just the medicine he needed.

"I'd like to stop at the hospital and see Brianne," she told him. "No, I *need* to see Brianne."

"Absolutely. I planned to stop there anyway and check that all the security arrangements are in place. Come on, darlin'." He reached for her hand. "We need to get going."

She wasn't sure who was more surprised at the endearment that slipped out of his mouth, the other men or her. But she took his hand and gave it a little squeeze. He was helping her get answers and making sure the people who hurt Dane and Brianne paid for it. She'd do something good for him, too.

Tonight.

Chapter Twelve

The first thing Peyton noticed when they approached her sister's room was the guard standing at the doorway, a gun in a holster at his hip.

"Is he hospital security?" she asked Blaze.

He shook his head. "He's one of Leo DeLuca's men. I talked to Nolan about it when I called him, and his suggestion that the man wear a guard's uniform seemed the best. That way there doesn't have to be any further explanation for why he's armed."

"Oh. Good idea."

The door to the room was partially closed, and when she opened it, she was stunned to see the number of people in there. Blaze had called his brother again once they were on their way. Nolan had assured him everything was okay and he'd see him there. He turned around as the two of them walked into the room.

"Everything's under control here," were the words he greeted them with. "She's in great hands. Leo's guy is set up outside her door."

"I saw that. The guard will change every eight hours."

"Good. Good." He handed Nolan a sheet of paper. "The list of medical staff assigned to Brianne. The guard has one, I faxed one to Leo, Chuck Wagner has one which he'll share with his brother. This one's for you."

Peyton spotted Chuck Wagner sitting in the armchair a slight distance away from Brianne's bed. He stood up as soon as he saw them.

"You take the chair, Miss West." He slid it closer to the bed. "Go on. Sit down. I don't need it."

She had to wait a moment while the nurse finished changing the IV bags that were feeding life-sustaining nourishment to Brianne until she could wake up and eat on her own.

If she could eat on her own.

No, Peyton. Optimism, remember? When *she wakes up and can do that.*

"She seems to be doing okay," the nurse told her. "I mean, considering the situation. Dr. Nolan ordered a daily massage to keep her muscles from atrophying. I think subconsciously it keeps her relaxed, too."

Peyton was all for anything that helped, even a little bit.

"I just took her vitals and all her numbers are good." She paused, tugging her bottom lip between her teeth. "I've cared for a number of comatose patients and I told Dr. Nolan I have a feeling she's going to come out of this pretty soon."

Peyton tried to control the little flare of hope that flickered.

"You think so?"

The nurse shrugged. "I'm not a doctor, and I could certainly be wrong, but I just have a sense of her. You get it when you've cared for as many as I have." She dropped her voice to a whisper. "But don't tell Dr. Nolan. He doesn't like to give false hope, just in case."

"I won't, but thank you."

As soon as the nurse left, Peyton tugged the chair closer to the bed, sat down and reached between the bars of the siderail for her sister's limp hand.

"Hi, Brianne." She said the words softly. "Sorry I was gone all day, but we're working on finding the people who did this to you."

She squeezed her sister's hand and continued talking in a low, soft voice. She was only marginally aware of Blaze behind her talking to Nolan, Chuck and another man who had just arrived. Instead she was totally focused on Brianne, holding her hand, squeezing it now and then, talking to her, looking and praying for any sign that this nightmare might be ending.

She turned when Blaze touched her shoulder.

"Nolan says she's doing very well considering the circumstance."

"I know." She sighed. "I just have this awful fear she's going to trapped in this state until her heart finally gives out. It kills me, because she was always such a vital, alive person."

"Just be assured she is getting the very best care possible. Come on, let's get out of here. Brianne is very well protected and you look exhausted. It's been quite a day and you need a break."

She wanted to tell him he was the one who needed it the most, but she'd take care of that when they got back to his place.

"You're right." She rose and leaned over to place a kiss on her sister's forehead. When she turned, Nolan was standing there next to Blaze.

"She's my number-one priority," he assured her.

She managed a smile. "Thank you for that, but I know you have many patients to take care of."

"And they all get the same attention," Blaze declared. "This is Wonder Doc."

Nolan chuckled. "Not really. I just love my patients. Go on, you two. Get out of here. Brianne is well-tended and well-protected. You two look like you fought the wars today."

Peyton wanted to tell him she felt like it, but her focus now was on Blaze. He had said little on the drive to the hospital and she could feel the tension radiating from him in thick waves. She could hardly imagine what he was feeling, knowing the man who had been responsible for the death of most of his team was mixing it up in his life again. She'd made up her mind that tonight it was her turn to take care of him.

After one last check with everyone, Chuck reminded everyone to check in regularly. Then, finally, they were headed away from the hospital.

"I want to make one last stop," Blaze told her as he pulled away from the parking lot.

"For what?"

"Let's take a moment to check you out of your hotel. I don't want you going back there for a lot of reasons. Besides, I guess you'd probably like to have some clean clothes."

She'd been thinking exactly the same thing. She'd showered that morning, but she felt less than fresh in yesterday's clothing.

"I'd really appreciate getting some things, but are you sure you want me to check out?"

He waited so long to answer that Peyton wondered if she'd even like what he had to say.

"Here's the thing," he said at last. "I'm going to be real honest with you."

"Good," she interrupted. "Honesty always works best."

"I don't know what's going on with us, but whatever it is has hit me harder than anything I've ever had with another woman. It scares the shit out of me, but at the same time I want it. A lot."

"Uh, okay." Where was he going with this?

"Besides keeping you safe, which is a top priority, I want you with me. In my home, in my bed. So I figure the hotel room is just a waste of your money."

Peyton swallowed a smile. He sounded as if he was sitting on the head of a pin, unsure of her answer, which she felt was an unfamiliar situation for him. She had the idea he wasn't ever unsure of anything. Until now.

His hands tightened on the wheel.

"If that's a bad idea, just say so." His voice was strained. "We'll do whatever you want. It's not an order. If I misread your reactions, I'll just drop you off at the hotel and pick you up in the morning."

For the first time that day, she relaxed and laughter bubbled from her mouth.

"That's not a problem, Blaze. I was just startled. I mean, I didn't think you wanted me around every minute."

He grabbed one of her hands and gave it a gentle squeeze.

"To be totally honest, I'm kind of shocked myself. I thought maybe in the beginning I was just horny and you were exceptionally attractive. But," he hurried on, "it's more than that. How can I tell in less than forty-eight hours? I don't know, but my gut tells me this is right. It also tells me this is probably the wrong time to get into this with all that's going on."

Peyton mentally shook her head. She was sure this was probably the least romantic proposition or whatever it was that she'd ever had, yet it warmed her the most. She pushed away the misgivings that wanted to crowd into her brain. If this turned out to be a mistake, when everything was over, she'd just walk away. She could do it.

"What about my car? If I check out, I don't want to leave it there and have to pay the fee for it."

"Where did you rent it?"

"Agency at the airport."

"Unless you think you'll need it, we'll get it taken care of. Give me the keys and I'll leave them in an envelope at the front desk. Someone will get it returned for you."

She quirked an eyebrow. "Someone?"

"One of the guys will take care of it."

"One of—"

"Unless I'm moving too fast here. If I am—"

"It's fine, Blaze." She touched the tips of his fingers to her lips. "I'm good with it. Let's just go ahead and get my stuff."

She sensed him relax just a fraction as they pulled up to the hotel entrance.

"We'll just be a few minutes," he told valet parking. "Keep it ready, okay?"

And that was all it took. She was an efficient packer and as anxious as he was to get out of there. She sensed the impatience rolling off him in waves while he waited for her to check out at the front desk. After putting her things in the car, they headed for his townhouse.

"I think I need a drink." Blaze stood in the doorway of his bedroom, watching her unpack. "Would you like one?"

She started to say no, but then realized she could probably use one as much as he did. The tension that had been building in Tom Hernandez's office was now almost a tangible thing.

"White wine?" he asked.

She started to say yes, then changed her mind. "Actually, I think I'd rather have whatever you're pouring for yourself. Bourbon, right?"

"Yes." A smiled teased at his mouth. "Something with a kick? It has been quite a day, hasn't it?"

"Pretty much so."

She closed the drawer on the last item of clothing and carried her toiletries into the bathroom. Scanning the long counter, she decided that if she kept everything in one corner, they'd be out of Blaze's way. What would he think if she told him she'd never spent more than one night in a man's apartment?

She turned to head back into the bedroom and nearly bumped into him standing in the doorway, holding two rocks glasses, each with a decent amount of bourbon. He handed one to her.

"Here's to getting past all this shit."

"Sounds good to me."

The smooth blend only burned slightly as it slid down her throat, and its soothing fingers reached to calm her frazzled nerves. Blaze took a healthy swallow of his own drink. The tic of the muscle in his cheek and the way he clutched the glass told her he was just as tense as he'd been in the law office, if not more so.

Peyton took another tiny sip from her glass, then set it on the nightstand, walked over to Blaze standing in the doorway and took his drink from his hand.

"You are wound up so tight your body twangs when you move."

He lifted an eyebrow. "And you think you can fix this?"

"I do. Come on." She managed a smile. "What can you lose?"

For a moment he resisted her, but then let her lead him to the bed, where she pushed him to sit down. Standing between his thighs, she tugged at his T-shirt, pulling it from his slacks and jerking it up until she had it over his head and could toss it to the side. He just sat there, no expression on his face, but in his eyes, she could see the smoldering embers of long-buried rage.

She took a moment to admire the sculptured line of his shoulders, the definition of muscle in his arms. The flat pecs with that dusting of dark hair that had so intrigued her last night. The tempting plane of his hard chest, eased just enough by the soft hair scattered over it.

"Relax." She climbed onto the bed behind him and began massaging his shoulders. God, he was so tight his muscles felt like cement. "You feel harder than a concrete pillar."

"Yeah? You want to feel something hard, come around in front and I'll show you."

She bit the lobe of one ear. "We'll get to that after a while. Close your eyes."

Blaze grunted. "Bossy little thing."

"Maybe that's what you need right now."

She continued to massage his shoulders and neck, occasionally placing light kisses along the nape or nipping an earlobe. Slowly, in tiny increments, he relaxed. By the time she worked her way down his spine to his waist, massaging slowly and steadily and punctuating her touches with a soft kiss now and then, his muscles began to soften. He sat less rigidly and his breathing was more regulated.

Okay, time for stage two.

She climbed off the bed and stood in front of him. "Now I want you to get up and take off your pants."

He actually burst out laughing. "You *are* bossy, aren't you? And I'm just supposed to do what you say?"

"I'm in charge." She managed a grin. "You want to argue with me?"

He studied her face for a long time before shaking his head. "Hell no. I want to see what you've got in mind."

He pushed himself up from the bed, kicked off his shoes and shucked his slacks and boxer briefs in seconds. Looking at him standing there in all his masculine magnificence, she did her best not to drool. Instead, she pulled the covers back all the way to the foot of the bed and patted the bottom sheet.

"Lie down on your stomach."

One corner of his mouth crooked up. "Still playing the boss?"

"Damn right. Now lie down on your stomach. And here's the rule. No talking and no movement. You have to lie absolutely still." She swallowed a grin. "Can you do that?"

"I was a SEAL," he grunted. "I can do anything."

"We'll see."

When he was stretched out facedown, she made sure his head was turned on the pillow and his arms were stretched over his head. Then she straddled him, keeping her own clothes on as a shield, which god knew she needed. She forced herself to ignore the flutters in her sex and the genesis of an orgasm that was trying to develop deep inside her. This was all for him. Placing her hands on his shoulders, she leaned forward and resumed the massage as before. All his muscles had tightened up again, but as she slowly worked her way down his spine, peppering kisses between her strokes, he relaxed once more.

By the time she reached the curve of his ass, his body, now warm, eased slightly beneath her. She slid her hands down past his waist, molding them to his butt, which she began to squeeze in a steady rhythm. If she hadn't been concentrating on him so intently, tuning herself in to every nuance of his body, she probably wouldn't have noticed when his breathing increased slightly and developed a raspy sound.

Good. All good.

As she shifted position, sliding backward so she could focus on his legs, she let the tips of her fingers trail lightly through the crevice of his ass. His groan was enough to turn up her own body temperature.

She started at one ankle then worked her way up his calf to his thigh, letting her fingers trail dangerously close to his balls before traveling back down the other leg. When she noticed his hands had curled into fists as he worked to maintain his control and a tiny groan rolled off his lips, she couldn't help smiling. By the time she'd finished with every inch of his back, tension rode every muscle, and it wasn't generated by anger as it had been earlier.

She moved off his body and nudged him with her elbow.

"Roll over, let out a breath and close your eyes."

He chuffed a short laugh. "Is this more torture?"

"Torture?" She lifted an eyebrow. "This is supposed to relax you. You were all tense and uptight."

"Yeah, well, now I'm tense and uptight for another reason. Take a look."

She ran her gaze over his body, pausing when she saw how swollen and rigid his thick cock was.

"If you climb on top of me now, sugar, you better center yourself on that."

"Well." She wetted her lips. "Let's see what we can do about it."

She went back to work on his body, loving the feel of his muscles beneath her fingers as she squeezed and kneaded muscles that were so tight, they felt like cast iron. She deliberately stayed away from his balls, but each time she moved up his thigh, always getting a little closer, his body tightened for a different reason.

"You're killing me," he groaned.

"At least I've got your mind on something else. Right?"

He didn't answer, but she could feel his response beneath her hands. She touched lightly as she worked her hands closer and closer to where he wanted them.

"For fuck's sake, Peyton. Have mercy."

"Mercy? You want mercy? Let's see what we can do."

She shifted so she was kneeling beside him, slid one hand between his muscular thighs and wrapped the fingers of the other around his cock that was so hot to her touch. Then she added her tongue to the movements that he seemed to take such pleasure from. She worked his cock so intently that Blaze nearly levitated off the bed.

Peyton looked over at his face, doing her best to swallow her smile. "Did I hurt you? Do you want me to stop?"

"Stop? Fuck, no!" He almost shouted the words. "I want you to do it faster."

"All in good time," she teased. "You don't want to miss anything."

Another groan.

She ran the flat of her tongue up and down his length, dragging it slowly over the heated flesh. As she continued to use her mouth on his cock, she squeezed and manipulated his balls with the fingers of the other hand. The sac fit neatly into her hand and she tried to time the movements of those fingers with those of her mouth.

A sideways glance at Blaze revealed the taut muscles of his face and his hooded gaze focused intently on her. She lifted her mouth from his rigid shaft and sat back on her heels, toying with his balls.

"For the love of god, Peyton. You're killing me here."

"Really?" She swallowed a grin. "That was not my intention."

"Could have fooled me."

He threaded his fingers through her hair and tried to push her head lower again, but she knocked his hand away.

"Uh-uh. I'm calling the shots here."

"Call them a little faster, will you?"

His cock was so hot to the touch, so hard beneath the soft skin, and when she placed her hand on his stomach, she could actually feel the strain in his body. She was sure he wasn't thinking of Warren Sulzberger or anything else right now. *Good. Time for the big finale.*

Taking the head in her mouth again and wrapping her fingers around him, she sucked as she stroked him, the tempo growing faster and faster. With each stroke she squeezed his balls, and his moans grew louder.

When he dug his heels into the mattress and tried to push himself against her touch, she knew he was ready. Now she stroked faster, sucked harder, again and again and again. Then he was there, his shaft like steel beneath her fingers as he spurted again and again into her mouth. She never stopped until he pumped the last drop and she gave one last powerful pull with her mouth.

At last his body went limp and his cock softened beneath her grip. She licked the head clean before lifting her head and looking at him.

"Good?"

"Are you kidding me? That's such a mild word for what happened. You have an incredibly talented mouth, sugar." He lifted his arms. "C'mere."

She moved until she was lying beside him, one of his arms circling her body, his other hand cupping her chin.

"Yes?" She curved her lips in another grin.

"That was incredible. That's the only word for it."

He pulled her mouth closer to his, enough so that he could skim his lips over hers. He drew a light line over the seam with the tip of his tongue before nudging those lips apart and slipping his tongue inside. It danced with hers before tasting every inch of the inner surface. She forced herself to pull back before her body began demanding more. This was all about Blaze, not her at all.

"Glad I could help," she teased, and started to slide under the covers next to him.

"You ready for sleep?" he asked, curving his arm around her. "You haven't had your turn yet. It's my rule not to leave a woman unsatisfied, although I think I'd need some recovery time before I could do you any good."

"Oh, I'm satisfied all right. Don't you worry. This one was all about you."

He shifted so that his face was almost touching hers, his tongue still doing its erotic dance. His was more than a kiss of passion, but she wasn't sure she wanted to examine exactly *what* it was. She slid her own tongue over his, the contact warming every part of her body. The fact that it was about more than passion made it all the more special.

At last he drew back, then shifted both of them so they were spooning, his body curved around hers. She was almost asleep when he whispered in her ear.

"Thank you, Peyton."

"You're welcome."

What she really wanted to say was, *Bet you're not thinking of Warren Sulzberger now.*

Chapter Thirteen

The ringing of Blaze's cell phone woke them in the morning. He fished it from his nightstand where he'd finally tossed it the night before, saw Eagle's name on the readout and punched Accept.

"What's up?" He looked at the time on the phone and frowned. "It's fucking six o'clock in the morning. This better be good."

"Would I call you otherwise? Rocket and I were working while you were snoozing. I downloaded some new software from a friend that helped me clean up the CCTV picture and he found out what happened to the car. We need to head to the plane. I don't want to discuss this where there's the least chance of eavesdropping. With Sulzberger mixed into this, he could easily have people watching all of us. The one place they can't tap into us is the plane."

In an instant Blaze was on full alert. "What's up?"

"Uh-uh. Not until we're on the plane. We already called Saint and told him to get everything ready. We'll pick up something for breakfast on the way."

"Okay. On it."

"I figured so."

He disconnected the call and saw that Peyton was already awake.

"What is it?" She frowned. "Bad news?"

"No, as a matter of fact. It's good. Let's get dressed and I'll tell you on the way."

She wrinkled her forehead. "On the way to where?"

"The plane." He dusted a brief kiss on her forehead. "We need to get moving."

They dressed quickly, foregoing showers, and in less than twenty minutes were headed to the hangar. On the way, he checked in with both Leo's man and Chuck at the hospital, relaxing a little when both reported no action at all. Peyton, meanwhile, called the charge nurse to get a report on her sister's condition.

"All quiet," he told Peyton when they both hung up. "Alan's there this morning and he says no action. I think having the two men there is discouraging anything overt. And Leo's man is checking the badge of everyone who comes into the room against the hospital's employee database."

"The nurse says she's about the same, but she continues to show signs of restlessness. I'm just praying very hard."

"I know you are. We'll stop by and see her after this meeting."

When they reached the hangar, he spotted two cars parked and the plane already on the tarmac.

"They must have called Saint very early," he commented to Peyton. "And since only Eagle's car is here, I'm guessing they all rode here together. Let's get going."

They climbed the stairs to the cabin and found the others seated at the same table arrangement as the day before. They were barely inside before Saint retracted the stairs and headed to the cockpit. Blaze was happy to see the others greeted Peyton as if she were an old friend, even if they did give him a quick side-eye.

He noticed that today only Eagle and Rocket had laptops sitting in front of them.

"You're not on the Show and Tell today?" he asked Viper.

"Nope. These guys have it all."

Saint's voice on the intercom interrupted their conversation.

"Buckle up, everyone. Here we go."

No one said anything as the engine noise increased and the big plane started to move. Then they were moving faster, rolling down the runway, the sound of the engines increasing as they picked up speed. No one said a word until they were in the air and they heard, "We're at thirty thousand," over the intercom.

"I'll get breakfast." Viper unbuckled his seat belt and rose from his chair. "Rocket and Eagle are doing all the talking."

"I'll go first." Rocket activated his laptop and tapped some keys. "The software my friend has can clean up almost anything. He's a programming nut and creates his own. After I ran the CCTV video through his program twice, I got an amazingly clear picture of the driver. At least enough to then run it through facial recognition software."

"But then how do you know who it is?" Peyton asked. "How do you identify the person?"

"What's the one thing that almost every legal citizen has in the United States?"

"I don't…" She snapped her fingers as the answer flashed in her brain. "A driver's license."

Blaze nodded. "Right."

"But can you get into that database? It's not accessible to the public, is it?"

Rocket's mouth tilted in a tiny grin. "We can get into anything."

Before he could continue, Viper was back with coffee and a plate full of donuts.

"Not as fancy as yesterday, but it's edible."

Blaze served himself and Peyton then gave Eagle a verbal nudge.

"Okay, don't keep us in suspense any longer. Who is it? Is it Owen Kendrick?"

"First, look at the cleaned-up picture." Eagle turned his laptop so everyone could see the screen.

Blaze was startled at the image he saw. He leaned closer, studying it. Had they been wrong all this time? "Damn! It's a woman."

Peyton rubbed her forehead. "I don't understand. We haven't talked about a woman at all. There hasn't even been a mention. Who is she?"

"I'll let Rocket show you," Eagle told her. "He's the one who worked the database."

"Okay." Blaze looked at the other man. "Let's have it. Who the fuck is it?"

"That's the kicker," Rocket told them. He clicked some keys on his laptop then turned it around. "Have a look."

Everyone stared at the driver's license displayed on the screen.

Finally Blaze cleared his throat. "Diane Kendrick? Is she Owen's sister?"

Rocket shook his head. "His wife."

For a long moment no one said a word as the name dangled in the air.

Peyton spoke first. "His wife? No one's even mentioned her before this. I mean, she's barely been a blip in the background. If she's the driver, do you think Owen knew about this and has been protecting her all this time?"

Blaze nodded. "That's my guess. But what about Peter Kendrick, Owen's father? Do you think he knows it's her? That she was the one driving the car?"

Tom shook his head. "Not from what I gather. I think we'd be seeing a lot different situation if he knew."

"You think he'd throw her under the bus?"

"Without a doubt. Word on the street is Peter Kendrick is building a long-term political campaign for his son. Having a murderer for a wife wouldn't do him any good. They'd ditch her like yesterday's trash and find him someone more suitable."

"Okay." Blaze looked at Rocket. "The car. What did you find out?"

"Tom helped with this." Rocket grinned. "Again, it helps to know people in low places."

"Yeah, I get it. Let's have it."

"Long story short, I found the last few pieces in a chop shop. How it got there is immaterial unless we need the info for leverage."

"But if it's his wife's car," Peyton said, slowly, "what's she been driving since then?"

"We're still working on that. But now we need a whole new game plan. We can't use regular police channels with this because we don't know who else is paid off."

"But we did a job for the police commissioner," Viper drawled. "He was very grateful. Said if we ever needed anything to ask him."

"Agreed." Blaze took a slow sip of his coffee. "But let's make sure we have all our shit together before we do. "

"We can't just go to them with what we've got?" Peyton's voice was edgy. "I mean, we have the picture and the driver's license. What else do we need?"

"We need to make sure of two things," Blaze told her. "That there's no way to dispute the identity in the picture for one."

"And that we have backup proof, which we need to work on."

Blaze clenched his fists in his lap, working on his control.

"And making Sulzberger face the music after all this time. Where the hell does he live, anyway? I thought he had that big estate in Maryland?"

"He does." Rocket nodded. "But he also has a place in Miami where he hides out. Tom says he only bought it less than a year ago. Apparently, he'd been up here helping his good friend Peter Kendrick solve his problems."

"Just realize," Viper told him, "you can't go off and shoot him, much as you'd like to. Much as we'd all like to."

"If you really want to destroy him," Viper put in, "let's get everything we can together. You know there's proof somewhere. Then send it wide to the media. He'll be as good as dead after that."

Everyone sat quietly while Blaze rolled it all over in his mind.

"Tom can help us with that. He's got connections."

"And we'll talk to him about it," Rocket agreed. "After we get our primary objective achieved."

"Getting the police to open the case again?" Peyton asked. "And giving them the info on Diane Kendrick?"

"Yes." Viper leaned forward, his face set in determined lines. "You can count on it."

"Are you contacting the police commissioner like you said before?"

"We are." Blaze answered her himself. "I promise you, this will get taken care of and Dane and Brianne will be avenged. That's what we do." He looked around the table. "Who's contacting the commissioner? Eagle, I think it should be you, since you were the lead on the case we did for him."

"No problem." Eagle picked up his cell phone and stood up. "Let me go in the back and give him a call right now. I still have his direct number."

Blaze looked at Rocket. "Did you retrieve any of the remaining pieces of the car from the chop shop?"

"I did. They're locked in the storage closet in the hangar. We also need to find out what Diane Kendrick's driving now. How did her husband get her a new car without arousing people's suspicions, especially her father-in-law?"

Blaze scowled. "Good question."

"Let me tap into my sources," Rocket told him, "and see what I can find out."

Viper chuckled. "I have to say, man, you sure look the part for someone who collects the creepy-looking characters you do as sources."

Rocket's mouth turned up in a big grin. "Why, thank you. I consider that high praise." Then the grin was replaced by a serious expression. "But if anyone can find out about under-the-table dealings no matter who's involved, it's one of my guys." He winked. "Or gals."

"Okay." Blaze slapped his hands on the table. He wanted to get moving on this stuff. "So we're good to go? Everyone knows what they have to do?"

The others nodded just as Eagle returned to the table.

"All set. I have a meeting with the commissioner at two this afternoon, at his home. When I explained the situation, he said we're better to keep it out of official places until we have everything locked down. I have all the files on my computer to show him. Rocket, make sure I have the couple of pieces of Diane Kendrick's car." He turned to Peyton. "We'll need Brianne's cell, also, so Rocket has the pictures she took."

"No problem. I've still got it with me." She pulled it from her purse, brought up the specific pictures and handed the phone to Rocket.

He scanned the table again. "I'd say we're good to go."

"We all need to be on the alert, though." Blaze looked around the table. "Rocket, if your meeting with the commissioner is successful, the Kendricks and Sulzberger are going to panic. We don't know what the hell they'll do."

"You don't think they'd try to get my sister again, do you?" The color had leached from Peyton's face and her voice was tight.

"I never know what desperate people will do, so it's best to be prepared. We'll stop by the hospital on the way home so I can double-check the security arrangements. I might even ask Nolan if he can move Brianne Hollister again."

"Oh, my god." Peyton clutched his arm. "Why won't they leave her alone? She can't tell them anything."

"They don't know that. Anyway, I'm just covering all bases. This is an unpredictable situation."

"And you?" Viper gave him a penetrating look. "What will you be doing?"

"Pulling the strings I have out there to hunt down Warren Sulzberger and make him pay." His face tightened in murderous rage. "I want to kill that fucker for what he did. And now he's been helping to hide the evidence of the accident that killed Dane and put Brianne in a coma."

There was a long moment of silence, broken at last by Viper.

"Be very careful what you do. I know exactly how you feel, but we have a good thing going here. Let's not fuck it up."

Fury raged through Blaze. "So I should just let him get away with most of my team being slaughtered? That's not an option."

"We're not saying that." Viper's eyes were filled with compassion. "Just choose your options carefully."

Beside him, Peyton cleared her throat.

"I, uh, might be able to help with this. I have an idea if you think it will accomplish the purpose." She turned in her seat to lock her gaze with Blaze's. "And keep you from going to jail for whatever it is you plan to do."

He studied her face with intensity. "What is it and exactly how would you do that?"

"Just listen to me and tell me what you think."

When she explained the plan to him, at first he wanted to refuse. The obsession with blood lust, with exacting vengeance, was too strong in him. But Peyton very carefully detailed how much more effective and long-lasting this would be. Then he listened as each of his friends told him why this was the best idea. At last he nodded.

"But how do we go about getting that information so we can use it? It's not like we can walk into someone's office and have them hand over the file, if there even still is one. We'd need help."

"I agree, but I just might be able to provide it."

"How?" Rocket wanted to know.

"I wrote an entire series set in Washington, DC, against the background of politics and I still have some very good contacts there. Let me reach out to the one I feel the most comfortable approaching about this. See if he's even agreeable to helping us get information from what I know are closed files. This could have a greater impact and he'd have to live through it."

It wasn't the same as exacting blood revenge, but maybe the others were right and this would be even better. "Peyton, you are a woman of many talents."

She winked. "And don't you forget it."

He deliberately ignored the grins his partners were giving him. "Go ahead and see if you can work your magic. You said you had contacts in Washington. You're sure whoever you plan to contact would have the info on what happened when Warren Sulzberger left Congress?"

"Yes. The man I have in mind is still pretty powerful. We connected, but I don't know if he'll want to do this. Depends on how much he hates Sulzberger. You'll have to give me all the details of what happened, at least as much as you know. I can take it from there."

"If you can get him to agree to see us, Saint will fly us to DC."

"Then let me call him right now."

She pulled her cell phone from her purse, scrolled through her contacts and punched a number.

"Senator Franz? Yes, this is Peyton West. I wasn't sure if this number still worked. How are you? Yes, yes, I do keep up with you in the media. You're doing some great things. Uh huh. Yes. You did? Well, I'm honored."

Blaze was doing his best to control himself as he tried to figure out what was happening on the other end of the conversation. He just hoped it was good.

"I have a specific reason for calling you. I don't know if you can help me or not, but I thought if anyone could, it would be you."

Another short silence. He was aware that everyone at the table was as intense as he was.

"I'm looking for some information about a thorny situation that happened a few years ago. I know you're still chairing the Armed Services Committee, so I'm hoping you can help me. What? Well, I'd rather not discuss it over the phone. It concerns a friend of mine. A close friend. He's very trustworthy and I really need to have him with me when I explain what I need. Will that work? Uh huh. Okay. I can be in Washington this afternoon and I wondered if you were free to meet with me? Us? Yes, I can explain it all when I see you. I just don't want to do it over the phone. What? Good. I'm glad you understand. Yes, I am. Right."

There was a long silence on Peyton's end of the conversation while Blaze did his best to hang on to his self-control. He had to bite his tongue to keep from asking her what was happening.

"Yes, sir. Right. That's not a problem. I'll call you when I land. Thank you again."

Blaze slid a glance her way in time to see her stick her cell back in her purse. Everyone else was waiting for her info, just as he was.

"Good news?" he guessed. *Hoped.*

"So far. He agreed to see us late this afternoon. Around four o'clock, at his home. I'm to call him when I land."

Blaze let out the breath he hadn't even realized he was holding and reached for Peyton's hand.

"Just like that?"

She shrugged. "He was a great resource for me, and he respected the fact that I didn't try to twist information he gave me. We struck up a friendship."

"Good work, Peyton." Rocket gave her a thumbs-up. "You might be our lucky charm. This thing has festered for a very long time."

"Let me just say this." Viper leaned toward her. "If you can pull this off, there's no charge for us taking your project."

"Wait. What?" She looked at each one in turn. "You can't do that. You have to get paid for your services."

"If you can do this," Rocket told her, "that will pay us in spades. What Sulzberger did was unacceptable and cost good men their lives. He needs to pay."

"I'll be sure you're properly rewarded." Blaze was aware his friends were watching the two of them carefully. He didn't care. This woman, hopefully, was about to help destroy the enemy, and he owed her everything.

Rocket let Saint know it was time to head for home, and laptops were closed and cell phones put away. No one said anything on the short flight. It seemed as if only minutes passed before he felt the plane descending from thirty thousand feet. Then they were on the ground and saying a quick goodbye to Saint.

"Stay ready and alert," Blaze told him when they deplaned. "Get something to eat. We'll be taking off for DC in a couple of hours."

"Got it. You all just be careful."

"Always." 'Careful' was their watchword.

"Be sure we all stay in touch." Rocket waved his cell phone. "Regular texts?"

Blaze nodded. They definitely needed to maintain contact and share information. Then he and Peyton were in his car and pulling away from the hangar.

"Where to?" Peyton asked.

"Home first to shower and change. Then I thought we'd stop by and see Brianne before we grab some lunch on the way back to the plane."

"Good. I need to lay eyes on her."

"I know. That's why we're doing it."

They had reached the townhouse by now and he wheeled the car into the garage and killed the engine. Unfastening his seat belt, he turned toward Peyton and took one of her hands in his.

"Keeping a lid on my rage has been the hardest thing for me. I've actually had dreams about catching up with Sulzberger and taking him apart with a knife one cut at a time." He paused. "But..."

"But?" she pressed.

"But I'd be the only one satisfied, and it would be momentary. I could always walk away from my partners to keep them out of the mess if I had to. But this…this plan is ingenious, if we can pull it off. I can watch him suffer for a long time." He put a finger beneath her chin and tilted her face toward him. "In two days, you've made a greater impact in my life than anyone else in the past twenty years."

"It's been fast," she commented. "But…"

"But?" he encouraged.

"But I'm getting the same feelings. Once we get the information, I'm going to pull whatever strings I can to make it happen."

He cradled her face between his palms and pressed his lips to hers. It wasn't a hot kiss. More like a sweet one, and full of promise. He just hoped to hell he was reading her right.

"You know," she said, when he broke the kiss, "for a change, I think my life might be moving in the right direction again."

"I damn sure hope so. Okay. Let's get moving."

They took the showers they hadn't had time for that morning, dressed for the coming meeting and headed back to the hangar.

"I'm glad we're stopping to see Brianne. I feel terrible. I haven't seen her since everything began to happen. Up to now I never missed a day. I keep praying she wakes up. Soon."

He reached over and gave her hand a quick squeeze. "Maybe when she does, we'll have good news to tell her."

"That's what I'm hoping."

Despite the two muscular male bodies camped in Brianne's room, it didn't seem crowded. While Peyton moved to sit in the chair next to the bed, Blaze checked in with the two men in folding chairs against the wall.

"All quiet," Alan Wagner told him. "We triple-check everyone who comes in here and it's not making us any friends. I think they'd toss us out a window if they thought they could get away with it and if your brother hadn't vouched for us."

"It may be overkill," Blaze admitted, "but the people who'd harm her are desperate and I wouldn't put anything past them. Just be alert."

"Not to worry. We've got this."

He moved over to where Peyton was sitting, holding Brianne's hand and speaking softly to her.

"Hate to do this, but we need to get moving."

She looked at her watch, nodded and leaned over her sister. "Hang in there, sweetie. I know you'll come out of this soon."

* * * *

When they pulled into the parking space by the hangar, they saw that Saint already had the plane on the tarmac.

"A little busy today, are we?" He nodded as they hurried up the stairway then retracted it and closed the door. "Well, have a seat and buckle up. We'll be taking off shortly. Oh, and no refreshments this trip. Sorry, but I didn't have a chance to pick anything up, and between yesterday and today, you guys drank up all the coffee."

"That's okay. I don't need anything." He looked at Peyton. "You?"

She shook her head. "I'm nervous enough already."

Flying time to DC was about two hours, and it was close to three o'clock by the time the Uber they'd ordered pulled up to the palatial home of Senator

Alston Franz. Blaze was stunned when the senator answered the door himself.

"Come in, come in." He waved them in, glanced both ways then closed and locked the door.

"Thank you for seeing us," Peyton told him.

"I always have time for you, Peyton." He shook hands warmly with her, then glanced at Blaze.

"This is Scott Hamilton, Senator. He's doing some investigating for me."

"Call me Blaze."

"What kind of investigating?" Franz asked.

"Something that tangentially involves a person you know. I'm hoping you can give me some help."

The senator shook hands with Blaze, a questioning look on his face.

"Well, I guess if Peyton vouches for you, you must be trustworthy."

Blaze swallowed a smile. "Thank you, sir."

"Blaze is a SEAL," Peyton told him.

"Okay." Franz nodded his head, trying to hide his confusion.

But Blaze saw the instant the man's brain made a long-ago connection, and again the senator looked from one of them to the other.

"I think we'd better go into my den to discuss this, if it's what I think it is."

The den was just down a short hallway from the entrance, a room paneled in aged oak and filled with books, photos and memorabilia that chronicled the man's life in politics. A tray sat on a low round table, containing a carafe of coffee on a warmer and a plate of what looked like home-baked pastries. They hadn't had lunch and Blaze was already salivating.

"Have a seat and help yourselves." When they were all seated, Blaze and Peyton on the couch, Franz in an armchair, and they all had coffee and pastries, he nodded at Peyton. "Okay. Let's hear it. Start at the beginning."

Blaze began by telling him who he was and his relationship to Warren Sulzberger. It was obvious Franz knew all about the situation, but he waited until Blaze told his entire story.

"Nasty business," he said. "Nasty and disgusting. The cover-up even more so. I'm sorry about your team. I just don't have words to explain the revulsion it created."

"I've been carrying this rage around with me for years," Blaze told him, "ever since it all happened. Good men were killed because of greed. You have no idea how many times I've visualized killing that man in any number of ways."

Even knowing that thirst for revenge held him in such a tight grip, Peyton was right. This was a better type of retaliation and lasted a lot longer.

"I can certainly understand how you feel. A lot of us felt that way at the time, although probably not as intensely as you."

He set his cup down. "I have to ask, sir. How and why was this buried like it was?"

Franz shook his head. "A lot of strings were pulled for that. Sulzberger had very influential friends. I'm assuming he still does, since he's made a killing as a lobbyist."

"Peyton came up with this idea we want to tell you about," he explained, "and she's right. It will be much more effective."

"I'm counting on that," Peyton told him.

"But why are you looking into it now?"

"Because Sulzberger has insinuated himself into our lives." She went on to fill him in about Dane and Brianne, Kendrick's efforts to bury the whole thing, aided by Sulzberger, and how it had popped him into Blaze's life again.

"Okay. What are your plans moving forward? I can tell you it didn't sit well with a lot of people to let him slide out the way he did. They'd be damned happy to see him finally pay for it."

"Peyton, why don't you tell him about it? This was your idea."

When she finished, the last thing he expected was for Franz to burst out laughing. The man laughed so hard they were afraid he'd choke, but eventually he settled down.

"Sorry, but that is going to make a whole lot of people very happy. Really, really happy." He leaned forward in his chair. "If you can manage to get a photo somehow, that would be a bonus. So what is it you'd like from me?"

"We need information." Peyton sat forward. "Just enough specifics that the media will dig deeper into it and find out the rest for themselves. Can you do it?"

Blaze watched the man turn it over in his mind then come to a decision.

"I can't give you everything, but I do know where some bodies are buried. I can get you enough solid information that the media can take it from there."

"I don't want you to get in trouble," she protested.

"Trouble is my middle name," he joked. Then the smile disappeared. "Hell, with all the stuff people are always leaking around here, there are at least twenty other people who'd be suspected. Besides, I think everyone would be cheering me on. I'm happy to do it. Believe me, this will be much more satisfying than killing him."

Peyton let out a breath. "We can't thank you enough. What are your arrangements? Can you stay over until tomorrow? I have to see if it's better to get the information tonight or in the morning." She looked at Blaze. "Can we?"

He nodded. "Not a problem. We have our own plane, Senator." He grinned. "It's also kind of our office."

"Office?" Both eyebrows went up. "That I'd like to hear about."

Keeping it short and sweet, Blaze told him about Galaxy, how it had come to be and what they did. And why their plane was their flying office.

Franz looked at him with a thoughtful expression on his face.

"So how does someone contact you if your services are needed?"

"They usually figure out who to ask and go from there."

"I'm sure you all don't have business cards, but how about writing down your cell number for me? The way things are these days, I might find I actually need your services."

Blaze chuckled. "Don't take this the wrong way, but I hope you don't. It means you've fallen into a whole shitpile of trouble."

"Well, I agree with you there. Let me call your cells so you'll have me in your contacts, also."

Fifteen minutes later, they were finished and ready to leave, the Uber they'd called for waiting outside.

"Thank you so much, Senator." Peyton shook his hand. "I really appreciate it."

"Happy to do it. Besides the fact that you're one of the few people I trust, I'm damn glad to see that fucker Sulzberger get his at last. I'll call you in the morning as soon as I have what you need."

Once they were in the car, Blaze relaxed a little.

"That was easier than I expected."

"I gather there was a lot of resentment and animosity when Sulzberger was allowed to slide out of Congress quietly and not pay for his sins." She glanced over at him. "So, what now?"

"Now we find a place to stay, have dinner and maybe…" He grinned at her. "Think of a way to work off all this stress."

She took his hand and gave it a squeeze. "I think I might have some ideas on just that."

Chapter Fourteen

Peter Kendrick paced the floor of his den, stopping every few seconds to look out of the window that faced the street. Owen had called that morning to tell him that he and Diane were on their way, so where in the hell were they? A strategy session was crucial right now. Every move the three of them made was liable to be under close scrutiny, so they could not afford even a tiny mistake.

At last he saw Owen's rental car pull into the driveway, and moments later the front door of the house opened. Owen walked in, Diane holding tightly to his hand. They were both dressed in casual clothes and wore identical expressions — as if the gallows were waiting right around the corner. They both looked pale as shit and stress lines bracketed Owen's mouth and eyes.

Something was definitely wrong. Peter had guessed there was a hell of a lot more to the situation than he knew, and a sour taste of fear washed through his mouth. *Shit and fuck. What now?*

"Let's go into the kitchen," he suggested. "That's where the coffee machine is and it looks as if you might need it."

They both nodded and wordlessly followed him into the kitchen. When they were all seated at the table, each with a mug of coffee, Peter looked from one to the other, studying their faces. *What the hell is going on?*

"Okay." He leaned forward. "Let's have it. What else is wrong? You both look like the roof fell in. Again. Did something more happen?"

Owen opened his mouth to speak, but Diane put her hand on his arm.

"No." Her voice sounded tight and scratchy. "This is all on me. Let me tell him."

"But—"

"For god's sake." Peter wanted to smack both of them. "One of you tell me, whatever it is, and do it now."

Diana inhaled a deep breath and let it out slowly. "Owen wasn't driving the car that night. I was."

Kendrick had thought that by now he was shockproof, but he was wrong. Her words froze his blood and for a moment he thought his heart had stopped beating. It took him a long moment before he could speak.

"Could you please say that again? I'm not sure I heard you right."

"I said I was the one who ran down the Hollisters, not Owen."

"What the hell?" He tried to find the right words to say, but his brain felt frozen.

Owen started to say something then stopped.

Kendrick looked from one to the other. "We'd better start at the beginning, wherever that is, because I've got a lot of questions. Let's start with where you got this crazy idea and why you thought it was a good one. Was it some misguided notion of protecting Owen? Didn't you think I could get him out of whatever vise Kellerman had him in?"

"I didn't want her to," Owen began but Diane interrupted him.

"Owen wasn't the one in trouble," she told Kendrick. "I was. I was in debt to Kellerman over gambling losses. It was me they were threatening."

Peter had thought he'd had the worst shock of the day, but apparently not.

"How the hell have you hidden all this?" His glance slid from Owen to Diane and back again. "And why? Jesus, Owen. This is a huge mess here."

"It was my idea," Owen blurted out. "After it was all over, I figured better it should be my mess, not hers. Besides, I was pretty sure you'd pull out all the stops for me, but I was afraid you'd throw Diane to the wolves." He took Diane's hand in his. "You know I'm right. I didn't even want her to tell you now, but she insisted. Said I was throwing away my life to protect hers."

Peter still felt as if he'd been run over by a train. He wasn't sure if he should praise his son for being so noble and protective or shoot him for fucking up his life. The political campaign was looking more and more unreachable. Political campaign? Hell, he'd be lucky if they didn't all end up in jail.

Diane sat a little straighter in her chair. "I couldn't let him do this any longer. Throw away his life like that."

Peter got up and refilled his mug then returned to his seat at the table. As he stirred cream into it, he realized what he really wanted was a shot of bourbon in it. It was only the discipline he'd built all these years that kept him from screaming his head off then throttling both of them.

"First of all, you'd better tell me how you got hooked up with Kellerman and his Tampa Mafia to begin with."

"I'll tell you." Rage flashed across Owen's face. "After you refused to represent them, they targeted her and waged a seductive campaign. Before she realized it, she was trapped."

"I don't understand."

He listened while his son told him a story that chilled his blood. How Owen had been swamped with work for new clients, leaving Diane to her own devices a lot. How she'd received an invitation to a luncheon supporting a local organization and been swarmed by Hayden Kellerman's wife and her friends. Of course, she had no idea who Kellerman was, so nothing seemed out of place to her. How they'd sucked her in and begun inviting her to afternoon cocktail parties, flattering her, making her feel welcome. Then, when Owen was out of town for a week on behalf of a client, she'd received the invite to a card game.

"It was slow at first," Owen said. "They told her sometimes they bet just for fun. But before long the card games became more intense and the stakes higher. She thought it was fun, never realizing she had a latent gambling addiction. Suddenly she found herself in debt for thousands of dollars and unable to pay. They thought for sure she'd come to me and I'd come to you.

Then they could use it as leverage to get you to represent them. Instead she kept it all to herself."

"What about those pictures?"

"A disaster out of the blue. I didn't know a thing about it until I got a call to meet a supposed new client at Maritime Drilling on Gandy Boulevard one day. That's where Kellerman's goons gave me the news and threatened me. Either pay up her losses, get you to represent them or they'd take their revenge in other ways. Jesus, Dad." He raked his fingers through his hair. "I didn't know what the fuck to do."

"They've done shit like that before," Peter pointed out. "With them it's all about leverage, and apparently you gave them plenty."

"I would have come to you at that point and begged you to help us," Owen told him, "but I never got the chance. It was fucking bad luck that Brianne Hollister happened to be driving by at the time and caught those goons with me. Her photographer's eye told her something was up, so she snapped some pictures and showed them to Dane."

Kendrick knew what had happened after that. Dane had come to him and the whole mess had exploded. *Fucking shit.* He wanted to beat his head against the wall.

"Diane, what in god's name made you decide to run over Dane and Brianne? That's the stupidest thing I've heard. What were you doing that night, anyway?"

He watched the two of them exchange nervous glances.

"We'd gone out to dinner," Owen told him. "Just the two of us. But Diane was feeling like shit and was drinking way too much. She was scared to death that Dane would keep sticking his nose into the mess with

Kellerman and it would all come out. I guess she thought she was protecting me."

Diane looked ready to cry. "Yes, I did. I was scared our whole life, his career, everything would be destroyed."

Peter stared at the woman. "So you thought killing the Hollisters would solve the problem?"

"I don't know what I thought," she cried, her face pinched with distress. "I just wanted to get rid of them because they were going to ruin Owen's life. Our lives."

Peter clenched his hands so he wouldn't reach out and throttle the woman. "You really must have been damn drunk to concoct this."

Her knuckles whitened as she intensified her grip on Owen's hand. "Yes, I was. Really drunk by the time we got home. Owen went into the den to do some work and told me to go into our bedroom and lie down. I just kept running it over and over in my head, though. I knew the Hollisters were going to dinner at Calypso, because Owen overheard Dane talking about it at the office. They were celebrating some new client Brianne got. It was a late dinner because Dane had a client meeting before then."

"So you, what, jumped in Owen's car and went off to run them over? What the hell were you thinking?"

Diane looked down at her feet. "I wasn't thinking. Obviously."

"And why take Owen's car?" He wanted to tell her it was a stupid move that had put them all in jeopardy, but again, he swallowed his words. Accusations weren't going to solve anything here.

"I certainly hadn't planned on it." She tried to lift her coffee cup, but her hands were shaking too much. "I grabbed his keys instead of mine and I didn't want to go back and exchange them. I was afraid Owen would hear me."

"I was out of my mind when I discovered she'd left the house." Owen looked at his father. "I knew she'd had too much to drink, but I never expected her to go out. I was about to go looking for her when she got back. Dad, she was a sobbing mess, shaking, hysterical. She could hardly get the words out to tell me what happened."

"I have no doubt. And you hadn't had anything to drink at all? Don't lie to me."

"One with dinner. Period. I swear. I wasn't drunk at all. When she told me what happened, I didn't know what the hell to do. I knew, though, if I put myself in the spotlight, you'd do whatever it took to bury it. I spilled liquor on my clothes and rinsed my mouth with it before I came to see you. I wanted my confession to be realistic."

Peter wasn't sure what to say anymore. This just kept getting worse. Bile surged in his throat as he thought of all the illegal things he and Sulzberger had done to bury this. All the favors they'd called in. All the dirt they'd shoveled. Now it was all for nothing. Owen was right, sick as it made him to admit it. If he'd known the truth, he'd have played the whole thing differently.

But now what the fuck did he do? Where had he gone wrong here? How had he missed the signs that Diane was in trouble? Why hadn't he pursued the situation where Kellerman's people had come down on Owen? Was he so arrogant that he—

Enough. No time for that now. He'd have to be the responsible adult here, but the ramifications if this got out sent unfamiliar panic racing through him, like a shot of ice water.

"We have some big problems to face here," he told the couple. "Owen, you know we have new players in the game. Men Peyton West hired who aren't going to be deterred or bought off."

"Whatever you were going to do for me, do it for Diane."

Kendrick wanted to throttle his son. Throttle both of them.

"The first thing I have to do is get both of you out of town now until I figure out how to fix this. These people Peyton West hired aren't your run-of-the-mill investigators. They've dug up things I thought were permanently buried."

"Can't you fix it?" Owen's voice was edged with strain. "You have a lot of power. So does Warren Sulzberger."

"If only. My plan when I thought it was you and the shit was about to hit the fan again was to act like you weren't involved at all. That's why I wanted you both here, so you could act normal and I could bluff the whole thing. And pray these new assholes couldn't find anything we'd buried. Jesus, Owen, we even got rid of your car. Told people the lease was up and we were getting you a new one. We've done everything we could to bury this."

"You wouldn't have done this for Diane." Owen's tone was rife with accusation. "I had to decide how we would handle this."

"Yeah? How's that working out for you?"

He needed to take a minute and think this whole thing through. Then he'd call Sulzberger to make sure everything was *really* buried so no one could find it. Not even these hotshots who seem to scare the shit out of Sulzberger.

"Go home. It's the weekend. Don't go anywhere or do anything. I have to make some calls and figure out how to get these Galaxy guys off our backs."

Diana lifted her chin. "I was just trying to protect Owen, but I'm ready to own up to it. I don't want this to fall on him."

"No!" Owen practically shouted the word. "That's not happening. We'll leave the country first."

"No one's going anywhere except home." Kendrick gave them each a hard look. "Let me figure out how to fix this."

"How is that even possible?" Diane asked. "Owen said Brianne Hollister is still in a coma and her sister is rattling every bush she can find."

"Just go home." He stopped, took a deep breath and lowered his voice. "I have to decide the best way to play this out. They don't have proof and all the witnesses have been taken care of. We're going to ride this out and hopefully put it behind us."

Owen swallowed hard. "But what about the sister?"

"I'll work on that. You both just go home and stay there. From now on, you do only what I tell you."

As soon as they had left, he punched a number on his cell.

"Warren? I know I'm the last person you want to hear from, and guess what. You'll want it even less after you hear what I have to say."

"This is just fucked." Sulzberger's voice over the phone was thick and scratchy. "How the hell did everything get out of hand like this?"

"We can argue that later. Right now, I need your help again."

"Really? Good luck with that. I can't put my neck out there anymore. I have to stay under that bastard

Hamilton's radar. He'd like nothing better than to kill my ass. Now that he knows I was involved in the coverup of the so-called accident, he's probably just waiting for this opportunity to destroy me. You'll have to take care of this one yourself."

Kendrick barely stopped himself from throwing the phone across the room. This was no time for anger. He had to come up with a plan. One that worked and didn't cost him everything he'd strived his whole life for.

* * * *

When Alton Franz handed an envelope to Peyton the next morning, Blaze felt as if it were a bomb waiting to go off. This could blow the lid off a lot of things, and finally, finally, avenge his team members who had been murdered.

"I didn't want to email it or text it to you," he told Peyton. "I had to do a lot of maneuvering to get this and too many people are very nervous about this coming out. Anything on the Internet can be hacked. It can also end up in the wrong hands. They don't want details of the coverup to blow back on them."

"I appreciate that, Senator, and this will be handled in the right way." Peyton smiled at him. "Those SEALs will finally get justice. Anyway," she assured him, "I know just the person I can reach out to with this. None of this will come anywhere near you. Senator, thank you so much for this."

He chuffed a laugh. "My thanks will come when I see the media coverage. Be sure to let me know when it's going to pop."

"I will. Thank you again."

"Keep the faith, Peyton. I know your sister will come out of this."

She shivered. "I hope you're right. I *pray* you're right."

They were halfway through their flight back to Tampa when Blaze's cell phone rang. "It's Rocket," he told her, checking the readout. "I'll put it on speaker." He punched the button. "Hey, Rocket. Peyton's with me. What have you got?"

"A promise from the police commissioner that he'll reopen the case of the hit and run. And do it right away. I mean like yesterday."

"Damn! You are good."

Rocket laughed. "You know it."

Peyton leaned a little closer to the phone. "Are you sure he'll keep his word?"

"More than sure. For one thing, after my phone call to him, he had his assistant search the cloud for the CCTV photos. Apparently, the idiot who said they were wiped didn't know it took two steps to wipe them from this particular cloud. He nearly had a stroke when I showed him the cleaned-up photos. That was enough to have him pull all the reports that were filed. Reports that are skimpy at best."

Peyton glanced at Blaze. "I'm sure he wasn't happy with the situation."

"He was damn pissed," Rocket told them. "He wants to do his best to prevent this from happening again. I'll bet there'll be some changes in procedure, not to mention a few people getting canned. He also made some phone calls while I was with him, to the precinct commander where the traffic detectives came from. Said he didn't care where they were on assignment, he wanted them in his office the next day."

Blaze slapped the table. "Damn good work. Thanks, Rocket."

"Did he say when he might have something?" Peyton asked.

"I'd say based on what he told me and the evidence he'll have, Diane Kendrick will probably be arrested within forty-eight hours. He just has to clean up the shit reports at the precinct so some scummy lawyer can't muddy the case."

Blaze was glad to see the frown smooth from her brow. "Rocket, thank you so much. Keep us up to date," Blaze told him.

"Will do."

He disconnected the call and reached for Peyton's hand.

"We're gonna get it done."

For the first time since the moment he'd seen her, the strain on her face eased a little.

"Oh, god, I hope so. At least the person who did this won't get away with it."

"I'm going to call the hospital just to give the guys another heads up that sometime in the next forty-eight hours, things could ratchet up. I already told them Sulzberger or Kendrick might just be insane enough to take this out on your sister. Now I want them to be doubly on the alert."

"Yes. Please. Good idea."

They made a quick stop at the hospital on the way to the townhouse. Blaze reassured both himself and Peyton that everything was in good hands, although he insisted on regular updates. It was early afternoon by the time they entered his townhouse. He was feeling a combination of jazzed and exhausted. They hadn't slept much the night before, too wound up about what was coming to relax. The sex had been frenetic but hardly satisfying. Now, the high-octane desire simmered just beneath the surface like an underwater bomb ready to explode. The news from Rocket had only added to the high.

"How soon do you think you can get this to one of your reporter friends?" he asked Peyton.

"I'll go through my contacts right now and see who would be the best one." She already had her phone out and was scrolling her list. "I have a good relationship with all the ones I've used as sources and resources, but there's one who will really make the big deal out of this if he'll help us."

"Good. That's what we want."

"I just have to figure the best way to get this to him. He won't move forward without this written proof."

He watched her sitting there, forehead wrinkled in concentration, thumbing through names.

"We can always have Saint fly it to him."

She looked up. "You'd do that?"

"I'd walk it there myself if I had to. Peyton, this man was responsible for the murder of most of my team. I'll do anything I can to make this happen."

"Okay. Then I think I have just the right person." She opened the contact name and hit the button to dial the number. "Dawson? Hey. This is Peyton West. Long time, no see." She chuckled at whatever he said. "Yeah, yeah, I know. Well, you always told me you wanted to be in one of my books so you'd be famous. I've got a better way if you're interested. It's the hot story of the year and I can't think of a better person to run with it than you."

She gave him a short, concise version of what she had for him. Blaze knew she didn't want to say too much over the phone. Cell phones weren't as secure as people liked to think.

"No, I'm not giving you a line. Yes, the information is authentic. I have proof." She laughed. "Yes, I know it's a big story. That's why I chose you to break it. I wanted someone I can trust. I wanted someone who I thought would do the best job with this and your name hit the top of the list. Listen. I'm going to put a man named Scott Hamilton on the phone. He'll tell you how and where you can pick up the written proof. Yes, he's one hundred percent solid."

Blaze took the phone from her and rattled off some information before handing the phone back.

"Dawson? Someone is flying to Atlanta to give you the proof. I didn't want to send it through the mail or try to do it electronically. But you have to promise me you will make the biggest splash ever. Yes, I know you do. That's why it's you I called. Okay. You'll be getting a call and a delivery in a couple of hours."

While she finished her conversation, he called Saint.

"Got another trip for you today." He grinned. "And yes, we're making sure you have enough hours in the air. The first thing you have to do is come by my place to pick up an envelope." Finished with the call, he looked over at Peyton. "You hungry? We haven't eaten since breakfast."

She shook her head. "I'm too jazzed to eat. Oh, Blaze, you'll finally get the revenge for your team members. Dawson's big for this—television, Internet as well as print. I am so glad I could be a part of this."

"A major part," he reminded her. "I could never have done this without you."

"Then something good has come out of this tragedy."

"No kidding. If not for the hit and run, Warren Sulzberger might never have come into my orbit again. If you hadn't hired us, I'd never have connected with the resources to finally make him pay." He winked at her. "I think you deserve a reward."

She looked up at him and grinned. "I think I do, too. But I think we'd better wait until after Saint picks up this envelope."

To Saint's credit, when he arrived, he didn't ask any questions, just took the envelope and the written instructions on how to deliver it, and beat it. Saint swallowed a grin as he headed to the door. Blaze figured the grin was his recognition of how important Peyton ahd become to him.

Go figure. He'd spent years avoiding entanglements, only to embrace one that had hit him out of the blue. Now he just had to convince Peyton that three days was enough for them to move forward with this. And that she should move here from San Antonio, or at least stay a while so they could see where this was going.

He hoped his partners didn't give him a hard time. When they'd formed Galaxy, they had all discussed what would happen if they developed a relationship with a woman that could turn out to be permanent.

'We don't exactly live a stable existence,' Eagle had pointed out. *'Most women can't deal with that.'*

'Most women,' Blaze had told him. *'But the right one could – '* Then he'd shaken his head. *'But you know that won't be me. Footloose is my middle name.'*

He swallowed a laugh thinking about it. He could imagine what they'd have to say.

"Finally." Blaze locked the door after Saint and pulled Peyton into his arms. "Now I can say thank you properly."

"Blaze, I'm all hot and sweaty," she protested.

"Good." He grinned. "Then I don't have to worry about getting you hotter and sweatier. Come on. I think you need something to take your mind off all of this."

He lifted her into his arms and carried her into the bedroom, sweeping back the covers on the bed and placing her on the sheets. He kept telling himself, *Go slow, don't rush things*, but he wanted her with an unfamiliar fierceness that he couldn't seem to control. He pulled off her shoes and tossed them to the side before lifting the hem of her silk blouse. Bending low, he placed a string of soft kisses along the strip of flesh exposed, then slid his tongue over the area.

God!

She tasted good everywhere, her skin soft as silk and tasting slightly of the peach body lotion she used. Teasing himself, he licked again, loving the way she squirmed, then slipped the fabric up and over to give him better access to her body. The breasts he'd come to love in such a short time plumped temptingly in a lacy gray bra. Traveling his tongue up over the fabric, he carefully licked the swells.

Peyton tried to grab the fabric to lift it up and over her head, but he wrapped his fingers around her wrists and forced her arms out to the sides.

"My party, my rules." He licked around the edges of her belly button.

She wriggled her hips in a teasing motion. "Oh. Is that so?"

"It is indeed."

"And just who decided that? Is that an order?"

He grinned, enjoying this side of her. "Me. And yes. The other night you took excellent care of me. Now I'm going to return that favor. Your only order is…don't move."

The pulse at the hollow of her throat beat harder as her imagination created all the things he might do to her. He maneuvered the blouse over her head, tossed it to the floor then pushed up the bra so her breasts plumped out beneath it. God, she had gorgeous breasts. The rosy nipples were already swollen, their color now a darker pink. He drew one into his mouth, scraping it with his teeth before sucking it hard again and again.

Peyton moaned and tried to raise herself up to him, but he pushed her back with one hand.

"Uh uh uh. My rules, remember?"

"Oh, we're having rules now?" Heat danced in her eyes.

"Yes. As many as we need."

What he really wanted to do was tie her to the bed and fuck her senseless, licking every inch of her over and over again, spanking her beautiful ass until it turned a gorgeous shade of dark pink. And fucking her until he wore out his cock.

But he was going to save that. Work up to it when he knew she wanted it as much as he did. Right now, he just wanted to do everything to make her feel very, very good.

He teased one nipple until she squirmed beneath his mouth then turned his attention to the other one. When they were deliciously swollen, he unfastened the bra and yanked it away, tossing it to the floor. Unhurried, he unzipped her slacks. He stood there for a moment, letting his gaze roam over every inch of her, drinking her in.

He eased the slacks slowly down past her hips, letting the tips of his fingers follow the curve of her hips and the line of her firm thighs, down to her ankles and her delicate feet. He'd been with all kinds of women — too many, some would say — but none of them held a candle to Peyton West. There was just something about her that set her about from all the others and pushed every one of his buttons.

And it wasn't just her luscious body that kept his cock in a continuous semihard state or made his balls ache when she smiled at him a certain way. It was everything about her.

When she was completely naked except for the tiniest lacy bikini panties, he pulled in a breath to steady himself, shucked his shirt and slacks, and crawled onto the bed, leaving his boxer briefs in place to keep some control over his very eager cock.

"Don't move," he told her. "That's an order."

Her lips tilted up in a wicked smile. "What happens if I do?"

He moved so his mouth hovered over hers. "I might have to punish you. Severely. I might not even let you come."

"Oh, god!" She arched her neck, eyes closed. "I'll behave. I promise."

Her words made him even harder, if that was possible. There was something so dynamic about sex with her, about being with her, an eroticism that he didn't remember feeling with other women, no matter how extreme the sex they had together. He knew at that moment he'd do whatever it took to keep her with him.

Positioning himself between her knees, he lifted one leg and began to string soft kisses from her ankle along her calf and inner thigh, taking little nips along the way. When he reached the little panties, he pressed a soft kiss to the fabric covering her sweet sex before trailing his mouth over to her other leg and slowly drawing a line down to the ankle.

Her breathing accelerated and her fingers gripped the sheet beneath her. He drew the line with his tongue again, scraping at the sides of her knees and tugging the fabric of the panties with his teeth. The more he did it, the more she squirmed, tiny sounds of pleasure whispering from her lips.

When she dug in her heels and tried to thrust herself up to him, he lifted her legs to bend them at the knees and planted her feet on either side of him. Then, instead of sliding off the tiny panties, he pulled the fabric of the crotch aside, pressed the lips of her sex open and drew a line tracing her wet flesh with the tip of his tongue. She moaned, so he did it again, and again.

He lapped the flesh over and over, loving the little sounds she made and relishing the sweet taste of her. Gently gripping her clit with his teeth, he tugged at it over and over, finally putting just the right amount of pressure on it to draw a small scream from her. He bit down a little harder, and just like that, she came, a small, shuddering orgasm, soaking his mouth. He swallowed it, and when her shuddering stopped, he licked the soft pink skin until he captured every bit of the liquid.

Peyton looked down at him, breath fluttering.

"God, Blaze. Just…holy god."

He shimmied up her body, cupped her face in his palms and took her mouth in a kiss that was both sweet and hot. He swept his tongue inside, licking the warm surface, and she met every thrust with one of her own. If it weren't for the fact that he was so damn horny, he could have spent the next hour just kissing her.

When the kiss ended, he grinned up at her. "Want more, sugar?"

"Are you kidding me? Damn straight I do."

He laughed, a low and soft sound. "I live to serve."

He grabbed the panties and ripped them off, tossing them to the floor. Then he pressed open the lips of her sex with his fingers again and plunged his tongue deep inside. God, she tasted so good. He pressed his face to her and inhaled her scent, his cock crying to be thrust inside. But this was for Peyton. For her. And he'd give her plenty of pleasure before he took his own.

He went to work on that very thing with a vengeance, licking and sucking, nibbling her clit, pulling back his tongue to thrust his fingers inside, curling them so with each backward pull, he scraped that special hot spot. Peyton pressed her heels into the mattress, pushing toward him, those delicious little sounds driving him crazy. He didn't think he'd ever get enough of her taste or the soft, liquid feel of her. Every beat of desire entered himself in his cock.

The second orgasm came without warning, just as he closed his teeth on her clit again and thrust three fingers inside her. She rode his hand, his fingers driving in and out, his lips and teeth teasing her clit. When she was finished, lying there panting, tiny quivers still teasing at her inner flesh, he pressed a kiss to her opening, licked her one last time and reached into the nightstand drawer, where he'd placed a new box of condoms.

By now he was so hard it was painful. Hands shaking with need, he ripped open a foil packet and sheathed himself. Then he flipped Peyton over and dragged her to her knees.

"This okay?" His voice was so hoarse he hardly recognized it.

"It will be if you stop talking and start moving."

God, but she was hot.

The sight of her upturned ass set his body on fire even more. He couldn't help taking a moment to place a kiss on each upturned cheek and give a slow lick to the rounded flesh. He was rewarded by the shiver that raced deliciously over her body.

Slipping a hand between her thighs, he used his fingers to test her readiness. *Wet! Soaked! Yes!* Those two orgasms he'd given her had only taken the edge off. He wanted her craving more, craving him, craving the feel of his cock inside her.

Gripping his swollen cock in one hand, he pressed the head against the entrance to her sex and gently pushed into her. Despite how tight she was, her muscles were loose from the two orgasms he'd already given her, making his entry easy and smooth. When he was fully seated inside her, he stopped to take a breath and gather himself.

He leaned forward and placed a soft kiss at the small of her back. Then he began the steady in-and-out movement, gripping her hips to hold her in place. Gathering himself, he began the familiar in and out, thrust and withdraw, again and again, all the way inside then back. When she squeezed him with her internal muscles, need strong as a hurricane rushed through his veins.

Her body matched every movement of his, her tight inner muscles clenching at him. Over and over he drove into her, the walls of her sex tightening around him and little flutters giving his shaft an erotic squeeze. He gritted his teeth, holding on as long as he could, until he felt her orgasm surging through her. He was so close to the edge and he didn't want this to be over before he even blinked. When her release exploded, drenching his cock, he could finally let go, pumping hard, his cock pulsing.

Depleted at last, he collapsed forward, taking her down with him, catching himself on his forearms. His heart was beating so hard he wondered they didn't hear it, and his breath came in harsh gasps. Peyton's body shuddered beneath him, her breathing as ragged as his.

He wasn't sure how long they lay there like that until he finally realized he needed to dispose of the condom.

"Now I think we can use that shower we didn't take." He chuckled. "We earned it."

"Mm-hmm."

Except pulling out of her body gave him an unfamiliar empty feeling. He had to make sure, when all this was wrapped up, that this woman stayed here. Sometime in the next forty-eight hours or so, everything was going to explode. Diane Kendrick would be arrested for Dane's murder and the attempted murder of Brianne. The story on Warren Sulzberger would break, with its expected fallout. And he had to pull out all the stops to convince Peyton to stay.

Chapter Fifteen

Peter Kendrick was up at five-thirty, ragged from lack of sleep and fighting a combination of fear and anger. In his head, he kept replaying the conversation from the night before with Owen and Diane. How the ever-lovin' hell had everything gotten so fucked up?

There was no way he could go into the office. He was agitated and on edge and needed to plug the holes in his suddenly leaky ship. He'd also be no good to his clients with his mind focused one thing only — how to make sure any remaining evidence against either Diane or Owen was destroyed.

He'd have to start fixing things all over again, beginning with the CCTV footage. Sulzberger had the contacts there, people he'd done favors for, people who also didn't mind taking a bribe or two. He had to make sure the tapes were wiped clean.

Paying off the cops would take a little more ingenuity, since Warren had handled it before, but he'd figure it out. He'd have to, because he had no choice. His family and everyone's future were at stake.

Warren might have bailed, but there were still powerful figures who were indebted to him. At his desk with a full pot of coffee, he spent the morning going through every name on his private list, figuring out who would be the best to contact. He was just about to ditch the coffee and switch to something that wouldn't erode his system when his cell phone rang. He looked at the readout. Owen. *Now what?*

"What is it?" he barked.

"Dad?" Owen's voice sounded like a strangled frog. "We need help."

Peter clutched the phone as a sick feeling washed over him. "With what?"

"The police are here, arresting Diane. Jesus, Dad. What the fuck are we going to do?"

Put everyone on a plane and hide on some isolated island.

How the hell had they done this so quickly?

Were the people the West woman had hired so powerful, so well connected, that they could make something like this happen? And where had the police gotten the proof that it was Diane? Everyone, including himself, had believed it was Owen until he'd gotten the news last night. What piece of evidence had they all overlooked?

"Dad?" Owen's hysterical voice pierced the fog in his brain. "She's freaking out. What should we do?"

With supreme effort, Peter pulled himself together.

"Where are they taking her? Get me the precinct number and I'll meet you there. As soon as I find out what's going on and what proof they used to make the arrest, we'll get the best criminal defense lawyer in the

Southeast. Just…pull yourself together. Your wife needs you now."

He noted the information in his phone as soon as Owen gave it to him and pulled himself together. Now wasn't the time to fall apart. He'd thrown on comfortable slacks and a polo shirt this morning to work from home. He'd better get changed and get his ass in gear. Right now.

* * * *

Peyton and Blaze were eating a late breakfast when his cell rang.

"It's Rocket. I'll put it on speaker phone." He answered and punched the button so they both could hear. "Hey. We're both on."

"Good," his partner said. "The deed is done. The arrest's been made. Diane Kendrick is on her way to the police precinct."

Peyton could hardly believe it. "Are you sure?"

Rocket laughed. "I parked across the street and got photos so we can show them to Peyton. What are you doing right now?"

"Just finishing breakfast. Come on over."

"On my way."

He disconnected the call and looked at the woman across from him.

"You heard, right?"

Her hands were shaking so badly she could hardly hold her coffee cup.

"I can't believe it really happened." She looked across the table at Blaze.

He grinned at her. "Believe it. Rocket's on his way with pictures."

She took another sip of coffee then had to set the cup down. "I know you guys have pull with the police commissioner, but—"

"But it wouldn't have made any difference," Blaze interrupted, "if the proof hadn't been solid. There was no disregarding the CCTV pictures. After Rocket gets here and shows us the photos, how about going to the hospital to see Brianne? Maybe telling her about this will help pierce that veil she's wrapped in."

Peyton's stomach turned over. "God, if only that were possible."

Fifteen minutes later, Blaze opened the door to Rocket, who had a big smile on his face.

"Wait until you see these." He took a seat next to Blaze. "Let me pull them up."

Peyton couldn't take her eyes away from the phone as Rocket scrolled through the shots. The police arriving at the residence of the young Kendricks. Owen opening the door looking disheveled in jeans, a T-shirt and bare feet. Diane behind him, looking equally in disarray. The men entering the house. Everyone leaving, with both Diane and Owen in handcuffs.

"They arrested Owen Kendrick, too?"

"Yes. My guess is he's going to be charged with covering up a crime. I wouldn't be surprised if Peter Kendrick will also be facing charges."

Peyton scrolled through them again and again, as if reassuring herself it wasn't a mirage. Finally, she looked from Blaze to Rocket then back to Blaze.

"I never would have believed this would actually happen. I owe Galaxy everything." Then she burst into tears.

"Hey, hey, hey." Blaze pushed out of his seat and came around to Peyton, pulling her to her feet and holding her against his chest while she sobbed. "I hope those are happy tears."

She nodded, her face burrowed against his chest, soaking his T-shirt but absorbing the comfort of his body. He stroked her back while she let it all out the tension—the despair, the anger, the panic—everything she'd felt since she got that first phone call. She clung to him until at last she calmed down and looked up at his face.

"Sorry to be such an emotional mess."

"Not to worry." His voice was like a warm blanket around her. "You earned a good cry. More than one, as a matter of fact. This has been a rotten time for you and your family."

She managed a smile as she looked up at him. "I can't believe you guys actually did it."

"It was a good team effort."

She hurried around the table to give Rocket a hug.

"Huge, huge, huge thanks. I wasn't sure this was even possible. You guys are worth every single penny you charge people."

"We like this kind of ending." He grinned. "It's the best kind."

Before she could say anything else, her phone sounded the signal for an incoming text. Her eyes widened as she read the message.

"Blaze? Turn on the television to any of the news channels. Do it right now."

He gave her a quizzical look. "Is the arrest already on television? I wonder if someone got wind of it and had a camera crew at the precinct."

She shook her head. "It's not that. Turn it on. Hurry."

He turned on the big-screen television in the living room and brought up the news channel he liked to watch the most. Immediately they saw a blowup of a photo of Warren Sulzberger, with the reporter doing a voiceover.

"…seems to be absent from both his home in Miami and his local office, as well as the one in Washington. Once again, former Senator Warren Sulzberger has been charged with treason for an event that occurred four years ago. This station has received proof that he received a cash payoff to leak information about a SEAL Team mission in Afghanistan. All but two members of the team were killed by insurgents. It appears this wasn't the only incident like this. The FBI at this moment has a nationwide search out for the man. Repeating, former Senator Warren Sulzberger… "

Blaze muted the audio and turned to Peyton, stunned.

"I can't believe you really did it! Holy fuck, Peyton, you actually did it."

She laughed, glad to be doing something besides crying. "Told ya. Let's boot up a computer and see every place that's carrying it."

While Blaze went to fetch his laptop, Rocket came over to her and gave her a bear hug.

"Woman, you just bought yourself a lifetime of service from Galaxy." He chuckled. "Although I have the feeling you're getting it anyway." His expression turned sober. "Joking aside, for Blaze to be getting this kind of satisfaction after so many of his men were killed is an incredible thing."

"More than incredible." He'd come back into the room, still wearing a dazed expression, and was booting up his laptop. "Let's take a look here, guys."

Peyton watched as he scrolled through news web site after web site — television, newspapers, digital publications, everything. Each one carried the story with bold headlines and pictures of the disgraced former senator.

"Dawson did good," Peyton commented.

"Better than good. Peyton, you were right. This is the best kind of revenge. He loses everything and will have to live with the fallout. In prison."

"I know you're still taking this in," she told him, "but now we have even more reason to go to the hospital. We have two pieces of good news for Brianne, even if she doesn't know you. Yet."

"Absolutely. Great idea."

"I'm gonna run along and leave you two kids to do your celebrating." Rocket picked up his phone. "Peyton, I'm sending these pictures to your phone."

"I'll probably spend a lot of time looking at them." She hugged him again. "Thank you, All of you. I want to thank Viper and Eagle, too."

Rocket looked over at Blaze. "Think we can put dinner tonight on the agenda? We should all celebrate together."

Blaze looked at Peyton, eyebrow quirked. "What do you think?"

"I think that's a great idea."

Blaze nodded. "Okay, then. Rocket, you guys pick the place and text me the location and time. Right now, we're heading to the hospital."

"And I'm out of here. See you guys later."

The moment he left, Blaze pulled her into his arms again, tilted her face up and gave her a kiss that seared her down to her toes.

"That's just a promise of what will come later. Let's get ready and get out of here."

They were ready in fifteen minutes and headed into the garage. When Blaze opened the garage door, she started to walk around the rear of the car when a vehicle pulled up and blocked them in. She turned, frowning, as a man jumped out and grabbed her before she could react. He wrapped one arm around her throat, his other hand holding a gun pressed to her temple.

"Hello, Blaze." The voice was hoarse and rough. "Look what I've got here."

The expression on Blaze's face turned hard, but her heart was pounding so loudly she almost didn't hear what he said.

"Aren't you in enough trouble, Sulzberger? Do you want to add premeditated murder to the list of charges?"

"You think I give a shit?" He pressed his arm against Peyton's windpipe. "You've ruined my fucking life."

"Yeah? That's nothing compared to the deaths of good men you caused because of your greed."

Peyton had never heard Blaze's voice sound so cold, so emotionless. Yet anger raged in his eyes.

"It was just a business transaction," Sulzberger told him. "The cost of war."

"Treason isn't the cost of war, you fucker. Now let the woman go."

"Not until you watch me kill her. You took my life from me. Ruined everything. Now I'm going to take something from you."

As petrified as she was, Peyton still remembered a scene she'd written in one of her books, one a former SWAT team member had described to her.

Be calm, she told herself, even though she was terrified. *You just need to give Blaze a chance.*

"Don't make things worse than they are," Blaze was saying.

"Worse than they are? How would that even be possible? My whole life is destroyed."

"But at least you still have it. Better than being dead."

Peyton looked directly at Blaze, trying to send him a message with her eyes. He was easing an inch at a time in her direction. Sulzberger was apparently so disturbed at this point that it didn't register with him.

Just a little more, she told herself. *Come on, Blaze.*

"You wouldn't think so if you were me."

Now, she told herself. She sagged in Sulzberger's grip, upsetting his balance, stomped on his foot hard, and when he jerked the gun away in reaction, dropped to the floor. She heard two shots and prayed none of them had hit Blaze, but she stayed curled into a ball until she felt gentle hands tugging on her arm.

"Come on, Wonder Woman. It's all over."

She let Blaze help her to her feet, wondering if Sulzberger was dead. When she looked, he was curled up on the floor, holding a hand with blood dripping from it, more blood seeping from a wound in one thigh, and he was moaning. The gun he'd been holding had fallen to the floor but apparently hadn't discharged.

"You're okay? Blaze? Let me see you." She tried to see all of him, checking for bullet holes.

"I'm fine, but Sulzberger needs medical attention, which someone other than me can give him. Are you okay if I take care of a couple of things here?"

"Yes. I'm good." Her laugh was a little shaky, but she was determined to keep it all together. The last thing Blaze needed was a weepy woman dripping all over him. "At least I think I am. Do what you have to."

He pulled out his phone and punched some numbers.

"Who are you calling?"

"Eagle. This piece of shit needs to get dumped at the Tampa FBI offices, but I don't want to be the one to do it. Someone else needs to deliver him. As soon as he's out of here, I'll call them on a burner phone I've got in the house. Go on, go inside and wait for me. This shouldn't take long,"

"Okay. I'm good." She'd say that even if she wasn't. "Do whatever you have to."

"You know where the liquor is. I'd say pour yourself a stiff drink. Now get going."

She hurried inside, heading for the bar, taking his advice about the drink. She forced herself to wait patiently, sipping at the bourbon, until Blaze was back inside. He came to her at once, crouching down in front of her and taking her hands.

"You okay? I hated sending you in here alone, but I didn't want you out there while we took care of the mess."

"That's okay." She drew in a deep breath and let it out slowly. "Is—Is he gone?"

"Sure is. Viper came along with Rocket so one of them could drive his car away from here. I called the FBI office and told them to get ready for some trash." He lifted her hands and kissed her knuckles. "You were incredibly brave. How'd you know to do that?"

Her laugh was shaky at best. "I wrote a scene like that in one of my books. The info was courtesy of SWAT and obviously it stuck with me."

He threw his head back and laughed. "I think I might have to read some of your books." He studied her face. "You still good to go to the hospital?"

"More than ever now."

He pulled her to her feet. "Then let's do it. But first…"

His kiss was hot and hungry and erotic and emotional all at the same time. When he stepped back, hunger flashed in his eyes.

"We'd better get out of here now or we might not leave at all."

She was grateful Blaze had suggested she have a drink, because that more than anything helped her steady herself on the ride. She wanted to be composed when she saw her sister, so she could tell her everything that had happened, even if she couldn't hear it.

But when they got to Brianne's room, she received yet another shock on this roller coaster of a day. The two guards Blaze had hired were standing against one wall and nodded at them when they came in. Two nurses, both of whom Peyton recognized, and a doctor were standing at Brianne's bedside. One of the nurses was adjusting the IV setup and she was smiling, something Peyton was not used to in this room. She recognized Blaze's brother at once.

"Nolan? What's going on?"

He turned and she saw he also had a big grin on his face.

"Come see for yourself. We've got a big surprise for you." He stepped aside and motioned her forward.

Her heart nearly stopped when she saw Brianne's eyes open. Her sister's face was pale, but a tiny smile played over her lips.

"Brianne? Ohmigod. Brianne."

They all made room for her to stand beside her sister and she took one of Brianne's hands in hers, noticing it wasn't as cold as usual.

"Hey, Peyton." Her voice was thin and ragged.

Peyton didn't care. The only important thing was she was awake. Alive and awake.

"Brianne." She couldn't seem to say anything else, and for the second time that day she felt tears running down her cheeks. She just stood there, holding her sister's hand.

"She woke up late this morning," Nolan told her. "The nurse was in checking her vitals and noticed some big changes, so she called me. Peyton, she's got a long road ahead of her, but I believe she's going to make a full recovery."

More tears fell. Peyton felt like the original waterworks.

"Thank you. For everything." Behind her she heard the murmur of male voices and she turned to motion to Blaze. "Come, let me introduce you to my sister."

"You sure? I don't want to upset any apple carts here."

"Maybe...he can tell me why I have two...men in my room." Brianne grinned. "Everyone else...keeps avoiding the question."

"Yes." Peyton swallowed. "I have a lot to tell you." She glanced back at Nolan. "Is it okay..."

He nodded. "She's been asking questions. I told her you had all the information. She needs to hear the truth, bad and good."

Peyton blew out a breath. "Okay. But please stay here in case, you know..."

He nodded.

Blaze pushed the chair close to the bed for her, so she sat, still holding Brianne's hand.

"Tell me about Dane first," Brianne begged. "No one will say a thing about him."

Peyton blinked back tears and searched for the right words to let her sister know what happened. Telling her was the hardest, most emotional thing she could ever remember doing. At the news about Dane's death, Brianne turned even paler and Nolan Hamilton moved forward to check Brianne's pulse and listen to her heart. When he nodded that it was okay, Peyton continued.

She related all the information about the coverup, about her push to get information, everything. Finally finding someone who would take her as a client and who'd uncovered the awful truth about what happened. The edge was softened, however, when she could tell her that Diane Kendrick had been arrested.

Nolan and the nurses were wonderful, checking Brianne's vitals and monitoring her condition. She introduced Blaze, who stood there with his arm around her, assuring Brianne that at least the people involved were being punished.

Brianne looked from Blaze to her. "I...take it this hunk...had something to do with all that."

Peyton nodded. "He and his partners had everything to do with it. They were the only ones who would help me. They uncovered everything that led to Diane Kendrick's arrest. And I'm pretty sure her father-in-law and her husband are going to be facing charges, too. And there's more."

She pulled up one of the stories about Warren Sulzberger on her phone and showed it to Brianne. "Not only did this guy do most of Peter Kendrick's dirty work, but he was also responsible for the death of almost every member of Blaze's SEAL team."

Brianne was shocked when Peyton told her the story, but managed a real smile when she got to the part about how they destroyed the man. By the time Peyton finished relating everything, she was emotionally exhausted, and she could see that Brianne's strength was fading. Nolan had left earlier, but now he walked back in to check on his patient.

He smiled at both of them. "She's doing great considering the situation, but I think that's it for today. Now she needs to rest."

"How long will she be in the hospital?" Peyton asked.

"If she continues to improve, I'd say no more than another two or three weeks. But if we send her home, she'll need someone with her until the arm and leg heal."

"I'll do it." The words just popped out of Peyton's mouth.

"You have obligations." Brianne's voice was weak but steady. "You can't put your career on hold for me."

"I can do whatever I want. Anyway, all I need is a phone, a tablet and a laptop and I can work anywhere."

Providing my agent and publisher haven't tossed me to the wolves.

"I'll be helping." Blaze's deep voice startled her.

"You have obligations too," she pointed out.

"Details," he told her. "Just details. Getting you to stay in Tampa is enough incentive for me to do anything you need."

Brianne's lips curled in a little smile. "You'd better hang on to him, Peyton. He's a keeper."

Peyton laughed. "I think I got that message."

Urged by the nurse to let Brianne rest now, Blaze and Peyton left the hospital and headed back to the townhouse. She didn't remember the last time she'd felt so relieved about something. She'd have to do some maneuvering and make changes to her life, but they were minor compared to what she'd be gaining. She just hoped she wasn't misreading Blaze's intentions about where they went from here.

But the moment they were inside the townhouse, he pulled her into his arms and kissed her with such intensity that her entire body flamed. He pressed her hard against him, one hand cradling her head as his tongue conquered her mouth. By the time he lifted his head, she was weak with desire and consumed by an unfamiliar emotion.

"Blaze," she began.

He touched a finger to her lips.

"Me first. I'm not asking, I'm telling, unless I'm reading this all wrong. I never had the urge to settle down, Peyton. I loved being unattached and uncommitted. Until I met you. Now I can't think of my life without you. So how long will it take you to get yourself untangled from San Antonio? Because you're staying here until Brianne leaves the hospital. Then we'll either bring her here or I'll move into her house with you."

"B-But she'll need—"

"Both of us. I'm telling my partners to take me out of rotation until she's back on her feet."

Peyton was astounded. She'd never expected anything like this. It shocked her that it had all happened in the space of just a few days, but she felt like Blaze did. This was it for her and she was thrilled that he felt the same way.

She smiled up at him. "Is it too soon to say I love you?"

"Hell, no. Not soon enough for me. When Brianne's well enough, we'll get married. Again, I'm not asking. I'm telling. But you can be damn sure I'll make sure the world knows you're taken. I love you, Peyton."

"I love you, too, Blaze. You make my life complete. No, scratch that. Remember how I told you my life was in retrograde? Well, now it's moving forward, and all because of you."

He startled her by lifting her in his arms.

"Then I think we'd better do something to seal this deal."

She laughed all the way to the bedroom.

Want to see more from this author?
Here's a taster for you to enjoy!

Galaxy: Critical Density
Desiree Holt

Excerpt

How fucking long can they keep me here?

Hannah Modell looked out of the window of her hotel suite to the esthetic view of…the parking lot. Beyond it, she could see other buildings in downtown Houston, accented by the sparkle of the evening's lights just coming on. Traffic filled the streets as people came and went, punctuated by the impatient honking of horns. She'd be happy to be in that irritated crowd. She'd be happy to be anyplace except this hotel. *Scratch that*. Anyplace except for Houston.

Fourteen days since it had happened, and she was still shocked by the whole thing. She and the rest of her GO-Team had been in a remote location, delivering explosives to take out a key terrorist figure who was hiding out in a house in upstate New York. The word was he was planning a strike on a major United States city and their assignment was to take him out first.

Her GO-Team had been flown to an isolated location to launch the drone, which was outfitted with special equipment because of the explosives, and had a long-range capacity. People from various branches of the government and the military would be back at Lowden, watching the feed from the camera on the drone. It was only the third time Hannah had been tasked with doing something this enormous and she'd spent hours checking and double checking everything to make sure nothing would go wrong. She knew she'd probably driven her team nuts, but she hadn't cared. There was no room for error in a situation like this.

She was stunned when the helicopter carrying Greg Kingsley, Lowden's vice president, had shown up at their site. Jumping out of the chopper, he'd told them they had to shut down the job. Right. Now. Right that minute. For a moment, she'd just stood there, stunned.

'But – why?'

'There's a situation, Hannah. Something went wrong big time with the drone delivery. A fuckup and we have a tragedy on our hands.'

'A tragedy?' She'd stared at him like he was speaking a foreign language.

'Worse than that. A disaster of epic proportions. We have to get everyone out of here while we sort this out.'

'But –'

'No buts. Lowden needs to see you ASAP, since this is your baby.'

What the hell?

She'd pestered him for details, but he had little to say beyond what he'd told her. Just said to wait until they were back at Lowden. She could not understand how this had happened. Misdirect a drone to dump its payload in a different place? Her? *Hell, no.* She was committed to her job, her country, her patriotism. That was why working for a paramilitary company that did black jobs for the government had been so satisfying, because she got to serve her country in a way a lot of people never could. She didn't even have friends outside of the job. How disgusting was that?

The moment they'd landed at the complex, they'd hustled her right to Eric Lowden's office, where he'd told her she was off the job until the situation was resolved.

Situation? This was a hell of a lot more than that.

'*Situation?*' She'd repeated the word.

'*Your drone flew off course.*' Lowden didn't mince any words with her. '*I don't know if the programming got screwed up or something else did. The fact remains that somehow that drone ended up at Senator Mark Hegman's summer house and blew it all to shit. Including the senator. We're just damn lucky his wife wasn't there at the time.*'

'*I don't understand.*' Her stomach had cramped and a chill slithered down her spine. '*How did this happen? I double and triple checked all my settings and we tested it several times.*'

"That's what we have to find out."

He continued talking to her in a low voice, but underneath it was hard anger at what a disaster this was for Lowden Tactical. She knew they had to fix this.

She could still hear his voice in her head.

Don't worry, Hannah. We need to keep you tucked away for your own good. We've got nice accommodations for you, Hannah. You'll be very comfortable while we sort this out. We just need to keep you away from the media while we figure out how it went wrong. You understand.

No, she didn't understand. She wanted to go home. Why couldn't she hide away there? *Oh, right.* The media. Lowden explained very carefully what a disaster that would be.

Although Lowden's voice had been even and reassuring, it left no room for argument as to what the plan was going forward. He was, after all, the boss. Someone had to take the fall for this, someone other than him. *Comfortable, huh? Yeah, right.* Why couldn't she be comfortable in her own apartment? She had the sickening feeling they were going to keep her under lock and key until they could definitively blame the whole thing on her.

You understand why we just need you out of the office, right? And available while we look into this? And as I said, away from the media. If you're not guilty, you have nothing to worry about. Besides, you might not be safe at home.

Not safe? Who would she be in danger from? Did they know? Or was the evidence not that conclusive? It was, after all, as Lowden had pointed out, her drone, her controls that had supposedly misdirected the drone to dump its payload on a vacationing ranking member of the Senate Armed Services Committee.

The stated target was supposed to be an ISIS leader who the government had gotten word was hiding out on the estate of a known sympathizer. Lowden had been tasked with delivering the payload because the government was afraid of leaks in its own system.

Were they looking to tie up the blame on her in a nice, neat package? Tell everyone it was her fault?

Mistake! This has to be a mistake.

That's all she'd thought of when she was standing in the Lowden offices. But if it really happened as they'd said, how did it all go that wrong? She always double checked her settings. And she'd never made a mistake. Ever. The drones were her life. Was it something with the equipment? Something she'd somehow missed? But that was verified and calibrated regularly. And all the questions. So many questions.

The fact there was so much they didn't seem to know was probably why they didn't stick her in a jail cell right away. Instead they hustled her out of Lowden to a room at the local FBI office and battered her with questions until she thought her head would explode.

Then, suddenly, it was goodbye depressing office, hello high-rise hotel.

What the hell?

They knew her. She kept thinking that over and over. They had to know someone else did this, committed what could actually be classified espionage. She got the feeling, however, that they wanted to make sure they could hang it on her. Keep her around while they sewed things up nice and tight. That was it. Also, there had to be something hinky about the whole thing or her accommodations would be much less appealing.

Espionage.

Just the word made her sick to her stomach, as she had been almost every day she was tucked away in this upscale jail.

She could still hear the voice of one of the federal agents who had brought her here. Two agents, actually, as if they thought she'd run away. Well, truth be told, if she'd had the chance she would have. This was so wrong. She had not done what they accused her of, although they did hedge a little. That was why she was in a hotel instead of stuck in a cell where no one could find her. Because either someone wasn't positive they could make a charge against her stick or they hadn't yet covered their tracks well enough.

This is just a precaution while we complete our investigation, Hannah. After all, national security is involved. If someone else did this, they may not want you to testify.

Someone else? She wanted to scream and tell them it had to be someone else because it damn sure wasn't her.

You'll be safe. We have people guarding you.

Guarding. Right. Someone sitting outside her door at all times. She snorted. Only it wasn't to protect her, no matter how polite they tried to be. It was to make sure she didn't find a way to slip the noose and get away from them before they made sure the case against her was wrapped up tight. Or to have anyone come talk to her.

Bodyguard my ass.

Despite what they said, they were more like jailers, and the comfortable suite, the cable television with streaming services and anything she wanted from room service didn't make up for the fact that she knew she was a prisoner. The windows might have drapes on them instead of bars, but the result was the same.

I'm sorry, Miss Modell. We just need you to be available and accessible while we finish the investigation. Thank you for being so understanding.

Available! Understanding! That was a joke. If she tried to leave this hotel suite, she'd end up in a place a lot less appealing.

She wondered what Lowden had even told the rest of its employees, and what they thought. She considered them her friends, sort of. It occurred to her she didn't have any kind of social life beyond Lowden, but until now that hadn't bothered her.

When they took her to her apartment to pack up what she'd need for what they called "a possible extended stay" elsewhere, she'd packed everything she could. Of course, her unsmiling guards had checked everything including her undies before letting her fill her suitcases. What the hell did they think she was hiding in them? Secret plans? A payoff? If she'd taken one, for the love of god, she'd have it in a secret offshore bank account where no one could find it.

She had no idea how things had gotten so fucked up, but she knew for sure she wasn't the one who had done it. She *never* made a mistake with one of her drones and she'd *never* do anything like this. She was meticulous with her setting, testing them repeatedly before every flight. Whatever happened, she knew in her bones someone else had screwed with the settings.

She was damn fucking good at her job as a drone operator and she'd never, ever make the kind of mistake of which she was accused. Or worse yet, do it deliberately.

Oh, wait! They didn't think it was a mistake! They thought someone had been paid to dump the load on a non-target and she was the most likely candidate.

Supposedly she wasn't "under suspicion." If she hadn't done this—big *if*—then she was possibly in danger from whoever the guilty person was. Or persons. Oh, yeah? She guessed that was why they were hesitant to stick her in a jail cell. If everything pointing to her didn't stick, Lowden could be in for a huge lawsuit.

Someone had recommended an attorney to her just in case, but since at the moment she didn't trust either the government or Lowden Tactical to recommend anyone not on their side, she'd passed for the moment. Right now everyone was still tiptoeing around the situation. If it got worse, though, and moved into the next phase, she'd figure out what to do then.

And no one seemed to want to give her any information. Three times a day when one of the "guards" wheeled in her food, she badgered them with questions, but they might as well have been mute for all the info she got from them. She spent hours going over every single thing that had led up to that particular drone launch and still she had no answers.

She turned from the window and began to pace the room, hands shoved in the pockets of her jeans. How in the everlovin' hell had this even happened?

She had been so excited to get the job interview with Lowden Tactical and it had gone well. She knew she had an unusually high aptitude for spatial awareness and action that made her an expert in the field of drones. Walt Lowden seemed impressed with her and soon, from the air-conditioned comfort of her control room, she was able to kick butt all over the world. Make terrorist strikes that politically the government could not get into.

When Lowden assigned her to one of their GO-Teams she could hardly contain her excitement and pride. These were the highly trained covert teams that took drones into enemy territory to surveille or deliver payloads in places where the government could not. Positions on the teams were considered highly selective. She'd made it through the rigorous training and managed to earn the respect of the others. She was one of only two women assigned to the Teams and she wore the selection like a badge of honor. She would *never* do anything to bring shame on it. Ever.

Someone had done this and manipulated things to place the blame on her. Someone who was going to make a lot of money as a payoff for getting the payload dumped on a different target. She was discovering in a most painful way there was a big difference between having brains and being smart.

She had to get out of here and try to figure things out, but how? She was never allowed out of the suite and both doors were guarded twenty-four seven. All her food came from room service, the trays minutely examined before she was allowed to receive them and even then, one of her keepers wheeled in the table. The waiters weren't allowed to enter. Did they think the staff was going to aid in her escape? When housekeeping came to clean the rooms, one of the men dogged her every footstep. She was surprised they didn't follow her into the bathroom, for god's sake.

She had her laptop, but she wasn't allowed internet connection. No cell phone and the desk had been told not to accept any phone calls from this room. She was completely shut off from the outside world. And she had become so immersed in her job that the only people in her life were those on her GO-Team and others at Lowden. How sad was that? And frightening. No one would be banging on doors asking where she was and what was going on.

She stopped pacing for a moment to look out the window again. It was darker now, the outside lights brighter, more people moving in the area filled with hotels and restaurants and shops. She might try to climb out of a window, except the windows were sealed and she was on the fifteenth floor. But there had to be a way out of here. No one was going to try to prove her innocence except her. *Could I just catch a break here, please?*

A knock sounded on the door, breaking into her train of thought…not that it was much of a train.

"It's Santos. Your dinner is here."

She opened the door, something that was just a formality. She was told — ordered — not to put the chain on the door in case she had a problem and they needed immediate access. Problem. Ha! They were the problem. She knew they didn't want any kind of barrier if for any reason they needed immediate access for her safety.

Right. She almost snorted when they told her that. It wasn't her safety they were worried about. They just wanted to make sure she couldn't disappear on them.

She opened the door and found Paul Santos standing there with the room service table bearing her meal.

"If you wouldn't mind stepping back from the door," he told her in the even, measured voice she'd gotten used to, "I'll just wheel this into the room."

Right. Step back. In other words, don't try to make a run for it. Everything they did made her feel more and more like a criminal and gave the situation an increasingly hopeless feel. She had to figure this out. She couldn't just wait here in this hotel while the government and Lowden Tactical gathered incorrect evidence about her and the person really behind this got away with it.

But for the moment, she stepped way back from the door while Santos wheeled the table in.

"Enjoy your meal, Miss Modell."

Santos backed out of the room and closed the door. Hannah had to restrain herself from throwing the safety lock. The lack of it left her feeling so exposed and vulnerable and she hated it.

As she'd done every night for the past two weeks, since she'd been locked away here, she lifted the lids on the dishes. Food had begun to lose its appeal to her, but she knew she needed to keep up her strength. She never knew when an opportunity would present itself. Tonight it was sliced steak and mashed potatoes with gravy, simple food but nourishing.

As she ate, she did what had become a habit with her—analyzed everything about her situation. Trying to figure out who could have set her up. Someone obviously who got paid a lot of money to drop the payload from a drone on a powerful figure who had been secretly aiding the United States on a critical project. How had anyone even had that information? And who would betray their country like this?

Her head ached, trying to find answers where there were no clues. And she certainly wasn't going to get any locked away in this hotel. But how to get out of here? That was the big question.

Okay, she'd seen enough movies, watched enough television to figure out how to do this.

Think, Hannah. You're not stupid so don't act like it.

Home of Erotic Romance

Sign up for our newsletter and find out about all our romance book releases, eBook sales and promotions, sneak peeks and FREE romance books!

About the Author

A multi-published, award winning, Amazon and USA Today best-selling author, Desiree Holt has produced more than 200 titles and won many awards. She has received an EPIC E-Book Award, the Holt Medallion and many others including Author After Dark's Author of the Year. She has been featured on CBS Sunday Morning and in The Village Voice, The Daily Beast, USA Today, The Wall Street Journal, The London Daily Mail. She lives in Florida with her cats who insist they help her write her books, and is addicted to football.

Desiree loves to hear from readers. You can find her contact information, website details and author profile page at https://www.totallybound.com